MONSTER

KING'S MEN MC
BOOK THREE

V.T. DO

CONTENTS

CONTENT & TRIGGER WARNING

This is a dark romance, and some readers may find it triggering.

Reader discretion is advised.

Trigger Warning includes:

- Dub-con/Non-con
- Unprotected sex
- Captive Romance
- Branding
- Breeding Kink
- Violence

1

EMMY

AH, HELL.

I ducked out of the way in time for the crumpled piece of music sheet to fly past my face, missing me by about half an inch.

A familiar voice shouted somewhere to my left—where the paper had been thrown from—

"Oh, shit!"

I looked over at Braxton Madden, a seventh grader, and put on my teacher's face that quickly had him looking down at his feet, muttering a half-hearted apology.

"Sorry, Ms. Wilde."

I opened my mouth to reprimand him about cursing in the hallway, but today was the last day of school, and I didn't think it would matter much, considering who the boy's father was.

I bet he heard all sorts of things back home.

Braxton's father was famous around this part of the city—or should I say, *infamous*?

There wasn't a person in this school who didn't know who Dominic Madden was, the notorious president of the

King's Men Motorcycle Club. I had never met the man, though I had seen him on school grounds for Braxton's football games and, once, at a mandatory choir concert I had directed for all the grades.

That was about the extent of my interaction with the man, and it was enough for me to know I should stay far away from him.

It was one thing to be attracted to bad boys and a whole other thing to be attracted to the kind of man Dominic Madden was.

With broad shoulders and the most mesmerizing blue eyes I had ever seen on any human, Dominic was beautiful.

Beautiful and untouchable.

I had been stuck speechless at first sight at the beginning of the school year when he first showed up to pick Braxton up on his bike.

I was so sure God had sent down one of his avenging angels to help save the world.

Then he flirtatiously smiled at one of the school's admins, and I realized he was more of a fallen angel—a devil in disguise. Even so, I had been fascinated with him from that day on.

My heart wanted to harbor this little crush. After all, who could an innocent little fantasy hurt? My head said Dominic wasn't good for anyone, even if I did nothing more than let him occupy my thoughts.

It was one of those rare instances in which I let my head win. I tried not to put myself directly in his path if I could help it.

Not that it mattered much. The man hadn't noticed me, and I doubted I was the kind of woman he usually went for. One look at him and I could tell he was experienced. And arrogant.

The last thing I needed in my life was excitement.

Especially with a man as rough-looking as him. Something told me I wouldn't be able to handle it. It also didn't help that I was wary about men his size.

Not that men with smaller statures were any safer.

I automatically gripped my hands together without conscious thought.

I had to focus on the present. And the present was something I should be proud of.

I was really enjoying the peace and quiet now.

I shivered as the dark memory threatened to surface and focused back on my reality.

I didn't know Braxton well, considering I taught sixth-grade choir, and this was my first year of teaching at Sacramento Public Middle School.

"Please pick that up."

We were in the middle of a crowded hallway. The kids had more energy now because it was almost time for school to be let out.

He nodded and picked up the paper before turning around, shooting me a sheepish smile that was quite charming on his face, and walking off, catching up with his friends at the end of the hallway.

He was popular in school.

Not only with the boys, but with the girls as well. And the last thing any of the teachers needed on any day was to hear from another adolescent girl just how "cute" Braxton was and how they wanted him to give them their first kiss.

That was a regular occurrence for me each morning before my class started, and I could get the kids under control.

I smiled a little.

Middle-schoolers were cute, in a very awkward kind of way.

Middle school was a unique time, and I had almost

forgotten how it was for me until I came here and interacted with these little kids.

I could hear Braxton's playful laugh even after he turned the corner. He was loud and drew attention wherever he went.

For now, it was because of his personality and likability. I had no doubt that things would be different years down the road when he would be known as more than Dominic Madden's second son.

Braxton was a wild little thing—or not so little. He already towered over the eighth graders, and I had no doubt he would be as tall as his father once he got older.

But if the gossip in this school was anything to go by, Braxton was considered tame compared to his older brother, Kai, who had just graduated from college last year.

Rumor had it that Kai had pledged to be a member of the King's Men and was set to inherit his father's criminal enterprise.

I tried not to pay too much attention to it, but the King's Men MC was an exciting topic around here. They were sometimes talked about on the local news as well, when they decided to set up some charity event, or if something terrible but unexplainable happened around the city.

I was sure that was nothing more than a front.

I couldn't really wrap my head around the fact that the parent of one of the students here would be involved in some sketchy shit.

Besides, the teachers in this school loved nothing more than gossip. It was like fodder for circus animals.

Frenzied and desperate.

I couldn't bring myself to join in the gossip, though that didn't stop it from getting to my ears. Not when the teachers all talked about it in the teacher's lounge.

I have been a sort of outcast for not joining in the *fun*.

And perhaps that was why, even after a full year of teaching music, I still hadn't made a single connection with anyone in this school.

Or perhaps the other teachers looked down on me because I taught music.

I wouldn't be teaching at all if my life had panned out the way I'd planned.

My hands shook, and I tightened my grip around the bottom of my shirt. I hadn't even realized I had been playing with it.

I automatically let it go.

The final bell rang, and as if by magic, all but a few students disappeared from the hallway, already outside and planning for their summer.

I sighed and headed back into the music room, looking at all the equipment I needed to put into storage, all the belongings I needed to gather, and everything I needed to clean before I could really enjoy my summer.

Being an adult sucked.

And there was no time for self-pity.

I quickly got to work.

By the time I got home, it was already six, and I was exhausted.

I trudged my way up to my small one-bedroom apartment on the third floor.

It wasn't exactly in the safest or most secure part of town, but it was within my budget, which was saying something considering how expensive California was, even if Sacramento was no Los Angeles.

Plus, I hadn't had any problems with my neighbors since I moved in.

I barely knew them. I had only seen some in passing as I left for work every morning, and that was the way I preferred it.

There also weren't any drug deals going down on the corner or a party in the building every weekend, so I found myself lucky to have found such a place.

It was my sanctuary.

It was everything I needed after moving away from everyone and everything I had ever known in my short twenty-five years of life back in Nevada.

I had been lost for a while, treading through life without a clear goal in mind and working odd jobs to keep myself busy. It wasn't until after I turned twenty-two that I realized I needed to do something with my life, so I decided to go to college and earn my teaching degree in music.

I was still new to the gig, but at least it provided some sense of purpose.

I unlocked the door and stepped into the quiet and almost-dark apartment.

I turned on the light and looked around.

It was a small but cute little place that I had really made my own, with a cool-tone theme of navy blue, maroon, and white.

I set my purse down on the small side table near the door and sat on the couch.

Some days, I didn't mind the silence.

In fact, I relished it.

I loved the peace, and I loved that I could be alone. Free from judgment.

But other times, the silence seemed to be too much, and I ended up not knowing what to do with myself.

Today was the last day of school, and everyone was out celebrating.

And I was stuck in this apartment.

I couldn't even remember how long it had been since I'd last talked to my parents, though it wasn't from their lack of trying.

Things used to be good between us before the incident.

We were a happy family, but perhaps we were too happy, because once tragedy struck, they didn't know how to handle it.

And I didn't know how to get back to the way things were —and what was more, I wasn't sure I wanted to. Not when the masks were off, and I wasn't sure I liked that side of my parents.

My gaze roamed over my small space.

These apartments had been renovated in recent years, so they followed more of the modern designs. I had an open floor plan, and I could see my apartment in its entirety, leading to the small kitchen in the back.

That wasn't what caught my attention, though.

Next to the kitchen was a small nook with a large square window that overlooked the side of the apartment building. The view wasn't great, but I liked the small, semi-private area, and it was also where I stashed my keyboard.

It was easily the most expensive thing I owned, having paid nearly four grand.

I had spent four summers in my teens working full time to save up for it and finally purchased it at the start of my senior year in high school.

It was one of my proudest achievements then, next to being accepted to Juilliard and receiving scholarships, covering about eighty percent of my tuition.

The rest would have been doable for my parents, and if not, I could have gotten a job while in school.

For a moment, it had been a wonderful fantasy I had revisited almost each night since receiving the news.

Then it was all shattered, everything taken away from me

—almost in a blink of an eye—and I didn't know what to do with myself after.

I didn't know how to pick myself back up, and it was a miracle I was even where I was today.

I looked down at my hands, at the slight tremors that always wracked me, at the thought of playing the keyboard.

I didn't even know why I took the piano keyboard with me to California. I should have left it in storage in Nevada—or, hell, perhaps sold it.

In the end, I couldn't bring myself to part with something I had worked so hard for, so now I had it on display in a corner, like a fucking memorial.

I stood up and slowly walked over to it, sitting down on the leather bench and looking down at the eighty-eight keys I had familiarized myself with since I was four, the same way I had familiarized myself with the back of my own hands.

I looked down at my hands.

Riddled with scars from all the broken skin and bones and a tedious thirteen-hour extensive surgery that hadn't been able to restore my ability to play like I used to.

Everyone had called me gifted.

My dream had been to play in Carnegie Hall.

I could still play.

With the help of physical therapy, bullheaded stubbornness, and sheer determination to prove everyone wrong, I could still play.

But not as fast, not for as long, and certainly not as well as I used to.

Not well enough to make a career out of it.

Not well enough to be the scholarship recipient for Julliard.

I couldn't even remember the last time I had sat down in front of a piano and lost myself to the music.

I pressed down on the A minor a few times before taking my hands away.

Taking in a deep breath, I slowly let my fingers drift along the keys before I hit the notes to "Moonlight Sonata," starting with the first movement, which I could play somewhat well.

By the start of the second movement, though, I could feel a slight twinge in my hands.

I forged on, sweat gathering on my forehead as I finished the second movement and transitioned into the third.

I hadn't been able to complete the third movement since the accident.

The notes were meant to be played faster.

The twinge I was experiencing before turned into more of an ache that was getting impossible to ignore until—

A sharp pain shot up from the wrist of my left hand and straight into the middle of my palm. I hit the wrong note.

I pulled my hands back. The silence that suddenly filled the space was hard to ignore.

I was breathing hard. The slight tremors in my hands weren't tremors, but shakes.

Tears of frustration burned my eyes, and I closed them, letting tears stream down my cheeks as I tried to control my anger and sadness.

Locked away.

I had many things to be grateful for in life.

Not being able to play piano wasn't the end of the world.

But sometimes, it felt like it.

2

DOMINIC

One of my brothers rode past me, patting his head to signal the bait had been taken, and I let out a loud fucking laugh that was drowned out by the noise of the motorcycle engine.

Fuck, yeah.

I revved up my engine and drove faster to keep up just as a cop car came into view in the side mirror.

The lights were flashing, and the poor fucker was trying to catch up.

He never would, not unless we slowed down, which we did. Marginally.

The California summer sun beat down on my skin, and I took in the open road spread out in front of me.

It was fucking freedom, and I couldn't imagine trading this in for anything else.

I revved the engine up again, shooting my bike forward before slowing down, teasing the cop in the back.

Up ahead, the road split, and I looked over at Axel, the huge fucker I was riding along with. He nodded when he caught my eye.

He was thinking the same thing I was.

When we got to the split, I took a sharp left, and he went right.

I was disappointed when the fucker chased Axel instead of me.

I slowed and turned my bike around, watching the empty road for a beat before the ground beneath me rumbled.

A huge semi passed by, and I recognized the faces in the truck.

They grinned and made obscene hand signals out the window, eliciting a small chuckle from me. I shook my head.

I had no doubt Axel had ditched the cop by now, and it would be best if I got out of there before backup arrived.

I hopped off my bike, dug into the small leather pack strapped to the side, and pulled out the license plate, quickly nailing it on before I drove away.

I didn't really have to be here, but fuck, did I miss the thrill and excitement of the chase. We'd distracted the cop to give our brothers in the truck enough time to cross the state line on its way to transport. There would be other brothers along the way to ensure the products would make it to their destination, making the King's Men MC very fucking rich, and Julian Levine, our biggest client, very fucking happy.

Julian Levine fucking owned the world.

Or, more accurately, he and three other men owned FHM Capital, one of the biggest monopolizing businesses in the world. They had their sticky little fingers in all sorts of depraved pies, most of which brought in an annual income of ten figures or more.

I wasn't fucking stupid.

The rich were corrupt, but it was still a shock when Levin approached me, wanting to collaborate with the King's Men.

We had a quiet and undisclosed partnership that was going on five years already, and I had brought the club to a state the fucking slimy former president couldn't even dream of.

It had been nearly a decade since I took the throne as president, and I had loyal men from all over the world who deferred to me to lead them, simply because they knew I would never lead them down the wrong path.

I rode back to the bar I owned in the corner of Sacramento.

It wasn't the most profitable business that I owned. Hell, it wasn't even that great to look at.

A small ugly building, really, but it was one of the first things I had bought when I first came into money, and it was the place where the local brothers liked to hang out and de-stress from all the shit in life.

Along with this bar, I also owned other bars throughout the city—far nicer than this one, mainly catering to the rich—various nightclubs, restaurants, and a few salons.

Some I owned with Micah and Roman Stone, my enforcer and my VP, and some I owned by myself.

Most of the businesses served as fronts to launder money made from the drug transportation business that I had set up with other men throughout the country. Men like Julian Levine and his three friends.

They resided in Chicago, so there should be nothing about these men and this organization to tie them to the King's Men.

It should make me feel better, not being connected to those fuckers, but they were some of the most powerful men in the world. If shit hit the fan, I was sure my club would be the first in the line of fire.

I shook away the thought and climbed off the bike, moving into the bar and hearing the noise, the laughter, the bustling of the employees, and the loud music.

It was like being at home.

Better than home, since my home was a perfect representation of the fucking American dream.

I lived in the nicer part of the city, something all my snobbish neighbors hated, I was sure. If it weren't for my boys, I wouldn't have fucking cared where I lived, but from the moment in the hospital when I first held my firstborn in my hands, I knew I would do anything to ensure they lived a better life than I did growing up.

Despite their neglectful mother, who left when Braxton—my youngest—was small, I made sure they knew they were loved.

I could only hope it was enough for them to know I loved them, but fuck if I didn't feel like I was fucking things up along the way.

My eyes scanned the entire bar, stopping when I found my oldest in the corner, nursing a beer.

Whereas Braxton took after his mom, Kai looked like me.

From his blue eyes to his stature to even his hot-headed attitude—all mine.

And my boy was an angry boy.

Shit happened.

Shit that I should have protected him from but I fucking didn't, and I would carry the weight of that guilt into my grave.

But now, my boy was no longer the loud, obnoxious kid he had once been, the kid who was sure the world was at his fingertips and that he simply needed to reach out and grab it.

In his place was a boy angry at everything and everyone.

A boy who didn't know what to do with all that anger, and a boy I fucking feared for.

We led dangerous lives.

And that danger could mean life or death in a blink of an eye.

I didn't want him to lose focus because his emotions clouded his judgment.

I rubbed my chest and walked over to him.

Kai looked up, and the corners of his lips lifted in the smallest of smiles.

That ache in my chest grew.

Fuck me, but I couldn't even remember the last time my kid had smiled fully at me.

"Hey, son," I said, patting his back.

"Hey." He eyed me carefully. "Did everything go okay?"

"Do you really have to ask?"

He rolled his eyes, but the small smile never left his face, and I could count that as a fucking good thing.

"Do me a favor?"

"Yeah, Dad?"

"I want you to find out everything you can about the men who head FHM Capital."

His eyes widened slightly in surprise. "The Four Horsemen of Chicago?"

I nodded.

"I thought they were allies of the King's Men."

"They are," I agreed. "Allies. Not friends. And even if they were friends, I'd still want to know as much about them as I can." The background check I had done on them when Julian Levine approached me only told me the bare minimum. But Kai had skills that even I couldn't dream of.

"I don't think they're easy to track."

"And that's why I don't trust anyone with this but you."

His blue eyes brightened a bit.

Things had been bad with Kai since the incident. For a moment, I'd thought I lost my son. It felt like I could no longer get through to him. But the more I involved him in my business—both legitimate and illegitimate—the more he seemed to focus.

It helped that I fucking created a genius.

Kai was a whiz when it came to computer shit.

I do all right myself, but hacking was on another level that went beyond my skill set.

My boy was fucking good.

"I'll see what I can do," he said, trying—and failing—to not sound too excited about the prospect.

"Just be careful. If you've heard of them, then you know who these men are. You know their connections, and I don't have to remind you what they can do."

"I always am. I'll be in and out before anyone even realizes I was there to begin with."

I smiled and ruffled his hair even though I would get a grumbling from him for messing it up. Sure enough, he pulled away and glared at me.

I laughed and grabbed his beer, chugging the whole thing, my eyes coming back to him, daring the kid to lip off.

He smartly kept his mouth shut.

He flagged the waitress for another beer.

I had to force myself to hold my tongue.

The kid was twenty-three.

Hell, I had done a lot worse than drinking in the middle of the day when I was his age.

My son hadn't been the same since that day in the fucking alleyway when my VP found him and his cousin, Jude, fighting for their lives after some bastards gunned them down.

Jude's body was taken, for who knew what kind of sick purpose, and three days after that, his hand was found in the Sacramento River.

"Have you been sleeping, son?"

He looked over at me but didn't say anything for a beat. The waitress came by and dropped off the beer, offering me a flirtatious smile that I returned.

Kai didn't miss it, but he knew I wouldn't do anything. I didn't fuck where I worked—or, in this case, where I owned and operated—and there was no attraction to the girl only a couple of years younger than my boy.

I might have been a young dad, having had Kai just a month after my fifteenth birthday, but I supposed an ambiguous line should be drawn somewhere in the sand.

I smiled a little at the thought.

My boundaries were fucking different from most people's, and I doubted anyone could really see that fine line I wouldn't cross.

Kai played the label on his beer before he looked at me again. "Some nights are better than others."

I nodded.

At least he was telling me the truth and not trying to cover all that dark shit with pretty words.

"Anything I can do to help?" I asked, my voice gruff.

He shot me his signature half-smile, and for a moment, it felt like I was transported back in time, looking into the mirror at myself.

Sometimes, I thought it was fucking harder that he looked so much like me.

I wanted nothing more than to ensure he got the best things life could offer. Better than me, and I didn't know how to offer that to him.

"I'm all right, Dad. If shit gets bad like before, I'll tell you."

I didn't say anything.

Unlike Braxton, who still somewhat clung to me, Kai was independent.

Had to grow up fast when you witnessed your cousin being murdered in front of you.

My fists clenched under the table, and he patted my shoulder.

I couldn't fucking believe he was trying to comfort me now.

I shook my head and reached over, squeezing his shoulder affectionately.

My old man was a piece of shit.

He didn't fucking know real emotions—unless that emotion was anger—and he barely showed any affection toward my baby sister and me.

I didn't want to be like that for my kids.

There might be certain… *qualities* that came with ruling one of the biggest one-percenter motorcycle clubs in the world, but I'd be damned if those qualities got in the way of my showing my kids just how fucking important they were to me.

The door to the bar opened and in came the two other men I trusted with the life of my kids.

The club life was all about brotherhood, and though I felt a sense of loyalty to all the men under my care, none of them was as close to me as these two brothers.

Roman took the lead and walked over to our table right away. His brother, Micah, followed close behind, protecting his back.

Always protecting his back.

I grinned at my VP and my enforcer.

Roman offered a cocky grin back while Micah grunted his greeting.

Both men took a seat, surrounding us.

The brothers looked like each other, both with tan complexions, brown hair, and—when Micah did smile—the same sarcastic tilt of their lips.

The only difference between the two was their eyes, from Micah's cold silver ones that showed the world the kind of monster that he was, to Roman's deep dark browns that hid the monster living beneath. Those who didn't know him well would say he was the more easygoing of the two brothers, and they might be right. Compared to Micah's cold and silent demeanor, Roman might be *easygoing*, but I wasn't stupid enough to not see the front that it was.

While Micah was meticulous in everything he did, making him perfect as the club's enforcer, Roman would kill you with a goddamn smile on his face.

Micah never bothered to hide anything. I thought he might enjoy showing his monster a bit too much. The man was easily the biggest motherfucker I had ever come in contact with. Taller than my six-foot-two height by three inches, he completed the unhinged, psychotic look with a brutal scar that ran down one side of his face and ended near the jugular.

I didn't know the story behind that scar, but I knew the stupid fucker who gifted that to him wasn't breathing anymore.

"How's Ryleigh?" I asked Roman.

He eyed me with an expression full of meaning. "Pregnant and hormonal."

I laughed, and Micah cracked a small smile. I could only imagine how that tiny little thing was torturing Roman with her mood swings and... *appetite.*

"Why don't you bring her around? I'm sure she's tired of looking at your ugly mug all the time."

He shot me a cocky smile. "She'll never tire of looking at me. And I'm sure spending time with you is the last thing she wants to do."

"Why is that? I'm nice."

I even smiled, baring my teeth.

Micah shook his head, and Roman rolled his eyes. Kai choked on his beer, and I patted his back.

"Oh, yeah," Roman said. "So nice. I'm sure she still

remembers you threatening to kill her the first time you met."

My smile widened. "I didn't outright threaten to kill the girl, and you know it. But we're good now."

Had to be, considering I invited the little Bambi to my house for Braxton's twelfth birthday not too long ago. I didn't invite a lot of people to my house. Very few people actually knew where I lived.

It was the way I wanted to keep it, considering my boys lived there—well, only Braxton, now that Kai moved to his own place a few months back.

I leaned back in my chair and looked across the bar.

The back table was reserved solely for us. It offered a full view of the bar and was closest to the hidden doorway beneath that only the people sitting at this table now knew about.

In case a quick getaway was necessary.

No one had dared poach on my territory yet, and I felt sorry for any sucker who wanted to try, but it was still better to be cautious than to pay for my arrogance later on.

This was only a small piece of my kingdom.

I fucking ruled California with an iron fist, a feat not many men could say they would be able to accomplish in their lifetime. And the useless piece of shit who'd ruled this section of the country was driven out by the King's Men when I moved the club from Las Vegas to California.

Las Vegas was the origin place of the King's Men.

It had been ruled by the slimy little fucker Brooks Tanner, also known as "Boomer" around the Strip.

He was rumored to have gotten his nickname because of his penchant for bombs.

Fucker was loud like one, too.

He ruled the club for nearly two decades, and things had been going well until the bastard got greedy and got into bed with all sorts of people, from politicians to corrupt officers and even the Italian mob in Chicago.

And he played double agent, trying to turn each of those powerful men against each other. Plus, fucker didn't just want the club to deal with drugs but skin.

I might be fucked in the head, but I didn't deal in skin.

I didn't deal in people.

I had been a new patch member in the club, and I could even tell shit was gonna blow up in our faces, and fast, if we kept on the trajectory Boomer was leading us down.

So I started an insurgent group.

Boomer was the first man I had ever killed.

I would have left the fucker alone if he hadn't threatened Kai, who had been no more than ten at that time.

I wasn't sure how much my boy remembered from our time in Las Vegas, but shit was bad for a while.

California was a way for us to start new.

To be better, stronger... *richer* than the old club, and I had more than accomplished that.

Beside me, Micah and Roman talked to Kai about the club, and I let the steady hum of their voices comfort me.

This was like being at home, with the classic rock music playing through the speaker, the bustle of the wait staff, and, hell, even the sticky floor beneath my black boots.

I wouldn't fucking trade this for anything in the world.

Micah caught the eye of the waitress, and he signaled for drinks.

It might be a little too early for drinking, but fuck, yeah, I wanted to join in on the fun.

I signaled for my own drink and leaned back again, taking in my kingdom.

3

EMMY

I WIPED THE SWEAT OFF MY FOREHEAD AS I EXITED THE CAR.

Even with the windows rolled down on the drive here, I was still hot.

Summer was officially upon us, and I should be excited about that, but very few things got me excited these days.

And this day was already ruined when I was woken up this morning by a phone call from my mom.

We talked for about five minutes, putting up the pretense that things were okay between us before slowly descending into an awkward silence that she finally ended by saying she had *stuff* to do.

It seemed that when I was growing up, my mom always had stuff to do that didn't involve being a mom.

The worst part about growing up wasn't the added responsibilities, nor was it the stress of adulthood, but the hard realization that your parents weren't the superheroes you had made them out to be in your head, but very flawed individuals who each year seemed to get more... *human.*

The realization that they had always been flawed people, only I didn't notice it until I was a grownup.

I didn't know when it was that I realized my parents were selfish people.

They weren't bad parents, per se. I didn't grow up abused, just slightly neglected. It still hurt to realize my parents had never really wanted to take on the role of parents in the first place, and I had been an inconvenience to them my whole life.

Until I finally had something to offer. To add value of my place in their lives. Too bad that had come to an abrupt end with the use of my own hands—and my music career.

I blinked against the blinding sun through my sunglasses and fixed my hair to make sure I was presentable before walking up to the two-story house that I would never be able to afford in my adult life, in one of the nicest parts of the city.

I rang the doorbell and there was some scuffling from inside just before the door opened to reveal a lady, probably in her mid-forties, wearing what could only be described as a housewife get-up.

Sleek brown hair came down to her collarbones and curved inward around a face with natural makeup that enhanced her features. Her clothes were impeccable and expensive.

She looked put together and happy.

I blinked up at her and forced a small smile onto my face.

"Hi, Mrs. Newman. I'm here for Freddy's piano lessons."

She offered a polite smile back. "Emmy. How nice to see you again. Please, come on in. Freddy is in the music room."

I nodded.

She always sounded pleasant, but with a note of condescension in her voice.

She moved out of the way for me to enter her beautiful home, and I went to the music room, trying not to let the weight on my shoulders show from the outside.

Despite the bad start in the morning, I had decided that today would not be the day I fell apart.

Exactly one hour later, Mrs. Newman came in to remind me the lesson was finished.

There was always a cold politeness that made me feel she might not like me very much. It wasn't really a problem whether she liked me, considering I only saw her once a week when I came to teach Freddy, and our interactions were always brief.

Still, I wondered why she didn't like me.

I patted Freddy on his little shoulder. "Good job today. I can see you've been practicing."

Freddy's chest puffed up in pride, and I wondered what his home life really was like outside of the weekly piano lessons.

He was a quiet, introspective boy.

It had taken him some time to warm up to me, but when he did, I could see the way he bloomed from my praises and compliments.

He seemed to love these music lessons, which was good because there was nothing worse than teaching music to kids who only did it because their parents made them.

I quickly gathered up my stuff, said my goodbyes, and walked out the door.

The heat seemed to have magnified tenfold since an hour ago, and I couldn't remember it being so hot in California this early in the year before.

I slung my backpack up over one shoulder and trudged to my car, not looking forward to getting in. It was probably roasting since I parked it directly in the sun. I opened the rear door and stashed my stuff before climbing in and starting the car, rolling down all the windows immediately.

I stared ahead of me, debating what I should do now that the only thing I had planned for the day was done when a boy zipped past me on his bike.

I followed him with my gaze, swearing that the boy looked a hell of a lot like one of my students.

It wouldn't be surprising. I lived in the same neighborhood as the school district. Freddy was an exception—he didn't go to my school because his parents wanted him to go to another private school, about forty minutes away. I heard the school had an amazing music program, and it was the first place I applied.

I obviously wasn't hired.

I put the car into drive and took off.

It wasn't until I was about a block away from Freddy's house that I found the boy on the bike once more, and this time, I was sure he was a student from school.

It was Braxton Madden.

He was hard to miss, not with his size and unruly chestnut hair.

There was a sudden noise at the rear of my car. I hit the brakes hard and let out a small scream.

Braxton looked behind him, first at my car, then further back. His eyes widened in surprise and—my blood ran cold —*fear*. He pedaled faster on his bike, away from me.

I looked in the rearview mirror, everything in me freezing, when I caught sight of a nondescript black car heading toward us—toward Braxton—with the passenger side window opened and a mean-looking man hanging out of it, holding a gun.

Fuck, the man had a gun!

For a moment, it seemed time had come to a standstill.

I had never even seen a gun in real life, much less held

one, and here one was, in the palm of a man with a determined look that told me he was out for the kill.

I blinked.

I didn't think.

I stepped on the gas and drove toward Braxton, stopping when I was slightly ahead of him.

I reached over and opened the passenger door.

"Get in!" I screamed.

Braxton hesitated for a brief second, and I wanted to scream at him because I could see the men eating the distance between us. Finally, he climbed off his bike, threw it off to the side, and rushed into my car.

I was driving off before he even had the door closed all the way. Braxton looked behind us at the car.

Another loud bang and something hit my car. I didn't need to see it to know it was a bullet.

My grip on the steering wheel tightened, and I didn't dare take my eyes off the road. "Seat belt!"

"Ms. Wilde—"

"Seat. Belt."

He clipped it on, and I zig-zagged on the street, trying to avoid getting hit.

All it would take was for them to blow out my back tire, and we would be dead.

"Do you know who those men are?" I asked.

From the corner of my eye, I saw him shake his head. "No. Probably someone who hates my dad."

Fuck.

Of course that would be the case.

"Do you live around here?" I asked.

"No. Alvin lives here."

I nodded. Alvin was a boy in the eighth grade.

I had seen them hanging out with each other a few times.

Those men had followed a twelve-year-old to his friend's house to—what?

Kill him?

Take him and threaten Dominic?

A small sound of panic bubbled up in my throat, and Braxton shot me a weird look as I drove out of the neighborhood.

The black car took a few seconds to appear behind me, but when it did, they gunned it, catching up to us. It wouldn't be long before they caught up, and then what?

What the fuck could I do?

My entire body shook from fear, and I looked over at Braxton to find he wasn't doing much better than me.

The boy was just that.

A boy.

No matter how arrogant he acted in school, he was only a kid, and I needed to protect this kid, no matter what.

But could I?

I looked up ahead at the red light, and when I found no cars coming down on the opposite side of the street, I made an illegal U-turn.

I drove past the black car on the other side, a concrete block separating us, and got a good look at the driver for the first time.

He had gray hair, tan skin, a five o'clock shadow that surrounded the scowl of his lips, and dark eyes that glinted in the sunlight.

Our eyes met, and it took everything in me not to throw up right then and there. The anger in his eyes would have been enough to bring me to my knees.

Even with his body partially hidden by the car, I had no doubt he was a big man.

He said something to me that I didn't quite catch, and I didn't care to.

I sped up and looked behind to find ongoing cars passing through and stopping the black car from following us right away.

Beside me, Braxton laughed.

I shook my head. "Don't celebrate too early. They haven't given up just yet."

Sure enough, the black car was able to make the U-turn and was heading right for us.

I moved in and out between lanes, trying to put as many cars between us as possible.

Somewhere to my left, a car honked at us, and Braxton gripped his seat belt, looking behind him with a fearful expression on his face.

What do we do?

What do I do?

No matter who Braxton's father might be, I was sure he wasn't used to dealing with things like this.

"Do you have your phone?" I asked.

He looked down at his lap. "No. It's strapped to my bike. I didn't think to grab it. I'm sorry."

I took a deep breath. "Hey, it's okay. Do you remember your dad's number?"

The bottom of his lip jutted out, and I thought I caught a hint of shimmer in them just as he shook his head.

I shot him a small smile I didn't exactly feel and looked at the gas gauge.

We were about to run into another problem.

I had been waiting until the last minute to get gas because of how expensive it was, and I didn't have enough money in my savings account. We were going to run out of gas soon.

The black car was only three cars behind us now.

How the fuck did they catch up so quickly?

My heart felt like it was just seconds away from clawing its way out of my throat, and I didn't know what to do.

How could this possibly be my reality at this very moment?

It felt like I was supposed to wake up any second now from a really bad dream.

It was, wasn't it?

The car in front of me slammed on its brakes for minor traffic, and my car jolted as I also suddenly braked. I looked back at the black car as I switched lanes once more and took the exit that would take us out to the highway.

Hopefully, we wouldn't run into any traffic there.

The man in the passenger seat hung out the window. "Get down!" I yelled at Braxton as I braced myself for the hit, and sure enough, a loud bang sounded from the side of my car.

Braxton let out a small scream. He didn't get down like I asked.

I reached over to reassure him that everything would be okay as I made the sharp turn and merged onto the ramp leading down to the highway, the black car following close behind.

I thanked my lucky stars that there didn't seem to be a lot of congestion on the streets.

I hoped Braxton couldn't see the way my hands shook.

The black car steadily followed us, but at least the man on the passenger side was back inside the car and was no longer shooting at us.

"Okay?"

Braxton nodded.

"Just hold on, okay? I won't let anything happen to you."

How I would be able to uphold that promise, I didn't know.

But I would not let anything happen to him.

No matter what.

I switched over three lanes to the fast lane, and the black

car followed like I knew he would. I looked to the side, and when I found an opening, I switched all the way back to the exit lane and took the first exit I came by.

I looked in the rearview mirror again. The black car tried to follow but couldn't. Horns rang out behind us, and I let out a small laugh.

Braxton smiled a little.

"Not out of the woods yet. Do you know how to get to your dad from here?" I asked.

He shook his head. "He owns a bar downtown that he likes to go to, but I've only been there two times before. I don't remember where it is, exactly."

I could tell from the tone of his voice he was moments away from losing it.

"It's okay. You know how to get to your house, though, right?"

He nodded.

"Okay. We just need to find a hiding place first and wait until they stop chasing us. Then I'll drive you home, and we'll try to contact your dad from there, okay?"

Braxton nodded.

"We need to call the cops—" I started, but Braxton shook his head sharply.

"No cops."

"Braxton—"

"You call the cops, and you'll be on the record. They'll know who you are and that you helped me. You'll be in danger."

"They can help us—"

He laughed. "No. They can't."

Since when were twelve-year-old so distrustful of the authorities?

"They won't be able to do anything about this. Those men

will either catch us before the cops show up, or we'll escape. But you call the cops, then we'll be involving a lot of people we don't want."

What the fuck?

Since when he sounded so mature?

And not call the cops?

"Please," he said, "Trust me."

I looked at him briefly before turning back to the road, torn.

Fuck.

"Ms. Wilde."

I nodded. "Okay. No cops. But we better get away from them."

He shot me a small smile and nodded. "Okay."

I closed my eyes and prayed I was making the right decision.

I found a small rural street, and we pulled onto it.

My car beeped, and the gas light went on.

Braxton looked at me.

Yeah. We were about to be stranded.

I looked around.

To my right was an open field of weeds.

We wouldn't be safe there.

To the left was a little better. It looked like some small, enclosed woods, with hundreds of trees lining closely to each other that should provide some coverage.

I looked at Braxton before I drove the car further into the side. There was a small hole there, the ground had crack opened for some reason, and the nose of the car touched the end of the hole. I winced, thinking about how much money this would cost me to fix once this was all over.

If we made it out of this alive, that was.

"Come on," I said. "We have to hide."

"Are you sure that's such a good idea?"

No.

"Yeah. This car is going to run out of gas soon. We don't want to be near those men when that happens. At least, this way, we will find someplace to hide."

I reached for my backpack, which had my purse and phone, and got out of the car. Braxton followed suit.

We headed toward the small woods, and Braxton grabbed hold of my hand.

I tightened my grip around his and drew him closer to me. I was sure he wouldn't want to be caught dead holding hands with the music teacher from his school, but he needed comfort from me now, and the truth was, I needed it just as much.

I didn't think I breathed properly until we got inside the safe covering of the trees, and even still, we kept going, trying to be fast but quiet at the same time. I didn't know how long it would take those men to find my car and start following us, but I would take advantage of this small lead we finally had.

We stopped when an old farmhouse came into view.

The roof on the left looked moments away from caving in. It appeared to be just waiting for the right weather to make it so. The paint had long peeled away from the wood, and one door looked like it was falling off on the hinges at the top.

It was abandoned, as far as I could tell.

Braxton and I looked at each other, and we made our way into the farmhouse.

I quickly closed the double doors carefully.

I was right.

It was close to falling off from the nail completely. I closed the latch and put up the bar that would keep the door locked from the inside. I doubted this would keep the men out should they find this farmhouse, but it would warn us.

I found a ladder on the side leading up to the small upper deck and, wordlessly, tested it to see if it could hold my weight.

Braxton looked like he weighed as much as me, if not a few pounds heavier. I indicated with my hand.

"Come on, Braxton. Climb up. We have to hide."

He bit his lip in hesitation.

I grabbed his shoulders and looked him in the eyes.

"You don't know me very well, but can you trust me? I promise I won't let anything happen to you, but I need you to trust me and do as I say. Can you do that?"

His bottom lip trembled, and I fought against the urge to cry. It wouldn't do us any good if I broke down, and right now, I needed to be the strong one out of the two of us.

He nodded.

I offered a small smile.

"Climb up, Braxton. I will be right behind you. I promise."

His throat bobbed from a hard swallow, and he turned and climbed up the ladder.

I waited until he was fully at the top before I climbed up, too, finding a somewhat sturdy wooden platform filled with hay and dust.

I didn't give myself time to think when I reached down and pulled the ladder up with us. I rested it against the wall and moved to the window, peeking out from the side.

Everything seemed quiet right now.

"We're just going to stay here for the night, okay?"

I pulled my phone out and looked at the service bars.

There were none.

It was just as well because, at this point, I didn't even know who I would call.

I had no one in California.

Braxton watched me silently from his spot in the corner. I looked over at him. "We're going to be okay."

"Okay," he responded quietly.

He took his shaky hands into his lap, and I watched him for a beat before I sat back against the wall.

"Tell me, do you have any plans for the summer?"

He shot me a look like he thought I was crazy for even talking about summer plans in this situation.

I just looked at him expectantly.

He let out a small sigh. "I'm not sure. Just play video games with Alvin, I guess."

"Your family isn't taking any vacations?"

He shook his head. "No. Dad's job doesn't really give him a lot of free time."

I didn't say anything right away. I didn't know how much Braxton knew about his father's job, but with the way he didn't seem all that surprised that those men were targeting him because of his dad must say something.

"Well, if you did have the chance, where would you like to go?" I asked.

"New Zealand."

I blinked before a small smile overtook my face. "Why New Zealand?"

"My aunt lives there," he said quietly.

"Are you close with her?"

"Used to be. We haven't talked in a while since… never mind."

I nodded but didn't pry. Obviously, that was a sensitive topic.

I looked back out the window, and when there was no movement from the outside, I said, "Well, I've heard nothing but great things about New Zealand. I might want to go there also someday."

"Why don't you go there this summer?" he asked, smiling a little.

I smiled as well. "Ah, it's an expensive trip."

"Oh."

I didn't think Braxton ever had to deal with money—or lack of it. I was sure the notorious motorcycle club brought in a lot of money each year—illegal and otherwise.

It was common knowledge that Dominic owned a lot of the businesses in Sacramento.

"Someday, okay?" I said. "We'll both get our chance to see that country. Yeah?"

His shoulders relaxed a little, and he moved closer to me. I wrapped my arms around his shoulders and held him.

"Yeah," he said with a sigh.

Two hours passed, and I thought we might be safe, but then I saw movement from the corner of my eye. I looked out the window, my heart thudding heavily in my chest, when I saw one of the men from the car heading this way.

Braxton was lying against the stack of hay, having fallen asleep about an hour ago after he played the limited games I did have on my phone.

I grabbed his legs and shook him awake. His eyes widened as I held a finger against my lips, shaking my head.

I moved back against the wooden deck and pushed us against the wall as the man started to push on the door from outside.

I covered my mouth as Braxton buried his face in my shoulder, and I held him tightly against me as another bang came from the door.

My body shook, and I closed my eyes, praying they wouldn't see us.

Braxton jumped when the lock finally gave way, and the doors were pushed open.

I didn't dare look down at the man, but I could hear some scuffling as the man walked around the open space.

I tensed when I thought I heard him get close to the side leading up to the platform where we were, but he would have a pretty hard time without the ladder. Not that it would stop him if he knew we were hiding up here.

Braxton peeked up at me, the blood draining from his face.

I held him tighter against me as the man's phone rang.

He answered it right away.

"Yeah?"

His voice was deep and unpleasant, with a slight New Jersey accent.

"No, they're not here.... Are you sure?... We can't lose the boy.... He'll have our head if we come back empty-handed. Do you know who that bitch with him is? Where the fuck did she come from? Yeah.... Okay, I'll meet you there."

I didn't know who the *he* was that this man was talking about, but it was obvious these men weren't in charge. No, they were just the retrieval.

I looked back at Braxton, hating what might have happened to him if I didn't leave Freddy's house when I did or what would have happened had I called off today's lesson like I had wanted to do this morning.

We didn't say anything as the man walked out the door, and I made Braxton stay where he was as I looked back out the window. The man was walking away from the house.

My shoulders sagged in relief, and had I been standing up, I might have fallen right here.

"He's gone," I said to Braxton.

"What are we going to do now?"

I didn't answer right away.

"Why don't we wait until midnight to leave? By that time, I'm sure they'll have given up searching for us, probably thinking you're safe back home. We'll find a place with some signal, and I'll call for a ride to get us. Yeah?"

He nodded. "Okay."

I smiled a little and leaned back against the wall, getting comfortable. We were at least several hours away from the sunset, then a few more until midnight.

We had a long way to go.

4

DOMINIC

MY FIST SLAMMED ON THE WOODEN TABLE, CAUSING THE MEN standing in a line before me to jump.

"Where. The. Fuck. Is my son?"

The sun had set, and Braxton wasn't safe at home, where he was supposed to be.

My boy was missing, and none of the useless fucks in front of me could tell me where the fuck he was.

My fists clenched, and I wanted to destroy the entire bar.

Fuck that.

I wanted to burn down the entire world to find him, starting with this city.

No one would be saved.

It would be fucking Armageddon until I had Braxton safely back by my side, I vowed it.

My eyes moved over each of the men, stopping on fucking Trent, the man I had tasked with escorting Braxton.

He startled when I stood and walked over to him, grabbing the collar of his shirt and dragging him close until our noses touched.

"If anything happens to my son, I'll make you fucking pay with your life."

"Prez, I'm—"

He didn't get the chance to say anymore.

I pushed him away until the fucker landed on his ass on the floor. I nodded to the men nearby to take him out of my sight, and I turned back to the table where Kai sat with his laptop in front of him. "Dad?"

"Found him?" I asked.

"His cell phone is about a block away from Alvin's house. I've already sent men out to search, but I think maybe he dropped his phone there."

The last part of his sentence was said quietly, and I was sure he was thinking the same thing I was. Did Braxton drop his cell phone because he was careless or because someone grabbed him and he dropped it in his struggle?

"His tracker?"

"I'm still trying to pin the location. I think he might be somewhere with a low signal because I can't get a good read on it."

"What about the last known location of the tracker?"

All of Braxton's shoes had a tracker hidden inside them.

Every single fucking pair.

With what I did, I needed to make sure he was well-protected, and that I was aware of his location at all times. Fuck lot of good that was doing now. I didn't know where he was and how that place could interfere with the signal.

Something pinged in Kai's computer, and he stood. "Got it! South of here, miles off Highway 99."

I grabbed my keys from the table. "Let's go. You take the lead, and we'll follow close behind."

About twenty minutes into the trip, I found something off the side of the road that shouldn't be there.

I signaled for the men behind me to pull over and honk at Kai before I turned my bike to the side and hopped off.

Kai came up to me moments later, and we looked down at the small red car parked off to the side, the tip of the front crashing down near the small dip—almost as if someone wanted to hide the car from view.

One side of the car was riddled with bullet holes.

All four doors were open, and it looked like someone had ransacked the car, looking for something.

I shared a look with Kai.

"Take a picture of the plate and have Roman look into it."

Kai nodded and did as I asked.

Both Roman and Micah were out talking to the local gangs to see if any of them knew anything or why the fuck my son was targeted.

I closed my eyes and took a deep breath.

Fuck, I knew why Braxton was targeted. Because of me.

But he was…

Fuck, he was just a child. My child. And my child was fucking defenseless.

And I was gonna kill whoever dared put a hand on him.

I tried not to think about how scared he was right now.

Kai turned to me and pointed to the area surrounded by tall trees. "Just about half a mile from here to there is where the tracker was last pinged," he said quietly.

An abandoned, ransacked red car, the fucking woods, and my boy hidden somewhere in those trees.

This shit didn't make sense.

I looked back at the men. Four, plus Kai and me.

"Have Axel and Blade stay here and keep watch. Everyone else, follow me."

We made the short trek across the field, reaching the edge of the woods.

I stopped and listened in carefully, but when there was no noise that seemed out of place, we walked on. I kept Kai slightly behind me, something I was sure he hated.

Kai might not be as defenseless as Braxton, but he was still mine to protect.

My skin itched even having him here with me, moving into a possible danger I didn't know how to prepare for.

The gun strapped on the back of my waistband burned through my skin, but I didn't reach for it.

Not yet.

We were quiet as we searched, not even knowing which direction to take.

Something flashed in the corner of my eye, and I placed a hand on Kai's chest to stop him from walking, letting my eyes adjust to my surroundings.

It was nearly pitch-black right now. The only light came from the full moon above, but even that wasn't enough.

"Right there," I said, pointing to a small flash of light through the top window of what looked like an abandoned farmhouse.

The light quickly shut off seconds later, but I saw what I saw.

Someone was in there.

Anticipation strummed along my skin as we quickly and quietly made our way over to it.

I signaled for the men to spread out and covered any possible exit, and Kai and I walked through the double doors.

One of the doors was almost falling off the hinges, and a broken lock hung off it in the middle as if someone had knocked it off.

We moved through the dark, and I approached a wall

leading up to a small platform just at the top of the farmhouse.

Kai didn't need me to say anything as he laced his fingers together and hoisted me up.

I quickly climbed up, bracing myself for whatever I might find. There was a chance there was someone here who could do a lot of damage to me with a surprise attack.

But I wasn't fucking easy to kill.

A scuffling came through the dark, then some movements.

It took a moment for me to make out the scene.

Two shadows sat huddled together in the corner.

One tiny shadow, and one not so tiny.

They flinched when I moved, and I doubted they were any match for me.

Slowly, I pulled out my phone and turned on the flashlight, pointing it at them.

I got a good look at two sets of wide eyes, one familiar one that sent relief straight to my heart, and one unfamiliar one—

The girl—*woman*, perhaps—jumped on me with a scream.

Jesus, fuck.

"Get away from us!" the little wildcat screamed.

I wrapped my arms around her flailing body and held her tightly against me. "I'm not gonna hurt you, girl, but you need to calm down before you hurt yourself."

She struggled more in my grasp until a small voice spoke. "D-Dad?"

Fuck me, but it was so good to hear his voice. "Braxton." I exhaled. "Are you hurt?"

He didn't say anything for a moment. Then, "No."

The girl was no longer moving, just breathing heavily against me. Slowly, I let her go, and she quickly backed off to the small corner, and the space she left was filled when Braxton jumped into my arms.

Fuck.

If I were an emotional man, I might have fucking broken down and cried.

I buried my face in my son's neck and held him close as his tears wet my shirt.

Every single one was like a fucking whip to my skin.

"It's okay, buddy. I got you," I said to him. "I got you, and I won't fucking let anyone hurt you, okay? You're safe, I promise. Dad's here, and you're safe."

He let out a small whimper that fucking killed me on the inside.

"T-they came after me. They were chasing me, and I didn't know what to do," he said into my chest.

My muscles tensed. "Who?" I asked quietly. My eyes moved over to the girl. It was too dark, but I was sure she hadn't moved since Braxton jumped into my arms.

"I don't know," he said, his voice thick with tears. I closed my eyes. "They had a gun," he added.

"It's okay," I said. "You're safe now."

I looked around the small deck.

I didn't know how long they had been here or how this girl was involved, but I would find out soon.

"How the hell did you get up here?"

"There's, uh, there's a ladder," the girl said, speaking up for the first time. I couldn't tell what she was thinking or feeling based on the tone of her voice, and it was too dark to see.

I let Braxton go, but he reached for me.

I paused for a moment.

Fuck me, but I was gonna skin whoever the fuck was responsible alive for putting this fear in my son.

My boys were nothing if not independent. Fucking fearless, too.

And now Braxton was clinging to me like he was scared something bad might happen to him if I wasn't close by.

My fists clenched, and I forced the anger from my voice, not wanting to scare him. "It's okay. I'm just letting Kai know."

"Kai's here?" Braxton asked.

I patted his head in answer. Kai was his favorite person in the world. I was sure he would feel comforted to know both his dad and brother were with him.

I leaned over. "Kai?"

"Yeah, Dad? Is he okay?"

"Yes. I need you to go outside and look for the breaker box. Or a backup generator. See if that still works."

Kai didn't say anything for a moment, but the relief was clear in his voice when he finally responded with a small, "Yeah."

I saw the ladder against the wall. I moved Braxton back to the girl and set the ladder back on the floor. "I'm gonna go down first. You guys follow, okay?"

I sensed some movement from them, but they didn't really say anything. Not that I blamed them.

Fuck.

I didn't know what they had been through—what my boy had been through—before we found them.

There was a small click from somewhere outside, and the lights came on just as my feet touched the ground.

I blinked and watched the two small figures climb down as my men walked in.

I examined Braxton, trying to assess any injuries he might have, but he looked fine. At least, from what I could see right now. Just a little shaken up. The rest would have to wait until we got home, and I asked him myself.

I closed my eyes briefly, trying to calm myself down and not give in to the urge to hold him close to me for the rest of the night.

My gaze moved to the woman who was with him. I didn't know what her role was in this whole thing or how she came to be with him right now, hiding out in an abandoned farmhouse, but I would find out soon enough.

I took in her back as she climbed down the ladder after Braxton.

She was a tiny little thing.

My first assessment was right.

Maybe an inch or two shorter than Braxton, and my boy might be the tallest in his class, but he hadn't hit his growth spurt yet, coming in only at five foot five inches. She was probably five feet four, tops.

I would tower over the little wildcat.

And she was all hair. Thick, dark, beautiful hair.

Braxton jumped to the ground from the last step and turned, rushing over to me.

I hugged him, letting my hand come down to his shoulder blades, feeling his solid form against me.

Fuck.

He was here.

He tightened his arms around me as Kai came into my line of vision, his eyes focused intently on his little brother as if he was afraid to look away.

I knew the feeling.

I patted Braxton's head and directed him toward Kai, whose arms were already open.

I might not be an emotional man, but I made sure always to show my kids how important they were to me, how much I fucking loved them. I'd hoped they would grow up to be men who weren't afraid of their emotions either.

I took a deep breath and turned to the girl, who was now on the ground, facing me. My breath caught.

Fuck. Me.

Who the fuck was this?

I felt blood roar in my ear, drowning out everything and anything.

She was tiny in every way. My two hands could span the entirety of her small back and then some.

She had small, delicate shoulders that were on display from the fitted black t-shirt, and dark gray jeans that hugged her legs.

There was something fragile about the girl that made me both want to be careful with her *and* test her limits. See how far I could push her without breaking her.

Her big hazel eyes stared up at me, and I noticed one of them was darker than the other, a small face that only made her eyes stand out even more, and that mass of dark hair that came down past perky, small tits that I would be able to cover completely with my own hands.

But there was something untouchable about her.

Not in a cold way, but in an innocent way.

In a way that told men like me that we weren't deserving of touching such sweetness.

"Who are you?" I asked quietly.

Her breath caught, and I noticed a hint of fear in her eyes.

"M-my name is Emmy Wilde. I, uh, I teach music at Braxton's school."

The music teacher?

She offered a small smile, but it looked more like a grimace, and she tucked her hands in her arms. I didn't miss the slight shake to them.

"Tell me what the fuck is going on," I growled, moving closer to the teacher.

Her eyes widened, and she took half a step back before she thought better of it.

"Dad, maybe we should head back home before we do any interrogating," Kai said.

I looked at my boys before turning back to the teacher, impatience making me want to shake the answers out of her.

But fuck, Kai was right.

This wasn't the place, and I didn't know if the fuckheads that came after Braxton were still around. I didn't shy away from a fight, but I didn't want to risk Braxton—and now, the teacher.

I nodded and took hold of the teacher's arm.

"Wait," she said. "What are you doing?"

"What does it look like I'm doing, wildcat? I'm taking you home with me."

She gasped in outrage, and I resisted the urge to smile. Fuck, but I didn't think I would be in the mood to smile right now.

"You can't do that!"

I nodded. "Yes, I can."

"Dad," came Kai's tight voice.

"Take Braxton home and watch him. I'll catch you up as soon as I can."

Kai looked like he was about to argue but changed his mind at the last moment, giving me a nod and leading Braxton away. He knew better than to argue with me in front of my men.

Braxton looked at me, and I shot him a reassuring smile. He relaxed a little, his eyes trailing over to the teacher until Kai took him out of there.

I waited until my boys were out of sight before I turned back to the little wildcat. Before she could say anything else, I hauled her up over my shoulders, ignoring her protest.

She struggled a bit in my arms, and I tightened my hold.

"Stop moving. I don't want to drop you," I said, pressing my hand down on her thigh and curving my fingers on the inside of her leg.

She froze, and I took advantage of her momentary distraction to walk back to my bike.

"I saved your son," she said quietly.

I nodded, even if she couldn't see me.

I might not know what was going on, but it was clear she'd tried to attack me to keep Braxton safe, despite knowing she wasn't a match for me.

Hell, I didn't think she was a match for anyone.

"You did. And I'm returning the favor."

"What the hell is that supposed to mean?"

I didn't answer her.

By the time we got back to my bike, Kai and Braxton had already left. Axel and Blade were still there, and they watched as I carried the little wildcat over to my bike and set her down on her feet.

I had an extra helmet hanging on the helmet lock on the back of the bike. It was meant for Braxton, but Kai had an extra helmet hooked on his bike as well.

This would hopefully fit the little wildcat.

I helped her put it on, feeling her eyes on me the entire time, and not knowing why the fuck my skin was buzzing from awareness from that.

I ignored it, hooked the helmet on, then wrapped my arms around her waist before she could even think about running away. She tensed in my arms. Even without being able to see her face clearly, I could tell she was scared of me.

Nothing I could do about that.

Nothing I could say that would help.

I was a big fucker.

And I was sure the King's Men MC was talked about in

that school. No doubt she'd heard about the more *unsavory* parts of the club… the unsavory parts about me.

"You're going to get on my bike, and you're not going to do anything stupid, got me? It's dark, and I don't feel like chasing you around. And if you make me, you won't like it when I catch you. Yeah?"

She didn't answer me right away. I could hear her breathing harshly, could feel the movements of her chest before she let out a small, "Yeah."

I grunted in response and hopped on the bike, pulling her up behind me.

She kept as much distance as she could between us, and I let out a small sound of annoyance before grabbing her hands and sliding her toward me until her front was plastered against my back. I wrapped her arms around me and said, "If you don't hold on tight, you will fall off."

"What about my car?" she asked. We both turned to it.

I figured that little red piece of shit was hers. It would explain how they got here.

And her car *was* that. A piece of shit. It didn't look like it would be worth anything.

I looked at Axel and Blade and pointed at the car.

They nodded in understanding.

"It's being taken care of," I said.

"But—"

I started the engine to drown out her voice, smiling a little when I felt her curl her hands on my chest in frustration.

Without another word, I took off on my bike, not looking behind to see if anyone was following us.

5

EMMY

I CLOSED MY EYES AS DOMINIC SPED THROUGH THE STREETS. The roar of the engine pounded in my ears, giving me a headache.

Some people describe riding a motorcycle as thrilling. *Free.*

Hard to feel any of those things when I was being abducted by the president of the notorious King's Men MC.

How was this the way my night was turning?

Whatever I imagined Dominic's reaction would be when I finally got Braxton home, this wasn't it.

I had imagined getting Braxton home safely and just leaving this night behind me.

I didn't think Dominic would find us so soon or that he would take me somewhere to *question* me. And then what?

What was going to happen after this? Would he let me go?

I tightened my arms around him without thinking when I felt him take an unexpected turn before I forced myself to relax my grip marginally.

There was just something so intimate about riding on the back of a bike.

I had never even seen a motorcycle up close, much less ridden one, and now I was in the back, my entire front pressed against him.

There was nothing I could do to put any space between us.

I jolted and opened my eyes when we came to the side of a huge building.

This was… not what I was expecting.

I didn't know where I'd thought he was taking me, but a huge fancy hotel was not it.

I couldn't see the hotel's name and realized too late that I should have kept my eyes open. I let my guard down, and now we were in a strange place.

I swallowed when he hopped off the bike and tapped out something on his phone.

I was debating whether I should try to make a run for it when the side door suddenly opened, making me jump.

Dominic glanced over at me briefly before looking back at the older man holding the door open for us.

Dominic reached over and assisted me off the bike. I struggled a bit until he squeezed my side and leaned down, whispering in my ear, "Don't cause a scene, wildcat. There are plenty of ways I can subdue you that the men who work here won't even bat an eye at. And with the way I'm feeling right now, you don't want to piss me off."

My bottom lip trembled, and I did something I hadn't done since the moment Dominic appeared on the deck. I begged.

"Please let me go. I had nothing to do with Braxton being shot at. I was trying to save him."

He didn't respond to me. I got the feeling he wasn't surprised that Braxton and I were shot at.

Then I remembered the bullet holes in my car. He probably guessed it.

I blinked and looked away.

When I didn't say anything, he led me to the door, his grip on my waist never loosened. I had no choice. Judging by the older man's expression watching us, I knew Dominic was right.

No one would come to my aid.

I blinked away the burning sensation in my eyes, trying hard not to cry.

I didn't want to appear weak.

The man pressed something into Dominic's hand—a key card—and Dominic handed over the keys to his bike.

Then we walked inside, taking the back way.

We ran into no one and took the service elevator to the fifth floor.

The hallway was empty when the elevator doors opened, and Dominic wasted no time leading me into the room. The tremors I had felt all day never really left, and they were making themselves known to me the closer we got to the door.

I didn't know what to do.

I struggled and dug my heels into the carpeted floor, and Dominic let out a frustrated growl and carried me up in his arms.

"No!" I screamed, but it was too late.

We were already inside the room.

He pushed the door closed behind us and turned on the light, setting me on my feet.

I took a small step back before I realized I was nearing the bed and stopped myself.

He pinched the bridge of his nose, walked over to the mini fridge without saying anything, and took out a bunch of small alcohol bottles.

He quickly downed one, turned to me, and opened a

second one, drinking all that before throwing both bottles in the trash.

I swallowed.

"Tell me," he demanded softly. I could hear the power in his voice.

I licked my suddenly dry lips and opened my mouth, but nothing came out.

I blinked at him.

He grabbed one of the bottles, opened it, and handed it to me.

Hesitantly, I grabbed it from his hands. It had looked tiny in his hand before, but now that I was holding it, I knew I couldn't drink the whole thing like he had.

With him standing over me like this, he was even bigger than I thought.

He was as intimidating as he was fascinating.

Slowly, I took a small sip, trying not to let it show how bad I found the burning taste to be.

"More, wildcat."

I took another sip, and he watched me intently, the unique hue of his blue eyes glinting in the light. I didn't know why a small flutter ran across my belly just from being the sole focus of his attention.

I shifted a little on my feet as I drank some more, the alcohol coating my tongue and making me feel warm from the inside.

I handed it back to him when I didn't think I could drink anymore without puking.

He finished off the bottle and let it join the first two in the trash.

One perfectly arched eyebrow rose expectantly at me, and I opened my mouth and tried again.

"I give private piano lessons to kids for some extra cash," I said. When his expression didn't change, I continued. "I was leaving the house of one of my students when I saw Braxton biking past. I recognized him from school. That's when a bullet h-hit my car."

I took a deep breath and tried to calm myself over the memory.

Now that the events leading me to where I was right now were over, the adrenaline was leaving my body, leaving only my useless limbs and dark memories.

I didn't want to get lost in the darkness.

Dominic shifted slightly, bringing my focus back onto him.

"The car," I said suddenly. "It was small and black, and two men were in it. The driver had gray hair, dark eyes, and t-tan skin, and the man in the passenger side, the one holding—the gun has..."

I shook my head, trying to remember what he had looked like. Fuck, but why couldn't I remember?

"Blond hair," I said finally. That was all I remembered.

I blinked furiously, trying to keep the tears from falling.

His eyes were still unreadable, but I thought I saw something in there that looked a lot like pity.

I looked down at the floor and focused on my feet.

My Converses were dirty.

They were an old, worn-in pair, and there was a small hole in the tip of my left sneaker, but they were comfortable. Looking at them now, though, I realized they had gotten dirty from my walk to the farmhouse.

I had the sudden urge to wash them off.

Dominic stepped closer to me, bringing his black boots into my line of sight.

He had big feet.

I was sure his feet were bigger than the average man, but compared to mine, they appeared ginormous.

He touched his finger under my chin. He lifted until I looked up again, meeting his blue eyes.

God, I didn't think I had ever seen eyes that blue.

The man was just too beautiful for his own good.

I didn't think I liked *rough* on a man, but he made rough look so appealing.

His brown hair was cut short to the scalp. He had a strong nose and a sharp, square jawline covered with little prickly-looking stubbles I was sure would feel rough against my palm.

His lips were full and, I imagined, would have the power to make my heart stop beating for a minuscule moment in time if he ever smiled at me. They were set in a straight line now, and I didn't think many things in life made Dominic smile.

I had the sudden desire to be the one to make it so, which was pretty stupid on my part.

I should not be fascinated with the man.

It was clear he was way out of my league. I wouldn't know how to handle any part of him, and what was more, I *shouldn't* want to.

"What are you thinking about, wildcat?" he asked, his voice gruff.

I blinked and shook my head. "What am I doing here?" I said instead of answering him.

"You're here because I need to keep you safe and figure out who the fuck was stupid enough to target my son."

"But you'll let me leave tomorrow, right?" I asked slowly, standing up.

He turned from me, and I could feel my heart jumping erratically in my chest.

"It's getting late. Why don't you get ready for bed?"

"Dominic."

His breath caught, and he turned to me, something animated moving in his eyes.

He stepped toward me, and I couldn't help but take one back.

He matched my step with his. He took another step, and I matched it, moving back one more step.

I froze when the backs of my legs touched the bed.

He closed the distance between us easily, and then he was so close to me I could smell him.

He smelled oddly like the outdoors and something woodsy.

It wasn't an unpleasant smell, and I might have been comforted in another lifetime, but not right now.

Not when he was trying to use his size to intimidate me—and he was succeeding.

I was fucking intimidated.

I didn't know where to look. Not into his blue eyes and not down at his hard body.

I focused on his Adam's apple, watching it bob up and down when he swallowed.

"Go to sleep, wildcat."

"Why do you call me that?" I asked. Of all the things, the little nickname shouldn't be something for me to focus on, but I was curious.

The corners of his lips curved up in the tiniest of smirks. I still didn't dare look into his eyes.

"'Cause you're like a little wildcat, showing your claws back at the farmhouse."

I frowned.

Was he talking about the way I'd tried to attack him?

Tried being the operative word, considering how embarrassingly easily he had been able to hold me off.

He cupped my cheek, drawing my eyes to his.

It was a bad mistake to look into them.

And now I was unable to look away.

We didn't say anything for a moment, and Dominic moved the pad of his thumb gently over my cheek, messing me up a little more with each swipe.

"Go to sleep. You look fucking exhausted."

It was on the tip of my tongue to ask what his plans for me were tomorrow, but something told me he wouldn't answer.

And I *was* exhausted.

I hadn't eaten anything since before the piano lesson, but right now, I was more exhausted than I was hungry.

I just wanted to sleep and pretend this day had never happened.

I was only moments away from crashing, I was sure of it.

I licked my lips, drawing his gaze to my mouth, and I felt very much like a curious little kitten staring into the jaws of a lion—and not running for my life, even though I should.

What would I do if he kissed me?

Push him away?

Slap him?

Or, worse, kiss him back?

I swallowed, and he stepped away from me suddenly, turning his back.

I took a much-needed breath of air and tried to keep from falling on my ass.

"Rest up. You're safe tonight."

I might be a little stupid because I believed him.

I was safe tonight.

I watched as he walked out of the hotel room, and it wasn't until the door clicked shut that I finally collapsed onto the bed—so, so exhausted.

6

DOMINIC

I HAD STOOD THERE AND LISTENED TO HER RAMBLE OUT AN explanation, putting the story together through the jumbled mess of her words and wild hand gestures.

Her flushed face—probably from the alcohol and all that had happened—and animated eyes played on my mind the entire time I drove home.

Her words were mainly nonsensical. The little wildcat didn't explain much that I found helpful, besides the fact that the car those bastards drove was black—probably stolen, and a brief description of the two men, but she might as well be describing a million other fuckers in the city.

It didn't matter. I had a pretty good idea of what happened, and I didn't like it one fucking bit.

The rest, I would find out once we hacked into the traffic cam, and hopefully, that would give me more information to go on.

She wasn't going to like me very much for what I would have to do to keep those under my protection safe, including her now.

But she had gotten involved in this situation. There was no getting out.

Not that I wasn't fucking thankful for her involvement. Braxton was alive and safe at home, thanks to her.

Fuck.

She should have never crossed my path. Should have lived her life without my interference.

The girl was just too fucking innocent to be thrust into club's life—into *my* life—but it seemed fate had other plans and placed the little wildcat right in front of me.

And I didn't know what to do with her.

I just… I had to keep her safe, no matter the cost.

Something told me she wouldn't like what that cost was.

My phone rang just as I got to the house.

The lights were on in the living room. Braxton was probably asleep now, or I hoped he was. I fucking hoped the nightmares would stay away.

But Kai was still here.

I imagined he might be there for a while, not wanting to leave Braxton out of his sight for too long.

I felt the same fucking way.

I picked up the phone and held it to my ear. "Yeah."

"Prez, you were right," Axel said. "Her entire place is ransacked. Whoever those bastards are, I think they got her information from the registration in her car because that was missing. And they got to her apartment and looked through everything."

"Fuck. Thanks for letting me know. Did they leave anything behind that might tell us who they are?"

The slight silence before he answered me told me everything before he did. "No. I'm sorry, man. They're either skilled, or they got lucky. There's nothing here. And everything in her place is ruined."

"They're not fucking skilled. They couldn't even catch a small woman and a child."

Not that I wasn't fucking grateful for that, but I didn't know who the fuck they were.

Who would be stupid enough to mess with the MC? Mess with me?

"Go home and rest," I said. "I'm calling church early tomorrow morning at the compound. Make sure you gather all the men. Call Roman and Micah and tell them to stop searching for clues and go home as well. I'm sure Roman wants to get back to the woman waiting up for him, warming his bed."

Axel's gruff laughter hit my ear before he hung up.

A plan formed in my brain, and I wondered if this plan was really as chivalrous as I *was* making it out to be, or if there was a darker intent hiding in the fucked-up recesses of my mind.

What was it about this girl that brought out all of my protective instincts?

Was it because she'd saved Braxton, and now I felt a need to ensure nothing and no one could ever get to her?

And I could do it, too. There wouldn't be a better protector for her than me.

The world was filled with monsters, but I was the biggest, meanest one of them all.

Or did I feel this need to protect her because she had made my dead heart tremble, and I fucking hated the feeling and was addicted to it, all the same?

I put my hand on my chest, rubbing at the small ache there.

I shouldn't feel anything for her.

Most of my humanity was fucking beat out of me by my parents, and what was left was reserved solely for my boys.

At least, I had thought so.

And if I went through with this plan I was forming, the little wildcat wouldn't fucking look at me and see someone human.

She would find me repulsive.

More monster than man. So many other fucking bastards had accused me of that. Usually, it was right before I sent them to meet their maker.

I didn't head inside right away. Instead, I sat on my bike, looking over at the house I tried so fucking hard to make into a home for my boys.

Did I succeed?

It felt like I was fucking it up every day.

There was a dichotomy between being a good father and being a good club president.

Most days, it felt like I had to make a choice between the two, and I always ended up choosing wrong.

It was the fucking life I chose that had now brought trauma to my youngest.

My fist clenched around the handgrip.

It was a little after midnight here, so it would be only nine o'clock at night in New Zealand.

She would still be awake.

But would she even pick up if I called?

I fucking wouldn't if I were her.

I put the phone call in before I could really think about it and held it to my ear. It felt like my heart was beating in the rhythm of the ringing tone.

Loud, long, and slow.

I released the handgrip a little when I heard a click on the line. For a moment, I was sure she had sent my call to voicemail. Then I heard it. The slight breathing on the other end. My heart was no longer beating too loud, too long, or too slow, but picking up speed.

I spoke first. "Jenny?"

My sister didn't answer right away. Then, in a cold and lifeless voice, she said, "What do you want, Dominic?"

I closed my eyes, trying to ward off the pain. She used to speak to me with affection. Once upon a time, I had been her favorite person in the entire world.

Now, I was the one she hated more than anything and anyone else.

"I need your help," I said, trying to keep my tone neutral.

She scoffed. "And why would I help you?"

I had expected her venom. It still slashed across my skin like a fucking blade. "Not for me. For Braxton."

Her breath caught. "Braxton? What's going on?"

I licked my lips and looked up at the night sky. How could I explain what was going on when even I didn't fucking know?

"I can't go into much detail, but I need you to take him for the summer."

"Are you serious?"

I shook my head. "It's the only way I can think to keep him safe."

"You know what would keep him safe? You not getting involved in the MC in the first place. You—" Her breath caught, and I hated the pain in her voice. "What would keep him safe… would have kept them all safe, was if you had listened to me."

"I'm sorry, baby bird—"

"Don't call me that."

I closed my eyes. "I'm sorry. I shouldn't have called."

I should have left her alone and let her live her life far away from me and all the danger and toxicity that I brought with me.

I was about to hang up when her voice rang out. "Wait."

I paused.

"Bring Braxton to me. I'll look after him, Dom. I'll do what you couldn't have done for me. I'll keep your son safe."

I closed my eyes. "Fuck. Thank you, Jenny."

"It's not for you," she said, her voice hardening. "He's my nephew. Of course I'll take him."

I blinked and looked away. "I know. I'm still grateful."

"Just send me his flight details when you have them."

With that, she hung up, leaving me sitting in the silence of the night, feeling the weight of the world bearing down on me.

Fuck, but I hoped this was the correct choice.

I hopped off my bike and headed inside the house.

Sure enough, Kai was sitting in the living room, messing around with his phone. He looked up when he heard me.

He opened his mouth, probably to ask if I knew anything, and I shook my head. "I'm calling for church tomorrow. Go to bed, son. You should—you should sleep here, tonight."

It wasn't just Braxton I didn't want out of my sight.

I didn't know how I would be able to keep both of my boys safe.

Fuck, but what would I do if anything happened to them?

Burn down the fucking world and everyone in it.

Kai nodded and stood up. I gently grabbed the back of his neck when he passed and held him close to me.

He looked at me questioningly with his blue eyes. It still fucking got to me just how much he looked like me.

Kai was my spitting image, but he was so much more than that. He was my better self.

I patted his back. "Night, son."

"Night, Dad."

I listened as he padded up the stairs to his old bedroom, and I waited there a beat before I made my way to Braxton's room.

He was sleeping soundly, and it didn't seem as though he was plagued by any nightmares.

Hopefully, things would be better once he was on the plane to New Zealand and far away from danger.

Maybe then, I wouldn't feel so fucking volatile.

I WALKED into the meeting room of the compound, a little building located on the same land as my bar, maybe about a mile or so apart from each other.

The bar could be seen from the window a small distance away, leading off to the open road.

I got here before everyone else and took a sip of my coffee as I looked out the window.

It was early.

Too early.

The sun had barely risen over the horizon, and after talking to Blue, a new patch member I had put in front of Emmy's hotel room, I learned she was still in there. Probably still asleep, exhausted from the night.

I knew the feeling.

I was fucking exhausted, yet I hadn't gotten any sleep last night. There was still so much shit that needed to be done.

Braxton's flight had already been booked, and I needed to decide what I wanted to do with the little wildcat.

I could do what I did with Braxton and send her far away until the danger passed, but people usually didn't like it when you sent them away against their will.

Something told me my little wildcat wouldn't like it either. The only alternative was to keep her close to me.

Fuck, but I could feel a small smile forming on my face at the thought.

It wouldn't be any fucking hardship.

But I wasn't like Roman.

I didn't take a woman simply because I became obsessed with her.

That shit seemed to be working out well for him though, considering he was set to marry his girl soon, but Emmy was… different.

I didn't want to marry the wildcat.

I couldn't, not with the shit I'd done and would do in the foreseeable and distant future.

Any woman I claimed as mine would be living with a target on her back.

And Emmy wasn't like my boys. She wouldn't grow big and strong like Braxton would, able to protect herself from danger. She wasn't big and strong like Kai.

The girl might be tiny, but she was probably in her mid-twenties. She was done growing.

Not that there was anything wrong with her body.

Fuck, but the memory of her curves pressed against me on the back of the bike was seared in my mind. The way her sweet pussy was pressed up against me every time I throttled the engine and pushed the bike forward…

I shifted in my seat.

It wouldn't do me any fucking good to get a hard-on before seeing my men.

Sure enough, the first bike on the road appeared through the window.

I watched as Micah drove in. The huge fucker was easy to identify.

I waited a bit for him to park his bike and come inside.

He sauntered in, his face expressionless as usual, the cold silver eyes of his glinting in the morning light.

If I didn't know I had his complete loyalty, I would have been wary of the bastard.

He rapped his knuckles on the table. "How's Braxton?"

"Still asleep," I said, noticing another bike driving in.

He nodded and took his usual seat at the opposite end of the table from me.

Roman came in next, grunted at us, and walked straight to the small table housing the coffee pots and cups.

He poured himself a drink and walked over to me, taking a seat on my left.

"Fuck, this is too early," he said, his voice gruff.

I laughed. "Sorry to take you out of your warm bed. You've gotten soft since you got the girl."

And fuck if that wasn't true. I remember a time when the fucker would come out with me and party the night away, only to come in to work early the next morning.

He took a sip of his coffee. "Do you know who's behind those fuckers targeting Braxton?"

I shook my head.

Of course, there would be someone behind it all.

I didn't think the ones who chased my boy down were the ones in charge, but the question was, who was?

The club was thriving.

We kicked out the older chapters around California when the King's Men came and took over the territory.

No one was strong enough to take us on.

Or stupid enough.

And there hadn't been any trouble.

I couldn't think of a single fucker… or perhaps I could think of a hundred other fuckers who were enemies of the club, but none of them fit the motivation,

Why would they suddenly act now?

That was a fucking anomaly.

I didn't fucking like anomalies.

My fists clenched on the table, and Roman looked at them before he patted my back. "We'll find them."

I nodded as more noise came through the doors, and the important players for the club arrived.

Blade and Axel walked in together.

The two were almost always together. They had joined my club around the same time.

Blade was the secretary for the club, and Axel was my road captain. He was also responsible for ensuring drug distribution made it across the state line, while Blade focused more on overseas operations.

They looked at me now, their faces serious. Blade walked over and placed a folder on the desk.

I nodded my thanks and grabbed it, looking through all the public records Blade had been able to dredge up on the girl.

I looked down at her full name.

Emmalyn Wilde.

I could feel a small smile tugging on my lips.

Wilde.

What a fucking coincidence.

My little wildcat.

I ignored the stares from my men as I focused back on the file.

What I knew of the girl so far: She went by Emmy. She had the most fascinating hazel eyes—the right one slightly darker than the left—a top lip slightly bigger than her bottom lip that made her look like she was perpetually pouting, an interestingly shaped nose that would have been altered had it been born on some starlet's daughter, but it was beautiful on her, and I was fucking drawn to it. It wasn't pointed or round but somewhere in between, a little upturned and a little crooked.

I would fucking break the hands of any plastic surgeon who dared touch it.

In her driver's license picture, she smiled widely and

showed off the small hidden dimples in the creases of her laugh lines.

I hadn't actually seen her smile at me… yet.

Her thick dark hair seemed to take over her small face and petite frame, and it was one of the first things anyone would notice about her at first sight.

I blinked and looked down at the copy of her driver's license once more.

I was right.

She was twenty-five.

I wanted to leave the meeting and look over everything in this thin folder, greedy for any information offered to me about the girl who had risked her life to save my son.

Instead, I closed it and looked around at my brothers.

Kai walked in and took a seat to my right, opposite Roman.

Everyone important was here. I looked around at my brothers, whom I trusted more than anyone in the world.

I cleared my throat, and the whole room quieted as my men looked at me expectantly.

"I called everyone here to keep you updated. Braxton is home safe, but we still don't know who the fuck targeted him or why." I looked over at Kai. "I'm sending Braxton to New Zealand for the summer."

Kai frowned. "New Zealand. You mean with Aunt Jenny?"

I nodded.

"She agreed to take Braxton?" Kai asked quietly.

I reached over and squeezed his shoulder. His blue eyes met mine, a shadow moving over them. I could only imagine what he was thinking right now.

"Yeah, son. She agreed."

He nodded but didn't say anything else.

"Do you think this could have come from the inside?" Roman said, drawing my attention.

I looked at him with one eyebrow raised.

We'd already suspected there was a rat among the ranks.

It was confirmed months before, when Ryleigh came to us with information that her dad and the dear old late mayor had known about the shipping arrangement being executed that night.

We were fucking lucky Ryleigh came when she did, or we would have been doing life in prison right now.

The reality of what I did, what I risked every single fucking day for the club, had never been more clear than when I realized how close we'd come to getting put away.

And we still hadn't caught the fucking rat.

He was lying low for now, but I was sure he would mess up sooner or later, and I could be fucking patient.

"You think this was an inside job?" I asked.

"Who else would know where Braxton was?" Blade asked.

I didn't answer him.

The fact that my son could have been taken away from me because of one of the brothers who'd sworn loyalty to me, who swore to protect my club and our brothers with their blood, had already crossed my mind.

"This stays between us," I said slowly, staring at every one of my brothers.

I might have dedicated my entire life to the club and to the men in it, but this was my inner circle.

Around me, my men nodded.

"I'm gonna find the fucking traitor," I said. "And if the bastard had anything to do with Braxton, they're gonna wish for fucking death before I'm done having my fun. It'll make Micah look like a fucking priest."

Across from me, Micah cracked a small smile, the promise of blood putting a glint in his eyes.

I WALKED down the quiet hotel hallway.

It was still early, and I didn't even think Emmy was awake.

That was good.

It was going to make what I had to do a hell of a lot easier.

Blue looked up at me when I got close and straightened.

The man was the newest patch member to be sworn in.

Like most of the men in my club, he came from a past filled with darkness he'd much rather forget.

Or take it out on someone else.

Lucky for him, my club provided the right outlet for that.

Aside from the thorough background check I'd done before I even let him become a prospect, I didn't know much about the kid.

And background checks only told me so much.

I relied a lot on my instincts and the words of other members who vouched for him. In this case, that member was my son.

I trusted Kai's judgment as much as I trusted my own.

As long as Blue was loyal to the club, I couldn't give two fucks about all he had done before.

It wasn't like I could judge, considering how much dark shit I had found myself in before. And it was about to get even darker.

"Any movement in there?"

He shook his head. "I'm pretty sure she's still asleep, or she's just really quiet when she moves."

I nodded. "Did you drive here by car or bike?"

"Car."

"Good. Go down and pull up to the side of the building. I'll be down with the girl in about twenty minutes."

Just as soon as I made sure she had something to eat.

Wouldn't want her to be sick when the drugs finally took effect.

He nodded and walked away without hesitation. I liked that from my men. I needed them to listen to me without question, and to go along with discretion with whatever I had planned. That was the only way my club had survived as long as it had.

I had men who didn't get uncomfortable or queasy from all the questionable things I asked of them, and Blue needed to be exactly that, considering I was coming in to abduct the music teacher.

I smiled a little at the thought and used my key card to let myself into her room.

It was quiet, and I found her on the bed right away.

She was still sleeping.

The events of last night must have really tired her out because she didn't even stir from the presence of a monster in the room.

Quietly, I made my way over to her.

I stood at the edge of the bed and looked down at the delicate girl, almost buried under the covers, her face free of makeup, and relaxed in a deep sleep.

She looked younger like this.

She looked like—

Mine.

I shook my head, shaking away the whimsical thought.

I wasn't a man given to whimsy.

I didn't give in to every urge, and I didn't protect sweet little girls who looked like they needed a hero in their life.

I was the furthest thing from a hero, but she'd played with fate when she decided to help Braxton.

Her life was now entwined with mine, and that was all there was to it.

I leaned down and let my fingers run gently across the soft skin on her cheek, taking in her fair skin before letting my finger drift upward to the tip of her nose.

Her eyes fluttered, and I straightened.

I waited for her to open her eyes, finding softness in them from whatever dreamland she was leaving.

Time seemed to come to a standstill for a moment, and it was just her in this room, breathing the same air as me.

Then awareness seeped in. Emmy's eyes widened in surprise, and she sat up so suddenly that she almost fell off the bed.

I grasped her elbow gently to keep her from falling, and she looked over at me, her hazel eyes light this morning.

"What are you doing?" she asked.

I didn't answer her. I watched her face.

I was really gonna do this. It wasn't a line I had ever crossed before, but I found myself *not* feeling conflicted over that.

Perhaps whatever humanity was left in my heart was reserved solely for my sons.

Unluckily for her.

"Go get ready," I said. "We're leaving the hotel."

"Oh." Something shifted in her eyes, but it was gone before I could really make out what it was. Disappointment, perhaps? Did she not want to leave the hotel room?

I didn't know.

I was usually good at reading people, but when it came to this girl, I found myself… lost.

I moved back from the bed when she threw her legs to the side and climbed off the bed. She was still wearing the same clothes as yesterday, and her hair was a mass of messy waves falling everywhere.

I watched her for a second, and a knock came just in time for me to get out of my thoughts.

I turned away and went to answer the door, vaguely aware of her making her way into the bathroom.

I opened the door to the chirpy face of a boy no older

than Kai, and watched as his smile slowly disappeared as recognition moved in his eyes.

I smiled and stepped aside for him to push the cart holding the breakfast I had ordered.

He hesitated, looking at the threshold of the room before bringing his attention back to me.

My smile widened when he noticeably swallowed, slowly stepping into the room.

What an amusing little man.

What did he think I would do to him?

"Enjoy," he said quietly, trying to head out the door.

"Wait," I said.

He tensed and turned to me.

"Don't you want your tip, boy?"

His eyes widened. "O-only if you think it's appropriate."

I smirked and reached into my pocket for a crisp hundred-dollar bill.

He seemed surprised when I slapped it in his hand. "T-thank you."

Then he was out the door, as if the devil himself was chasing him.

I chuckled and closed the door.

Movements from behind caught my attention, and I turned to see Emmy standing there.

Her eyes seemed brighter now that she was able to wash away the sleep, and her hair was a little more tamed. I almost missed the just-got-out-of-bed look on her, but the little wildcat was coming home with me.

I was sure there would be plenty of opportunities for me to catch her like that.

"Why are you smiling like that?" she asked timidly.

I wondered if she was a timid person by nature, or if she was timid by the situation and by me.

It was probably the latter.

I shook my head. "Come eat, wildcat."

She bit her lip, hesitating.

I walked over to the cart and removed the lids of the two plates of two eggs, roasted red potatoes, and bacon strips.

It wasn't much, but it would be enough before transporting her back to my home from the hotel.

"Aren't you hungry?" I asked.

Her stomach answered for me when it growled loudly. A fascinating blush took over her face, and I wondered if that blush went anywhere else.

The urge to find out was strong, but I held in some control.

I wasn't that much of a monster.

I wheeled the cart over to the bed and sat on the edge of it, patting the seat next to me.

She eyed the space as if she thought I would take a bite out of her if she got close enough.

I looked at her expectantly and waited. My patience was already running low, and if she waited any longer, I would get up and grab her.

Luckily for her, she walked over and sat down, trying to put as much space between us without making it obvious.

I rolled my eyes, wrapped my arms around her waist, and pulled her close enough that our thighs were touching, and I could feel the heat of her pressed against me, making my dick twitch, wanting to play.

Fuck, but since when did I react this way to a woman after such a short amount of time?

She gasped and tensed in my arms.

I looked sideways at her.

"Don't want you to fall off," I said, like the helpful man that I was.

"I wouldn't have."

"Are you sure about that?"

She didn't answer me, and I pushed one of the plates in front of her. I handed her a fork. She looked at it like she wasn't sure what she was supposed to do.

"Eat, wildcat, or I'll feed you."

She quickly grabbed the fork, and something that resembled disappointment moved through me as the image of feeding her while she sat on my lap dissolved.

I blinked and focused back on my own breakfast, taking a huge bite of the bacon and feeling her eyes on me.

I pretended not to notice, but fuck, I loved her eyes on me.

I didn't mistake the brief heat that I'd seen in them yesterday.

Whatever this... *connection* I was feeling between us was, the little wildcat felt it too, and that would make what I was going to do a lot easier.

We ate in silence.

I finished mine before she did, and I leaned back against the mattress, my hands braced behind me as I watched her. She was aware of my eyes. That blush that I had been so fascinated by was back on her cheeks. This time, a deeper shade of red.

My finger jerked with the need to reach out and touch her cheek, to see if it would be as hot as it looked, but I resisted.

There should be a fucking reward for having this much self-control.

Once she got in the last bite, she grabbed the napkin nearby and wiped her lips delicately.

Everything about this girl was delicate.

A perfect little doll.

"Done?" I asked.

She nodded and cleared her throat before she spoke. "Yeah. I'm done."

I stood up and held my hand out to her. She didn't do anything for a moment, then carefully placed her hand in mine. I looked down at it, taking in the stark contrast between us, from her pale skin to my tan skin, from the gentle curve of the back of her palm to my own hand, once filled with blood.

Innocent to monster.

I helped her up, and she tilted her head back to look me in the eye.

I focused on the light brown and green swirl of her irises before I led us out of the room.

"Where are we going?" she asked, running a little, trying to match my pace.

I wrapped my arm around her waist, bringing us to the elevator and pressing the button.

She tensed, but I didn't give her a chance to think about it, squeezing her to my side and making sure she stayed firmly put. There would be no doubt in anybody's mind that she was with me.

The elevator doors opened, and I quickly ushered us inside, watching the numbers blink as we made our way down to the lobby. I led her out the same way we had come in last night and found Blue in his black Cadillac Escalade.

She tensed.

"Dominic?"

"Come on. We don't have all day to just stand around."

I opened the back door for her and helped her climb in, letting my hand curve around the swell of her ass.

I heard her suck in a sharp breath and I pretended not to notice. Before getting into the car, I reached into my pocket for the drug I had prepared.

"Take me back to my house," I said to Blue.

He nodded.

Emmy tensed and turned to me. I knew she was getting ready for a fight. "Your house? What are you talking about?"

I turned to her and made quick work with my hand. The needle pierced the skin on her neck, and her eyes bulged out from the sensation.

"Dominic," was all she managed to say before her eyes closed, and the drug quickly took effect. I drew her into my arms, letting her head rest on my chest and ignoring the feeling of rightness that washed over me from having her so close.

Blue looked back at me in the rearview mirror before facing forward once more and taking off.

7

EMMY

THERE WAS SOMETHING PRESSING AGAINST MY EYELIDS THAT made it hard for me to open them.

I let out a small groan and turned to my side, only for a slight headache to bloom at the back of my head.

Using my hands, I tried to take the weight off my eyes, but there was nothing there.

It still felt nearly impossible to open my eyes.

I didn't want to.

I couldn't remember the last thing that happened before I went to bed last night.

I frowned a little at the thought.

I couldn't even remember going to bed last night.

How did I even go to bed?

I felt like there was something important for me to remember, but… what?

Slowly, awareness seeped into my consciousness.

The hotel… the abandoned farmhouse… Braxton… bad men with guns…

Dominic.

I gasped and sat up on the bed quickly, which I regretted

right away when my vision spotted in the corners of my eyes, and I felt faint.

I closed my eyes and pulled my legs toward me, hugging them. I leaned forward and buried my face in my knees.

Fuck.

The bastard drugged me.

He drugged me, and he brought me back to his house.

After all I had done, risking my life to save Braxton, this was how he treated me?

My fists clenched as I battled with a barrage of emotions.

Anger, frustration... *fear.*

God, but I was fucking scared shitless.

Beneath all the other potent emotions I tried to battle through, there was fear, even if I didn't want to think about it.

Even if I didn't want to admit to myself just how terrified I was. I did not want to give in to the fear. If I allowed myself to do that, I would be rendered immobile.

I took a deep breath, tears blurring my vision for a brief moment, before I blinked and the room came back into focus once more.

I was in a nice, enormous room.

It looked like a master suite of a house. The décor was done in navy blue and black. The furniture was strong and masculine and simple.

It wasn't something I would have picked out myself, but it was tasteful in its simplicity. I wondered just who this room belonged to.

I was afraid of the answer.

This didn't look like a prisoner's room.

I was on a king-size bed, with dark blue comforters and a thick black blanket.

It was summer, but the house was cool, and I found

myself wanting to burrow deep into the covers and go back to sleep. To hide from this reality I suddenly found myself in.

God, what the hell was I supposed to do?

I climbed off the bed, my vision hazy as if I were in a dream, and I went to the door.

I tried the doorknob.

Locked.

I knew it would be. Had already suspected it. And still, I couldn't stop myself from reacting to it.

I looked up at the door and found another lock on the inside just several inches higher than my head. This one didn't look like it was locked, but I had a feeling it might be once I found myself trapped in here with *him*.

I shivered at the thought.

What the hell was I going to do now?

The tears seeped out from the corners of my eyes.

I felt stupid, but given a chance to do this again, I still would have chosen to save Braxton.

Despite his monster father, Braxton was innocent, and he didn't deserve to have gone through something so traumatic.

I turned around, leaning against the door, unsure if my own two feet could possibly hold me up any longer, and looked around the room.

At my new prison.

I DIDN'T KNOW how much time had passed, but it couldn't have been very long, considering it was still morning.

There was a clock on the nightstand, but I had flipped it facedown, unable to bring myself to watch the minutes tick by, counting down my execution.

Apparently, my time was up, because the doorknob

twisted a bit before I heard the key being inserted into the keyhole, making my heart run into overdrive.

I felt light-headed, and I was afraid I would keel over, despite the fact that I was sitting down on the bed.

Don't faint, don't faint, don't faint.

The door was slowly pushed open, revealing the big man standing there.

My, what vicious eyes you have.

I swallowed as he stared at me with his blue eyes, his face impassive and his arms relaxed at his side.

He looked at me as if I were an anomaly. As if he didn't understand me.

I swallowed and looked down at the comforter, unable to hold his stare.

What the hell did he want with me?

"People will look for me," I said, my voice almost a whisper. I was afraid if I spoke any louder, the fear would get to me, and I would either cry or puke.

I didn't know which I hoped for the least.

He didn't answer me right away, and the silence was somehow even more unnerving than if he had been angry or screaming at me.

At least with anger, I would know how he felt.

This silence told me nothing about the man.

"No, they won't," he said finally. I flinched at his blunt words.

Aside from the phone call from my mom the previous morning, it had been months since I'd last talked to my parents.

My going even longer without talking to them wouldn't raise any red flags, but how would he know that? How would he know I was alone in California?

"My job—"

"You're a teacher. You're off for the summer," he said casually, as if the words he spoke weren't so fucking creepy.

I blinked and shook my head. "I told you, I tutor in the summer."

"And do you think those rich, entitled bitches whose kids you tutor will really be looking for you? They would just think you flaked on them. You might not have those jobs anymore."

He didn't sound sorry about that. I hadn't expected him to, but for him to sound so casual while talking about it...

I had no retort to that. I thought back to Freddy's mom, trying to think of her looking for me once I missed a lesson with her son without notice.

No, she wouldn't be worried.

If anything, she would fire me and look for a new piano tutor for her son within the same hour.

My bottom lip trembled. Screw trying to be strong. I looked up at him with wet eyes. "Why are you doing this?"

For a moment, there seemed to be some sort of emotion in his eyes that wasn't blank. Something that told me the man standing before me was human.

But it was gone in a blink of an eye. I didn't think he felt anything, doing this to me.

I was wrong.

Dominic Madden wasn't human.

He was a fucking monster.

"I'll have Lucy bring some food for you," he said, and with that, he turned around and walked away. The click of the lock was the final blow it took for me to lose it completely.

I buried my face in my knees and cried.

THE ROOM WAS BATHED in darkness.

I didn't bother turning on any lights.

I'd much prefer looking out the window, watching as the streetlight came on just a few feet away from the window. Looking at the darkened sky, and beyond that to the hidden stars.

I was sure they were out there, but I couldn't catch a single one in this room. The food Lucy had brought me remained untouched.

She worked for Dominic.

It was strange to think of the rough biker employing a woman to cook and clean for him, though it made sense. He was probably too busy doing all sorts of illegal things to bother taking care of his kids, so of course, he would hire someone else to do it for him.

It was funny, because when I met the man, my first impression was that he was a good father. Braxton had clung to him at the farmhouse, seeking safety in his arms and knowing his dad would take care of everything for him, but perhaps that wasn't a reflection on the kind of father Dominic was and more that Braxton was young and scared, so of course he would cling to the only adult in his life.

Dominic wasn't a good man.

How could I see him as a good father?

Lucy probably did everything.

I looked down at the tray of food placed on the floor by the door.

I hadn't eaten breakfast or lunch, and though I was getting hungry, I didn't know how I could eat anything without it coming back up.

Lucy was a short-statured woman, almost as wide as she was tall.

She had brown eyes and caramel-colored hair. She didn't talk to me at all. When I tried to speak to her, she looked at me as if I were a different species—an alien invading Earth.

Under her sharp gaze, I was unsure how to convince her that I had come in peace.

I didn't know where she was from or what language she spoke, but I guessed it was something European or Mediterranean.

She looked like she had spent most of her life on a tropical beach, so what the hell was she doing here in California, and why was she working for such a man?

She didn't even bat an eye over the fact that I was being kept here against my will, a testament to that when she didn't enter this room—my prison—by herself when she delivered the food, but instead with a mean-looking older man, tattooed from head to toe.

Lucy didn't speak to me, and this man didn't look at me.

Neither wanted to, or perhaps had been instructed to not interact with me.

Just a small smile from Lucy as she placed the food down, then they both left, and the lock clicked into place.

My stomach grumbled, and I was half tempted to eat something, but that meant I had to turn the lights on and move away from my safe spot on the small recliner facing the window.

I wasn't ready for any of those things.

I wasn't ready to face my reality just yet.

It didn't seem I had a say in that because the door clicked open once more, and though I didn't look to see, my skin pricked with awareness and the hair on the back of my neck rose.

It wasn't Lucy coming back with dinner.

Not with my body's natural response to a predator in the same room as me, I was sure.

I held my breath and kept my gaze on the window when he just stood there and watched me in the dark.

At this point, I wouldn't really be surprised if someone told me he could see in the dark.

Then he let out a small audible sigh that nearly had me jumping out of my skin before he reached over and turned on the light, encasing the entire room in a soft orange glow and taking away my view of the outside.

I blinked as I gazed at my reflection from the window.

I didn't look any different from how I did when I left the house… two days ago?

I felt different.

It felt like a lifetime had already passed.

He walked further into the room and his reflection came into view. He was carrying a tray of what looked like a grilled-cheese sandwich and tomato soup.

My stomach grumbled a little at the sight, and he paused.

"Jesus, girl. What were you thinking, starving yourself all day? Do you really believe that will help?" he grumbled, his voice gruff.

I cleared my throat. "My name's not *girl*."

The corners of his lips lifted marginally into a small smile. "Wildcat."

I frowned at him when he sat on the edge of the bed and faced me. He set the tray down on the bedside table, and I tried not to squirm from his attention.

"What do you want?" I croaked. A part of me didn't want to know, but the bigger part was so fucking scared of the unknown, I would much rather have him tell me than keep me in limbo.

"For starters, how about you eat dinner?"

I shook my head. "I'm not hungry."

One eyebrow raised at that. "I'm sure your stomach says otherwise."

My stomach was a traitorous bitch.

As if to prove the point, it growled once more. Dominic smirked.

As if we were friends sharing a joke.

The smirk just revealed more of the face of the monster. Did he not feel bad for all the things he did?

"Just let me go," I said. I didn't know what more I could say. I didn't know what he was doing, trapping me in this room, or why. It wasn't like I was his enemy or the King's Men's enemy. I didn't even know about them until I moved to Sacramento, and I could probably count on one hand how many times I had seen him at the school.

"I'm afraid I can't do that, wildcat."

"I saved Braxton. I didn't have to. Doesn't that count for something?"

He nodded, agreeing with me. "It does. That's why I'm keeping you."

I blinked. "What?"

"I'm keeping you."

"Y-you can't *keep* me."

"You sure about that? I'm doing that right now."

"I'm not a fucking stray on the street. You can't just take me home and decide you're going to keep me."

He didn't say anything for one long second, and that long second seemed to stretch out for an eternity.

It felt like I was drifting away from Earth, drifting away from reality.

This couldn't possibly be my life at this very moment, could it?

"Come eat," he said. "Lucy said you haven't eaten all day."

I shook my head but didn't answer him. I didn't think I could. Not with the lump the size of a golf ball forming in my throat.

He studied me. Then, without saying a word, he reached over and pulled me into his lap.

I struggled to get away, but he tightened his arms around me.

"Stop moving," he said, leaning down until his lips touched my ear.

"Let go of me!" I screamed.

He tightened his grip even more, and I stilled when my thigh brushed up against something hard.

My breath caught, and I looked at him with horror in my eyes.

He wouldn't…

He drew me closer to him, and confirmed I didn't mistake that.

I let out a small cry, and he shushed me as if he was trying to offer me comfort.

But a fucking monster couldn't comfort anyone.

He only knew how to destroy, and right now, he was destroying my sanity, one small shred of it at a time.

"Please," I whispered.

I was so fucking scared. The last time I had been this scared, I was lying on the ground, broken and bloody, watching as a pair of black Oxford shoes walked away.

This somehow felt so much worse.

He hadn't broken me yet, but it was only a matter of time.

He cupped the back of my head and pushed my face toward his chest. I could feel and hear the steady strum of his heart.

I stilled.

What kind of game was he playing?

He placed his other hand on top of my thigh, his long fingers curving almost around it casually as if he weren't aware of doing it.

What did he think would happen now that he was holding me in his arms like…

Like…

Like lovers did?

I closed my eyes, and I surrendered to him.

For now.

He was just so much stronger than me, so much bigger.

How the hell was I supposed to fight him off?

I didn't know how.

His hand moved down from my head and between my shoulder blades and finally settled on the small of my back, near the swell of my ass.

I tensed and looked up at him, waiting to see what he would do, but when he just left his hand where it was, his eyes focused on the wall in front of him, I found myself back in a relaxed posture, trying to get used to the fact that a man I didn't know was touching me so intimately.

Why the hell was he touching me intimately?

I wished I could read minds. Wished I knew what the hell was going on with him and what his intentions were for me.

I closed my eyes and tried to pretend I was anywhere but here.

Tried to pretend I could be anyone else.

But I was me, and I was stuck in this room with the president of the King's Men MC, and he had his hands on me.

When he finally moved, I realized I had nearly fallen asleep.

He leaned back so he could look at my face, and all I could do was stare at him with wide eyes, wondering what the hell I was on to have relaxed in his arms like this, as if I was safe here.

I leaned back a little also, trying to put as much space between us as possible, and he wrapped both hands around my waist.

"You lean back any further and you'll fall right off, wildcat."

"The floor is probably better than being in your arms," I hissed.

One corner of his lips lifted in a small smile, and he pretended to let me go, leaving me off balance and nearly falling off his lap.

I quickly wrapped my arms around his neck and held him to me, my heart racing at the near fall.

The bastard's chest shook as he laughed at me.

My grip around his neck tightened, trying hard not to give in to the urge to slap the smirk off his stupid face. Or choke him.

My arms *were* conveniently around his neck.

Something told me he wouldn't be so receptive to that, and I didn't know what the repercussions would be if I pissed off the beast.

He shifted me on his lap and let me sit sideways, my legs falling to one side of him over the edge of the bed, almost in line with his legs. Then he carefully reached over for the tray and set it on the bed beside us.

I watched him curiously.

What was happening?

He picked up the spoon, scooped some tomato soup, tested it against his lips, and brought it to mine.

I shook my head, refusing to eat.

He didn't say anything.

Just looked at me.

"You can be as stubborn as you feel like, wildcat, but we're not leaving this position until all the food on this tray is gone. You really think you can out-stubborn me?"

Yes. Yes, I did think that.

But the hardness in his eyes told me not to test him, and I didn't want to spend the night on his lap.

Did I?

I shook away the stupid thought and opened my mouth slowly. He fed me some tomato soup. I barely tasted it.

Satisfaction entered his eyes, and he scooped up some more.

"I can feed myself," I croaked, trying to grab the spoon from him.

He held it away from me.

"And now you don't have to."

I frowned.

"What's wrong with you?" I asked before I could think better of it.

Dominic was quiet for a moment. Then he let out a booming laugh, and I jumped, not expecting that reaction.

"Lots of things," he answered, taking advantage of my slightly gaping mouth and feeding me another spoonful.

I quickly swallowed, looking over at him warily.

We didn't speak for the rest of the meal.

Dominic didn't eat.

He also didn't look away from me.

There was something unnerving about having his blue eyes on me the whole time while I did something as vital as eating. While he did something as nurturing as feeding me.

He dipped the grilled-cheese sandwich in the tomato soup between every other spoonful.

I looked up and met his eyes as he got to the last spoonful.

We didn't look away when I finally swallowed, and he placed the metal spoon down against the ceramic bowl.

The small clang it made sounded loud in the silent room.

I didn't flinch. I didn't move. I didn't even think I was breathing.

He reached up and swiped his thumb across my bottom lip, taking away some of the crumbs I had there. My breath caught when he brought his thumb up to his mouth and sucked on it, the act strangely intimate.

I couldn't even remember the last time someone had fed me.

I was a grown adult woman. Of course, it had been a while since the last time someone had fed me.

"Good?" he asked softly.

I wasn't thinking when I nodded. I paused, thinking better of it, and pushed away from him, standing up when my feet touched the floor.

I crossed my arms over my chest, feeling vulnerable under his gaze.

I didn't like it.

Not one bit.

"Go shower and get ready for bed," Dominic said.

It was still early, I was sure of it.

I didn't know what time it was, but it didn't feel like much time had passed since the sunset and since Dominic made his appearance.

I didn't want to argue.

I didn't want to think about this reality anymore, and what was more, I didn't want to disrupt the peace I suddenly found us in.

I turned and walked to the bathroom without another word.

This morning, when I had taken my time exploring this room, I found a toothbrush still in its package on the bathroom counter.

I assumed it was left there for me, and that was what I picked up when I crossed the threshold.

I looked at myself in the mirror.

Dark circles ringed my eyes.

I blinked and looked down at the counter, avoiding my reflection.

My hands shook as I went through the motions of brushing my teeth.

I would like to say it was because I was scared of the monster sitting out there, but since the accident, my hands always shook randomly, often while I was doing the most mundane things.

I locked the bathroom door and stripped, getting into the shower.

I probably shouldn't have risked it, but I was sweaty from the night before, and even if Dominic wouldn't comment on the way I smelled, I didn't think I could stand it anymore.

I chuckled softly to myself as the water rained down on my skin.

As if right now, the thing I should be worried about was whether Dominic found my scent repulsive.

It would have been ideal.

It meant he would leave me alone.

Or, at least, it should, but the thought of spending time by myself in this room held no appeal.

Besides, where would he go?

The bastard had put me in his room.

That was what I figured out while I was looking around for something to help me escape.

The walk-in closet was filled with men's clothes in Dominic's size.

Unless he put me in some other man's room, they were his.

I stayed under the shower a little longer than necessary, trying to wash away all that had happened since the morning I woke up and drove across town to give piano lessons to a kid whose mom didn't even like me.

What a fucking mess.

My throat clogged, but I held the tears in.

I only allowed myself once a day to break down, and I had already done so this afternoon.

I would not break down anymore.

When the temperature turned tepid, I turned off the water and reached out to grab a soft, fluffy white towel.

I stopped when I found some clothes neatly folded by the towel.

I glanced at the door.

I knew for a fact I had locked it before I hopped in the shower, but now there were clothes laid out on the counter for me, and the door was unlocked.

I took a deep breath, locked the door again, even if it was fucking useless, and quickly put on the clothes.

I stopped short at the sight of his black boxer briefs.

The thought of his boxer briefs touching me so intimately…

I shook away the thought.

If I gave myself more time to think about it, I might not leave the bathroom tonight.

I left the bathroom, stopping short, when I found him sitting on the bed in the same spot he had been when I left, but it was clear he'd left and returned.

His hair was slightly damp, along with the skin on his face, neck, and shoulders. He was shirtless, displaying the tattoos he had, and he was donning a pair of fitted black boxer briefs, showcasing curves and steel and…

I quickly averted my eyes, not wanting to be caught staring at him, and looked down at the floor at my bare feet.

It had only been about three days since I was home at my apartment, attempting to do something as simple as painting my toenails pink.

It didn't look so bad from far away, but up close, I could see where I had messed up the paint, when my hands had shaken so badly, I had a hard time staying inside the cuticle line.

My eyes blurred before another pair of feet came into my line of sight.

I blinked away the stinging and noticed the obvious size difference between us.

His feet were probably twice the size of my own, his skin a shade or two darker than mine. His feet were much hairier than I had expected men's feet to be, and his toenails were cut neatly, short and round and free of color.

He placed two fingers under my chin and lifted until I met his eyes.

"Time for bed, wildcat."

He led me away from the bathroom door before I could really process his words. I dug my heels into the floor when my brain finally registered what he'd said, and I grabbed onto the hand holding my other hand captive.

"Dominic, wait!"

My heart jumped in a panic. I didn't want to go anywhere with him, but I especially didn't want to go near the bed with him.

The harder I struggled, the more I realized just how fucking *easy* it was for him to manhandle me.

He wasn't listening to me. Frustration made my chest burn, and I just… I just wished I was strong enough.

Fuck, how could he be so strong when I was so weak? It wasn't fair.

He plopped me down on the bed, pulled back the covers, and pushed me under before he walked around to the other side and got in as well.

He wrapped his arms around my middle.

It took a while for me to realize all he intended to do was hold me. His hand splayed across my stomach, the size of it covering the entirety of my belly, and he used that hand to draw me toward him until there was no space left between us, until I could feel the heat of him on my back, and I didn't know what to do about it.

I tried to put some space between us, but all I did was tired myself out.

He reached over me and clicked off the lamp, bathing the room in darkness save for the streetlamp just outside his window.

I wiggled against him.

He tightened his arms around me even more, making breathing almost impossible.

"Go to sleep, wildcat."

"Dominic—"

He squeezed me.

I took in a deep breath, unsure of what I was supposed to do.

"Sleep."

Was that all he could say?

Was that all he was going to do?

This whole day had been unexpected. I had been plagued with turmoil for hours, filled with so many emotions I thought I was experiencing whiplash at one point. And now he was holding me.

And that was all he was doing.

I wasn't sure about anything anymore.

Or—just one thing.

Dominic Madden was a strange fucking man.

8

EMMY

Dominic Madden was a fucking monster.

That was what he was.

That was what I had concluded when the terrible beast took me back to his house and held me against my will.

It was only confirmed this morning when I woke to his arms still around me.

I knew he was awake.

He had been awake for a while, and he was still lying in bed, holding me as if I were his *lover* rather than his captive.

When I turned around and met bright blue eyes free of sleepiness or fatigue, the man had the nerve to smile at me as if everything was fine between us.

He placed a swift kiss on my forehead and got out of bed, heading into the bathroom.

I could have attempted to leave the room, but what was the point?

It was locked. Otherwise, he wouldn't have left me alone.

I confirmed my suspicions when I looked at the door and found the inside lock in place.

I could hear water running from the bathroom, and the

little movements Dominic made as he got ready for his day, ready to rule it like the king that he was.

I wondered what that felt like.

To walk around the world as if you owned it, because he did—at least, a small but very significant portion of it.

The shower turned on and I could hear Dominic opening the glass door and climbing in.

Intrusive thoughts entered, and for the life of me, I couldn't rid myself of the image of Dominic naked, lathering his skin with soap.

I shook my head.

I should not be attracted to the man.

He was, by far, the most good-looking man I had ever encountered in my life, but that didn't mean his insides weren't pitch black.

And it didn't mean he could do whatever the hell he wanted, like keep me trapped in his room.

Why the hell was I even in his bedroom in the first place? Didn't he have a dungeon for all his prisoners?

I took a deep breath, trying to shake out the thoughts.

I should not be thinking of a possible dungeon he might have in his house—or wish to be placed in it.

Dominic might be beautiful, but I knew better than to trust a man just because he was good-looking. I was sure Lucifer was depicted as beautiful in some stories.

I stared up at the ceiling. I had spent the entire day within these four walls. Even so, it felt like I was looking at it with new eyes now.

I closed my eyes when I heard the shower turn off, resisting the urge to yank the blanket over my head. I wasn't seven. Hiding wouldn't make the monster disappear. But how great would it be if that were the case?

The bathroom door opened, and I didn't move when I heard him walk over to me, his bare feet padding across the carpeted floor. He stood at the edge of the bed, just in front of me.

"Aren't you going to look at me, wildcat?"

I let out a small sigh. "Stop calling me that."

I could hear the smile in his voice when he asked, "Why?"

"Because I have a name."

There was a slight pause on his end. I was almost tempted to open my eyes and read his face. Not that it would tell me much about what the man was thinking.

"Emmy."

My skin tingled at the sound of my name in his voice. I had never reacted so strongly to my own name.

"Emmy," he said, and I felt him shift closer to me. The heat of his body radiated toward me, making me uncomfortably warm underneath the covers. My cheeks flushed, and I was sure he could tell.

My eyes sprang open when I felt a callused finger run up and down my cheek.

I looked up into mesmerizing blue eyes.

The color reminded me of the ocean. Of hope and freedom and beauty.

It reminded me of everything he took from me.

I turned away from him, only for my eyes to come upon an expanse of bare skin.

Fuck.

I sucked in a sharp breath, my eyes tracking down all the tattoo colors, from the floral design that decorated his right bicep down to his elbow, to the kneeling angel on his right pec. My eyes took in the angel, wondering if it was the trick of the light or if that angel really look as tortured as I was making her out to be.

I swallowed and settled my gaze on the other ones, just as beautiful, from the realistic feather on the side of his left forearm to a broken old-fashioned pocket watch on the opposite side.

My lips felt dry.

I had always been fascinated with men's forearms, and Dominic had nice ones. Veiny and tan, and I was hot. Too hot.

The man was built like a tank. A huge, muscular tank, with defined muscles that told me he did more than spend a few hours at the gym every week.

No, this body was a work of art that took decades of training to achieve—and how well he achieved it.

His shoulders were broad, his neck thick—the only place on his upper body that wasn't covered in ink—and he had massive arms that were wider than my thighs, a hard stomach that housed an eight-pack, and a happy trail that led down into the towel that covered his lower half.

Even like this, I could tell he was big.

Fuck, but he was big.

Too big.

And getting bigger.

My gaze jumped to his and was met with a light amusement on his face.

I pulled the covers up further to hide the bottom half of my face.

I couldn't believe he had just caught me ogling him.

I couldn't believe I *was* ogling him.

He threw his head back and let out a deep laugh that vibrated deep within my skin.

If I wasn't blushing before, I was sure my entire face and ears were now red.

He bent down until his face was mere inches from mine.

Like this, I could make out the individual golden flecks in the blue of his eyes.

"Do you like what you see, Emmy?"

I didn't know how to answer him. It was obvious that I did, but I wasn't going to admit to it. I would die first.

It didn't seem like he wanted an answer, anyway.

"Be a good girl today, okay?"

I frowned at him.

What the hell did that mean?

He reached over and patted my hair. I could only watch him silently, and after a while, he stood up and turned away, heading to the walk-in closet. I caught sight of the realistic wings that spanned across his shoulder blades.

Just before he walked into the closet, he dropped the towel.

I couldn't be sure, but I thought I let out a small squeak in surprise, and Dominic laughed at me.

Dominic left the room soon after that, with that stupid smile plastered across his face.

I would be fucking smiling too, if I was allowed to leave my prison.

I might have been embarrassed about this morning, but now that he was gone, it was replaced with anger and frustration.

I quickly got ready for my day and settled back on my usual spot, in the recliner and looking out the locked window.

The door clicked open, drawing my attention. Lucy came in. Her gaze automatically moved to me, and she shot me a friendly smile.

I didn't smile back.

"You're up," she said, her voice soft and airy.

My eyes widened in surprise. She did not sound the way I had expected. She had a very soft feminine voice.

She laughed at the look on my face, and I schooled my features back to neutral.

"Why are you looking at me like that?" she asked.

I shook my head. "Just surprise you're actually speaking to me."

"You are?" she asked, and I couldn't tell if she was being serious or coy. The small glimmer in her eyes told me the latter, but her expressionless face suggested otherwise.

I shifted in the recliner, not knowing how to answer her or react to such an odd woman.

"Would you like to see the house?" Lucy asked.

I narrowed my eyes at her. "You're allowed to let me out of this room?"

She nodded. "Of course. Dominic wants you to be comfortable here."

I didn't know whether to laugh at that or not. He wanted me to be comfortable here? How comfortable did he imagine me getting?

Lucy tilted her head to the side, and I knew better than to look a gift horse in the mouth. And that was what this was. A messed-up gift.

I quickly got off the recliner, and Lucy walked outside. I looked down at an invisible line at the threshold, unsure why my heart was pounding so hard. It wasn't like I had been in this room all that long, but I had believed I would be here longer, until Dominic…

I didn't exactly know why Dominic took me or what he planned on doing with me.

I should be scared, and though I was initially, a sort of numbness had settled over me now. I was just taking it one day at a time.

Lucy looked back at me when she got to the stairs. "Coming?"

I sighed inaudibly and quickly followed her to the stairs, touring the house for the first time.

"How many bedrooms are there?" I asked when I walked past a room with the door open. A look inside had me thinking it was probably Braxton's room. I wondered how he was dealing with everything that had happened. I also wondered where he was.

"Four, including the office downstairs," she answered without looking back. I paused on the stairs.

So there was room for me to be somewhere other than with Dominic?

What. The. Hell.

We came downstairs, and I could only look around with wide eyes.

This... was not what I was expecting.

Not for the president of the King's Men MC. The man was rough with sharp edges that cut, and he lived in a nice, luxurious house with a housekeeper?

"How long has he been here?" I asked.

"About thirteen years," Lucy answered.

"And how long have you been working with him?"

"A few years longer than that," she answered, and something about her expression told me not to pry. "Since he was living in Las Vegas."

"Las Vegas?"

She nodded. "That's where the King's Men originated. It was started by a man named Brooks Tanner. When Dominic took over, he brought the club to California."

There were so many questions swirling inside my brain. I kept my mouth shut, afraid I might say something that crossed a line with her.

My focus shifted to the front door.

"I wouldn't," Lucy said.

I turned to her. She wasn't that much bigger than me.

Plus, I was much younger than her. Did she think she would be able to keep me here if I decided to make a run for it?

"Our closest neighbor is about a mile away," Lucy added. "And Dominic has men posted outside the house. You wouldn't even cross the property line, and the privileges you have right now would be gone."

My lips snarled. "Privileges? You mean my freedom has to be earned?"

Something softened in her eyes, something that looked a hell of a lot like pity, before she schooled her expression. "I don't make the rules, Emmy. But don't do anything stupid until you know more."

"Know more about what?" I asked. When she didn't answer, I laughed. "All I did was save Braxton. Dominic should be getting on his fucking knees and thanking me, not holding me here. I have a life outside this house, and he just decided to take it away?"

"Calm down, Emmy—"

"I am calm!"

She didn't say anything to that. My fists clenched, and I took a deep breath.

We were silent for a beat. "I'm going to make some breakfast and maybe do some baking. Would you like to help me?"

I blinked, trying to will the tears away. I did not want to break down in front of her.

"I'll be in the kitchen if you decide to help," she said.

She turned and walked away from me.

I considered my options: risk going outside and running into Dominic's goons, go back up to my prison in Dominic's room, or help Lucy.

None of those things held any appeal.

I walked into the kitchen.

9

DOMINIC

I PARKED MY BIKE IN THE DRIVEWAY AND LOOKED UP AT THE darkened house.

The men I had guarding the place nodded their heads at me before they went back to their car, back to their home.

I didn't usually have guards around here, and these men weren't really guards… more like prison wardens, keeping one small woman inside my house.

It was late.

Well past the time for anyone to be up and about, and though I was fucking tired as hell, I wasn't sleepy.

I couldn't remember the last time I had a full night's sleep, even with the little wildcat in my arms the night before.

It hadn't been my plan to put her in my room, or to sleep in my bed.

Hell, Kai's room had been empty for a while now. I could have put her in there.

The windows had already been nailed shut, a remnant of my son's wild high school years, when he would sneak out in the middle of the night and get into all sorts of trouble around town.

I was a young dad, and I probably had more energy to deal with a teenage boy than the other old fucks in my position, but Kai's teenage years were ones I was so fucking grateful had passed.

I shivered just thinking back on it.

Now I didn't have a wild teenager in my house, but a woman held against her will.

I should fucking feel bad about that.

I was just fucking confused, wondering what it was about the little wildcat that got to me so much, or why the hell I had been thinking about her all day.

I was sure Roman and Micah knew my mind was elsewhere today, because Roman was looking at me with a shit-eating grin on his face for most of the day, and Micah was looking at me with the same expression he had given Roman when shit with him and Ryleigh had just started.

Fuck me.

I turned off the ignition on my bike, and a sudden silence filled the air.

I hopped off my bike and made my way inside the silent, dark house. Lucy should be back at her own home by now, with Colt, one of my club brothers—and her husband.

I came up to my room first. I knew it was empty before I even opened the door. Only the fact that there was no way for Emmy to have escaped with my men outside kept me from panicking.

Where the fuck could she have gone?

I went to the room next to mine—Braxton's, who was now safely under the care of his aunt—found it empty, and went to Kai's old bedroom.

I found her curved into a small ball under the covers, sleeping soundlessly.

Like a small child, so sure of her surroundings.

She didn't even know a monster was in her midst, wanting to claim her and own her completely.

I shook my head and tried to calm my heart.

What the fuck was that?

Why the hell did she affect me so much?

Fuck, but I didn't even feel this way about Veronica, Kai and Braxton's mom.

I had been ready to make her my old lady and give her all the benefits of being mine.

But the time we were together, the club was just taking off.

I was fucking busy, and any free time I had was dedicated to the boys.

It was something she should have fucking accepted, but she hated it. She hated coming in second to the boys, and I didn't fucking put up a fight when she told me she wanted to leave everything behind, including her sons—her fucking *sons*—and go back to Las Vegas.

I might be a lot of things, but I would never abandon my kids, and I couldn't fucking understand how she could. Braxton was just a baby at the time. He barely remembered her, but Kai sure as fuck did.

And both of my boys were hurt over that.

No one mentioned Veronica in this house.

It wouldn't have mattered because the only reason I had allowed her to be as close to me as she had been was for the boys.

But I didn't fucking feel the need to claim her as mine, to protect her from all the bad shit in this world, even if I was that bad shit happening to her.

I didn't feel like my fucking dead heart was trying to beat at the sight of her.

I stepped closer to Emmy, and from the light in the hallway, something silver glinted on the bed.

I frowned a little and extracted the kitchen knife she had hidden under her pillow.

Fuck me, but if I wasn't trying to be quiet and let the poor girl sleep, I might have fucking laughed over the ridiculousness of this.

What did this girl think would happen?

I towered over her by about a foot and outweighed her by more than a hundred pounds.

How much damage did this little wildcat really think she could cause?

She was like a little kitten trying to take on a lion.

And I fucking ruled this jungle.

I smirked at the little innocent and dragged the covers off.

She was in my clothes.

She fucking looked good in my clothes, but the image of me dressing her up in pretty, girly shit took hold, and fuck, but that had its appeal, too.

I could present her like a fucking queen to the outside world, gifting her with all expensive and pretty things, but behind closed doors, dress her up like my own little whore.

My pretty little sex doll.

Shaking away the thought and trying to keep my hard-on under control, I lifted her into my arms.

She shifted and made a small noise before turning her head and burying her face in my chest.

She didn't wake up when I brought us back to my room and put her on her side of the bed, furthest from the door.

My heart finally calmed at the sight.

She belonged in my bed.

And that was where she would stay.

Taking her was to keep her safe from the men who tried to take Braxton.

But it was her fault for looking so fucking appealing.

For looking like she was mine.

Did she think I could let her go once this shit was over?

Did I think I was capable of it?

I shook my head and moved to the bathroom, quickly getting ready for bed.

She didn't stir when I finally peeled the covers back and climbed in. I wrapped my arms around her middle and pulled her to me.

She had been using my shampoo and body wash, yet there was still a unique floral scent to her that fucking got to me.

I buried my face in the back of her neck, my hand coming up and settling between her perky tits.

Fucking mine.

I WAS up before the sun had even peeked through the clouds.

A look at the clock on the nightstand told me it wouldn't be long until that.

I didn't have shit to do this morning. Most of my work was done at night.

When all the good citizens of Sacramento were asleep.

That was when the real monsters came out to play, and here in this city, in this state, I was the biggest one of them all.

Yet here I was, lying in a warm bed with a soft woman in my arms.

Dawn came through the window, giving enough light for me to make out her features.

Did she know how peaceful she looked like this?

Peace was something I knew very little about.

My life, since the day of my birth, had been nothing but chaos.

I was born to a crack whore of a mother who cared more

about her next fix than her children, and a dad who pimped out his wife for money in the same house his children slept in at night. Everything was noisy and chaotic and fucking scary.

I realized early on the only way to survive, to fucking protect my baby sister in such a dark, cruel world, was to be an even bigger monster than the people who brought me into this world.

It wasn't without pain.

It wasn't without loss.

Now my baby sister barely spoke to me, having moved to another fucking country to get away from all the bad shit I brought to the table.

And my nephew was dead at fifteen.

But with Emmy in my arms…

I still felt like a fucking monster, but perhaps that was okay.

I tightened my arms around her, and her face scrunched a bit, her eyes fluttering before slowly opening.

She focused her gaze on me, the sleepy softness in her eyes very much present this morning.

It took a second for awareness to come to her, but when it did, her eyes widened, and she looked around the room.

"Why the hell am I here?"

"I carried you back to my bed last night," I answered casually.

Her eyes shifted about the room, and I watched the fascinating hazel irises change with her thoughts. "Why?"

"'Cause this is where you sleep."

Her eyes narrowed. "With you."

One corner of my lips lifted in a small smirk. "That's right."

There was a slight pause on her end. "Why?"

Fuck if I knew.

I didn't answer her. I didn't know how. Instead, I reached over for her, and pressed my thumbs against her full bottom lip.

She had the most fascinating lips.

Soft and supple, they settled in a natural pout that made me want to kiss her.

Fuck, but I really wanted to know what she tasted like.

I licked my lips, drawing her attention to them, and she froze.

"Dominic—"

Her words were cut off when I pressed my lips against hers.

Electricity traveled across my skin from our lips, bringing forth a prickling of awareness.

I groaned against her and pressed my lips harder against hers.

Fuck, but she was everything I had imagined her to be. I could be fucking addicted to this. To her.

I tightened my arms around her and shifted over her body, pressing her down on the mattress.

She froze beneath me for a beat, a small sound of protest coming out and vibrating the skin between us. Her hands came out from between us, pushing at my chest and trying to get me away from her.

I grabbed her hands and pressed them down against the mattress, deepening the kiss and molding my lips over hers.

She struggled underneath me, but I could feel the fight leaving her the more I kissed her.

I pulled back slightly so we could both catch our breath.

"Dominic…"

I bit her bottom lip.

She gasped, and I took advantage of that. I moved my tongue in between her lips, pulling her closer to me until there wasn't an inch of space separating our bodies.

Fuck.

I kissed her harder, deeper, rougher.

I felt her relax against me, then another sound came out—and this one didn't sound like protest, but pleasure.

The hands that were pushing against my chest were now on my shoulders, clinging to me.

I gentled my movements, savoring the taste of her.

My hands slowly explored the curves of her body.

I didn't know what it was about this girl that got to me so much, but I couldn't bring myself to question it. Couldn't bring myself to stop.

I wanted to take everything from her.

I molded one hand around one tit through her shirt and played with it, massaging the pliant flesh before plucking at her hard nipple with my fingers.

Her back arched, and she wiggled beneath me, her hips rocking against my body.

Fuck.

Stars danced behind my eyes.

I played with her nipple, wanting to taste it so fucking bad, but not wanting to stop the kiss.

I spread her legs with my hips and crawled between them.

I thrust against the fabric of the sweatpants she wore, letting her feel my hard-on against her soft pussy.

That seemed to be the thing that brought her back to reality.

She gasped, bit my lip hard, and angled her head away.

I leaned back and looked at her, from flushed cheeks to dark pupils and swollen lips. Slowly, my tongue peeked out, and I touched the spot she had bitten, a slight metallic taste hitting me.

She watched me carefully before she placed her hands on my chest and pushed me away.

I let her win and watched as she moved out from under me, off the bed and to the bathroom.

She closed the door with a loud bang before I heard the lock click.

Did she think that would keep me out?

I had the key, but I let her have this moment to herself.

I was still fucking reeling.

My hand came to my lips as I thought about the kiss.

Fuck, but what was that?

I LEFT THE HOUSE EARLY.

Earlier than I usually would unless I had to, and this morning I didn't have to, but I didn't know how to stay in the same house as Emmy and think straight.

There were a few people here at the warehouse, having worked through the night.

I didn't greet anyone as I walked straight to my office and looked out the glass window that separated my office from the work area.

Fuck, but I needed to get my head on straight.

I was acting like Roman had when he tried to hide Ryleigh from the club.

I couldn't afford the distraction.

Not as president.

Not when there were so many people depending on me.

My mind had been fucked since the moment I decided to bring the little wildcat home with me, and I couldn't reason why I had done this, even to myself.

I could have thrown some money her way and told her to stay out of California, out of the country, until this shit got resolved.

But I wanted her close, even if her closeness did fuck with my mind.

I leaned back in the chair and tried to focus on what was important.

My club. My business.

My brothers and my boys.

There was always some shit that needed to be done, and I couldn't let the prim-and-proper piano teacher mess with my mind, even if I was the one who brought her into my messed-up world.

She might have gotten close to my world when she helped Braxton, but I was the one who dragged her fully into it, ignoring her kicking and screaming, and keeping her in my house under the fucked-up guise of protecting her.

I still didn't know who the fuck had tried to mess with my son.

There was nothing to go on, and the idea of this being an inside job came back to mind.

Who would have known about Braxton's schedule, where the hell he would be that day, other than my brothers in the club?

Perhaps I had gotten too soft over the years.

Too fucking lenient.

I used to think I ruled this club with an iron fist. How could that fucking be true with a traitor in the midst?

But that was going to fucking change.

It was time to set some rat traps.

10

EMMY

LUCY LEFT EARLY—AROUND SIX O'CLOCK—ONCE DINNER WAS made and the kitchen was cleaned.

She made roast beef and brussel sprouts, and though it smelled amazing, food was the last thing on my mind.

My emotions had been flying all over the place all day.

I envied her freedom to go home. I was getting cabin fever.

I was sick and tired of looking at the walls in the huge house, sick of the men I caught sight of loitering out front, whose one job was to keep me here until Dominic came home, and I was—

I took a deep breath.

I fucking hated my reaction to his kiss.

I should not have reacted at all, unless that reaction was disgust, but that was far from the truth and Dominic knew it, and I knew it as well.

I hadn't wanted him to stop kissing me.

To stop touching me.

And the worst part was, I couldn't stop thinking about it all day.

How far would we have gone if I hadn't pushed him away?

I didn't think I was ready for anything with him.

The last relationship I had been in was when I was eighteen, and saying it had ended in disaster was an understatement of the century.

I looked down at my scarred hands.

I didn't think Dominic knew, or if he did, he hadn't said anything about it. The surgeon who had taken care of me at the hospital had done a good job of reducing the number of visible scars. I could still feel the indents caused by what scars were left, though. If Dominic looked closely enough, he would see just how disfigured my hands were.

It wouldn't have mattered to me if they were the ugliest hands in the world. I would have taken ugly hands if it meant I could have the ability to play the piano again.

I would have given up almost anything.

But that was the least of my problems right now.

I was still trapped here, and I had kissed Dominic Madden, a man so wrong for me in every way, it wasn't even funny.

Yet my lips tingled in remembrance of the kiss, and my clit throbbed as I thought back to him pushing his erection against me.

I had been battling with two different emotions all day.

Pleasure and anger.

Right now, anger was winning, but not by much, and I wanted *out* of this house.

I paced the small hallway that separated the kitchen and the living room. I had a full view of the front door, but it wouldn't have mattered. If his schedule from last night were anything to go by, Dominic wouldn't be home until late.

Still, I had the kitchen knife I had been able to sneak in with me last night tucked into my pants.

I pulled it out, my hand touching the metal blade, warm with my body heat.

I swallowed.

Could I use this on another person, even if it was to ensure I could get away from my prison?

The only time I had ever touched a knife was when I was cooking, and that was rare.

I didn't know how to cook, and what was more, I hated it.

I hated the feeling of slicing into raw meat, and now I was willing to use this on another human being?

My hands shook, and I realized too late that I should have been more aware of my surroundings when a thick voice called by the front door.

"What are you doing, wildcat?"

My breath caught. Dominic was standing there, his face partially hidden in shadow.

My heart felt like it was going to fall out of my throat, and I didn't know how to answer him.

He took a step toward me.

I took one back, holding the knife in front of me. He paused.

"Put that away before you hurt yourself," he said.

I shook my head. Did he really think I was stupid? Now that he'd caught me with a weapon, did he think I would just put it away and surrender to him?

"Let me go, Dominic."

He shook his head. "Can't do that."

I hated how calm he sounded right then, especially because of how not calm my heart was.

I felt light-headed, and I didn't know how much more of this I could take.

"Why not?" I asked. "I won't tell anyone. Who would I tell? Who would believe me? We both know the King's Men MC rules the state, and I am just an insignificant woman."

"I wouldn't call you insignificant," he said quietly. I couldn't tell what the tone of his voice meant or what he was thinking or feeling.

It was one thing for the monster to be angry; it was another for him to be so… emotionless.

"P-please," I begged, and I hated myself just a little bit more. "I just—fuck. I just want to leave. You don't have any right to keep me here. Just let me fucking go!"

And that anger came back, overshadowing the fear.

Anger and desperation only led to one thing.

Bad and impulsive decisions.

I didn't think before I threw the knife at Dominic. I regretted my decision almost instantly, as the knife flew out of my hand. But it was too late. I was watching this in slow motion, and I wanted to yell at him to get out of the way.

I didn't say anything. I couldn't.

Dominic ducked in time, and it hit the wall with a loud bang before falling to the carpet by his feet.

His eyes were incredulous.

Mine were wide and fearful.

We didn't say anything for one… two… three long seconds.

I didn't know who had moved first, and I didn't care.

I turned and ran out of there, and he gave chase.

I dashed up the stairs, my heart plummeting to my stomach as I heard his heavy footsteps behind me. I didn't know where I was going, and I didn't care, just as long as I got away from him.

I hesitated at the top, looking to my left at Dominic's room, and to my right, at the room I had spent a part of my night in before he'd carried me out.

I tried to head right.

But that small hesitation was all it took for him to catch up to me.

He wrapped his arms around my waist and lifted me, my back plastered up against his front.

I struggled in his hold, my arms and legs flailing to get him to release me.

"No! Let me go, you sick, terrible, creepy monster! Let me go! Let me go!"

He shook me against him, his lips grazing my ear and making fear run up and down my spine. I was going to be sick.

"You started this, little girl. You could have killed me with that knife."

"That's the point!"

He shook me again. "Well, now you've done it. You've unleashed the monster."

I cried out when he turned us around and brought me to his room.

"No, please," I begged, tears dripping down my chin.

"I might be a monster," he said, kicking the bedroom door open. I flinched at the noise. He threw me on the bed, not too gently. I turned around and looked at him. "But I'm your monster."

I shook my head and tried to back away from him. He grabbed my legs and pulled me toward him. I kicked his hands, but he was much too strong and much too quick. It didn't seem to have any effect on him.

"Let go of me!" I screamed, panic in my voice.

He shook his head. "No. Now you have to fucking deal with *your* fucking monster."

"I don't want it. It's not mine."

He wasn't mine. Not the man, and definitely not the monster.

He crawled his way up my body, pushing my legs apart and settling between my legs, bringing us to the same position we had been in this morning.

Unlike this morning, I didn't feel desire mixed with fear and a hint of apprehension.

No, right now, all I was feeling was unadulterated fear.

I struggled beneath him, and he pushed his body weight down on top of me, trapping me against the soft mattress and his hard body.

"Dominic!"

"Say my name again, wildcat," he said roughly, his eyes wild.

He pushed against me once again, his hard erection pressing against me in the most intimate position possible.

My legs trembled. "Please, I'm sorry."

"What a fucking stupid thing to do."

"Please."

He held still but didn't lessen his weight, letting me feel the hard press of him, feel the way he covered my body with his. Letting me feel the solid man on top of me, an immovable burden that wouldn't lessen unless he decided to lessen it.

I was helpless beneath him, unable to budge under his weight.

I met his eyes. The blue irises swirled in an electric fire that I didn't think I had seen on any other men.

My lips trembled, and his expression changed marginally.

It was slight, and I almost wouldn't have noticed it had I not been looking at him closely enough.

My mouth opened but nothing came out, and I didn't know why it suddenly felt like the weight of the world was piled onto my too-small shoulders.

His face relaxed, apathy etched into every line, and somehow, that only worked to calm me down. He wasn't looking at me with pity.

Not the way people back home had once they found out what happened to me.

The hushed whispers of "What a shame. And she was so talented," echoed in the empty spaces, and I had to pretend I didn't hear them.

It was one of the reasons I chose to move a state away. I couldn't handle it anymore.

And Dominic was different. Monsters couldn't feel empathy for others, could they?

Somehow, it made it so much better.

Slowly, I raised my arms and wrapped them around his neck.

He didn't stop me.

He didn't say anything.

For a moment, I didn't even think he was breathing.

I let my hands settle on the back of his neck, my fingers playing with the short hair there before I drew him down to me. He came willingly, then I buried my face in his neck.

The tremors came first.

Then the tears.

Dominic tensed above me for a quick second before he became almost pliant in my arms.

"Shh, it's okay, wildcat," he said softly. His soothing voice only made me want to cry harder.

"I'm sorry," I said. God. I almost hurt someone. I almost hurt him. What would I have done if he hadn't ducked in time?

Nausea bubbled its way to the surface, and I quickly pushed it down, not wanting to think about it. I couldn't.

"It's okay," he said. I couldn't believe he was trying to comfort me. There was something messed up about us, because I was feeling comforted.

He shifted us around until he was lying on his back on the bed and I was on top of him. I unfurled my arms from his neck and placed them on his chest, moving my face up until I had it buried in his neck again, inhaling his scent.

He was just so solid beneath me.

So real.

There was something reassuring about his form, and as stupid as it might be, I didn't want to let go.

Not yet.

I couldn't even remember the last time someone had held me in their arms like this.

I couldn't even remember the last time someone had the ability to make the world cease in significance for me, even for an infinitesimal moment in time.

I closed my eyes, and he ran his soothing hands up and down my back.

I didn't know how long we stayed like that.

I didn't care.

I just…

I just wanted to stay.

WE DIDN'T TALK MUCH as Dominic led me by the hand downstairs and to the kitchen.

I didn't have the strength to say or do much of anything, so I didn't mind when he took control and started preparing our plates for dinner.

He set me on a barstool by the huge kitchen island, and I watched as he moved with ease.

He glanced over at me briefly before he went back to what he was doing, and I wondered what it would be like to be this kind of man in the world, confident in his role in it.

It took me a moment to realize he had only piled one plate with a mountain of food, not until he placed it in front of me. Did he think I could finish all that on my own?

I frowned and looked at him questioningly.

He didn't answer as he held out his free hand to me.

I instinctively placed my hand in his before I really thought better of it, and he pulled me up from the chair.

Then he sat.

Did he want me to stand there and watch him eat?

I narrowed my eyes at him at the thought, and I swore his lips twitched a little before he grabbed my waist and lifted me onto his lap.

I stiffened.

I shouldn't be surprised at this, considering we'd been in this position before.

He slid the plate closer to us.

"Dominic?"

"Yeah?" he asked, forking up some roast beef and holding it against my lips.

I took it, chewing slowly before I spoke. "What are you doing?"

"What does it look like I'm doing?"

"Giving in to a feeding fetish?"

He chuckled lightly and shook his head. "Believe it or not, I don't make it a habit of feeding women."

"Or not," I muttered. He was just too comfortable with this. I watched as he took some food for himself.

I should have stopped him.

I didn't.

I let him feed me dinner and watched as he took his own bites between mine. We finished the plate quickly. He gently helped me onto my feet and brought the dish to the sink.

I silently watched as he turned around and walked to me.

He picked me up and made his way toward his room.

The man obviously didn't know the definition of personal boundaries because he apparently had none.

And I was so tired from all that had happened, the crying and the anger and the fear.

I was so tired.

If his plan was to wear me down and make me compliant…

Well, he was succeeding.

I wrapped my arms around his neck and rested my chin on his shoulder.

I felt him pause on the stairs for a fraction of a second before he continued.

He set me on the bathroom sink, my back to the mirror, and watched me with those unreadable blue eyes of his.

"Get ready for bed," he said gruffly.

"What, you're not going to help me brush my teeth?" I said, only half joking.

One eyebrow rose at that, amusement glinting in his eyes, and he made a move to grab my toothbrush, calling my bluff.

My eyes widened, and I snatched it up before he could.

He smirked at me and I hopped off the counter, pushing him away and eliciting a small chuckle from him.

The sound affected me more than it should have, and I shivered. I didn't do anything until he walked out of the bathroom.

I turned to the mirror and examined my reflection, only to find a stranger there.

I didn't know if that was a good thing or not.

11

EMMY

By the time I woke up the next morning, Dominic had already left for the day.

Since he'd brought me to his house, there wasn't a single night I had spent by myself, and I was starting to think it would never happen now.

I didn't know what to think about that.

Why would he want to spend most of his nights with me?

I wished Dominic wasn't so hard to read. Perhaps I wouldn't be spending most of my time in a state of confusion.

One look at Dominic, and it was easy to see he was experienced.

Far more experienced than me, and there wasn't a doubt in mind that he didn't lack willing bed partners, so why take me—an unwilling one?

Are you really unwilling? a small voice whispered in my mind.

I quickly shook it away and climbed off the bed. I made my way to the bathroom, squinting at the bright morning light around me as I brushed my teeth.

My mind was lost somewhere far from reality, and perhaps that was why the morning was going by so slowly.

Finally, when I made my way downstairs, I found Lucy in the kitchen, sipping on a cup of coffee and looking like she was waiting for me.

Her eyes brightened when I walked in.

I paused in my step and eyed her warily.

I might have gotten a little closer to her in the past two days, but I hadn't forgotten who had her loyalty, and it wasn't me.

"You're up," she said, getting off the kitchen barstool. The same barstool Dominic had sat on last night with me in his lap while he fed me.

I didn't think I would be able to see that stool without thinking about the memory from now on.

"I'm sorry. I didn't know you were waiting for me."

She waved away my apology and shot me a soft smile. One I couldn't help but return. "We're going shopping today."

"We are?" I asked, confused.

She nodded. "Wouldn't you like to be in your own clothes?"

I could be in my own clothes if Dominic let me go home, but I didn't say that out loud. The look on her face told me she could tell what I was thinking.

She tilted her head to the side. "What do you say, Emmy? Don't you want to get out of this house and spend a whole bunch of Dominic's money?"

I couldn't help but laugh at that. "Fine. You make an appealing case. And I wouldn't mind putting a small dent in his bank account."

She laughed. "That wouldn't be accomplished with just one shopping trip, dear. But we'll still have a lot of fun."

Right.

I was sure Dominic was pretty well off.

If the rumors I had heard about him were even half true, then he really did rule California.

I didn't want to know how he obtained his money, as I was sure most didn't come from legitimate businesses.

I looked down at myself. I was in Dominic's black sweats that were way too long for me, and his hoodie.

I looked comfortable.

"You look fine," Lucy said as if she could read my mind.

I nodded.

Vanity should probably be the last thing I worried about, given my situation. "Let's go."

THE SHOPPING TRIP took up most of the day.

We stopped for lunch, and the man who had come in with Lucy my first day here accompanied us, along with a couple of men I was sure had the job of watching the house and making sure I didn't leave.

I didn't really see them, not unless I was paying attention, but the knowledge that they were there, shadowing us closely, was a stark reminder of my situation.

Things had been… chaotic with Dominic last night, but that didn't mean all my emotions had suddenly disappeared just because he had held me in his arms as if I was something precious.

So I did the only thing I could do in situations like this.

I spent the bastard's money as if there was no tomorrow.

Anything I touched, I bought.

It didn't matter that I might not like it once I had it, or that I might never have the chance to wear it.

It didn't matter.

If it was pretty in some way, it came with me, and I didn't pay attention to the price.

I was a woman on a mission.

Lucy and Colt—the man who accompanied us—looked on with amusement in their eyes.

I didn't care, and there was some satisfaction in finding out I had spent more in one store than I had in the previous ones.

It became like a game.

I hoped Dominic would think of me when he received his credit card bill and realized just how much useless shit I'd bought.

My hands came to a stop on a pale pink silk scarf. There was no price tag. But we were in a nice little boutique that didn't have price tags on any of their things.

I shot Lucy a small smile and grabbed the scarf. I would never have a chance to wear it, since I didn't know where I might go that would be appropriate for me to wear it, but it was soft, I liked the color, and at this moment, I hated Dominic Madden with everything in me.

UNLIKE LAST NIGHT, Dominic didn't come home early.

I didn't know if he was coming home tonight at all. If something had happened to prevent him from coming home...

I should wish for him to get hurt. Wish for something to stop him from coming back home to me. Instead, the thought of it made it almost hard for me to breathe.

I took a deep inhale and let it out slowly as I lay back down on the bed and turned off the lamp in Dominic's room.

I debated whether I should sleep in the room I had been in before, but what would be the point if he would just carry me back to his room in the end?

So now I was lying on his bed in his room, in one of his

shirts and a pair of boxers, because despite the shopping trip, I didn't think to buy any sleep clothes.

The shirt smelled like him.

Everything in this place smelled like him.

I looked out the window and stared at the streetlight I had been so fascinated with since day one, wondering how the hell I was supposed to fall asleep when my mind seemed to run a million miles an hour.

I was alone in a big house that wasn't mine, in clothes that weren't mine, and here I was, worrying—

I jumped when I heard the front door open.

He was home.

The weight on my chest lifted as I heard his footsteps coming up the stairs. The door to the room slowly opened, revealing a huge shadow in the doorway.

I could only make out some of his features, but I could tell his eyes were on me.

"Are you asleep, wildcat?"

I didn't answer him right away. I didn't know if I should pretend I was asleep or not.

"Yes," I said.

A small laugh escaped, and he fumbled with the light switch and turned it on.

I blinked against the intrusion of light.

He was in a black leather jacket over a plain white T-shirt that I knew from memory molded against his muscular form perfectly, fitted dark blue jeans that looked well worn, and black boots.

He brought with him the scent of grass, outdoors, and cigarettes.

I didn't think Dominic smoked since I hadn't seen any cigarettes or ashtrays around the house or in his room, but someone was smoking wherever he had just been.

It wasn't an unpleasant smell.

I blinked up at him again, and something strange flashed over his eyes as he gazed at me lying on his bed.

He walked over and slowly reached for me, as if he was afraid of scaring me off. He set me in a sitting position and tucked a strand of my dark hair behind my ear.

"Come on. I want to show you something."

"What?" I asked as he pulled the blanket away from me.

His eyes heated their way across my skin when he realized what I was wearing.

I pretended not to notice. Acknowledging Dominic's attraction to me was dangerous, especially since I was certain he knew I was also attracted to him, despite the whirlwind of my mostly negative emotions regarding him.

He walked to the bureau, withdrew another pair of black sweats, and threw them on the bed before going into the walk-in closet.

He came out moments later with a gray sweater in his hand.

I was still in a small daze when he returned to me and slid me toward the edge. Then, he proceeded to dress me.

My eyes widened. "I can dress myself."

He shot me an amused look. "I know."

But he didn't move away as I expected. He hauled me to standing and pulled the sweats all the way up, pulling at the strings so the pants stayed on my hips before wrapping the sweater around me.

Once he had it zipped up, he grabbed my hand and led me out of the room.

I had no choice but to follow.

"Where are we going?" I asked.

"You'll see," he answered cryptically.

He led me outside the house.

The property seemed to be a little different during the

nighttime. The streetlamp I had been looking at stood off to the side of the house.

Dominic brought me to his bike.

I pulled on his hand and shook my head. "No way. I'm not getting on that deathtrap again with you."

He looked at me, his lips curving into a small smile. "Scared, wildcat?"

"Absolutely."

There was no need for pretense. The fact that there wasn't anything between me and the open road was unnerving enough.

The first time I was on his bike, I had no choice. And with all the shit that had happened with Braxton, I hadn't given myself the time to think about it. I had been terrified, but not as much as I had been terrified about coming face-to-face with the president of the King's Men MC. This time was different. I didn't want to get on his bike a second time.

"Do you trust me?" he asked.

I narrowed my eyes at him. "Nope."

He laughed and, cupping my shoulders with his hands, bent down until we were eye to eye. "Fair enough. But I won't let anything happen to you, okay?"

He placed a helmet on my head despite my protest. I must be really out of it because I hadn't even noticed the helmet on the bike.

I doubt he would wear one as well.

I shook my head.

"Get on the bike," he said. "The last thing I want to do is stand out here arguing with you."

"You're the one who dragged me out of bed at this godforsaken time."

"Baby, it's barely ten o'clock at night."

Not everyone functions on so little sleep the way he

seemed to. It wasn't late when I went to bed, but I wouldn't exactly call this early, either.

He climbed on the bike and held his hand out to me.

I hesitated. The streetlamp provided enough illumination that I could make out the expectant look on his face. One way or another, I would be getting on the back of this bike, letting him drive me wherever he wanted.

I just...

I grabbed his hand and let him help me climb on.

I just wanted the illusion of choice.

But it was a fucking joke.

I had no choice in this, not when it came to Dominic Madden, but I didn't want to fight him either. I would surely lose.

He wrapped my arms around his middle, bringing me close to him. So close, I was pressed up against him in every way possible, and could feel his powerful muscles tense with every movement he made.

He turned on the bike, and I jumped a little at the noise.

I hadn't forgotten how loud the engine was, yet it still surprised me.

"Hold on tight," he said loudly. "When I turn, you lean with me, got it? We'll be in sync."

He turned slightly, and I could see his lips curved in a devilish smile. "It's like sex. And something tells me you'll have no problem keeping up."

And with that, he drove off, my gasp of surprise blending with the wind and his laugh.

Bastard.

He drove fast but not recklessly.

I should have been scared, but I felt oddly safe with him.

I shouldn't trust him, yet a stupid part of me believed him when he told me he wouldn't let anything bad happen to me.

But what happened when *he* was the bad thing happening to me?

Dominic expertly weaved through the almost-empty streets, and after a while, I could see the appeal of riding. I could see why so many people loved it, and I began to understand the freedom that came with being on the back of a bike that offered very little protection.

It was nothing like the last time. Perhaps it was because I knew what to expect, but I wasn't as scared.

I was… having fun.

It was titillating. I grinned when he made a right turn, leaning with his body as he'd instructed, my eyes meeting his in the side mirror.

I smiled, and he chuckled, his body vibrating against me.

He revved the engine and went a little faster.

The wind blew by my ears, my hair flying away from my face, and though it was summer, I was still glad Dominic had put a sweater on me beforehand.

This was amazing, and I enjoyed myself much more than I thought.

This probably explained why I didn't realize he was taking me on a familiar road until we came to a stop in the parking lot of my apartment building.

I looked up at the place, and my heart thudded heavily in my chest.

I didn't know if my reaction was a relief to be coming home or…

Or disappointment.

Perhaps both.

A huge part of me was happy to be back. To get back to the home I'd tried to build for myself and to the freedom that was taken away from me.

Yet the disappointment was there, and I couldn't figure out why for the life of me.

I should not feel disappointed. I had wanted to go home since he'd drugged me and taken me back to his home.

But this made little sense.

Why would he bring me back here without any of the stuff I had bought this afternoon?

Unless he was planning on returning everything.

Then why the hell did he have Lucy take me shopping in the first place?

Dominic turned off the engine and held his hand back for me. Quietly, I grabbed it and climbed off the bike. He followed suit, and gently—much more gently than I would have thought he was capable of—he took the helmet off my head.

I looked up at him, and we didn't turn away from each other for three long seconds.

I broke the spell and turned to my apartment building first.

He did the same.

It hadn't been that long since I'd left, but it felt like ages ago.

The building looked different, like I was coming back to a life that wasn't my own.

Dominic also looked up at the building. No doubt he knew which apartment was mine.

It seemed very little went on in this city that he didn't know about.

He wrapped his arm around my shoulder before leading me to my apartment.

I didn't know why he was acting like this, and why he'd suddenly decided to let me come home.

But the closer we got, the more excited I became, and the easier it was for me to forget about the disappointment. I might reflect on it once I was in my bed tonight, wondering if I would see him again because whether or not I wanted to admit it to myself, I was attracted to Dominic. There was no point in denying it to myself.

For a moment in time, there had been some change to my monotonous life.

It felt a little fucked-up that I thought I would remember my time with him with some fondness, but then again, *I* might just be a little messed up.

I shook my head a little at the thought as we arrived at the door, my eyebrows pulling down a little at the beginning of a frown. It took a second for my brain to comprehend that there was something off about the door.

I glanced at Dominic from under his arm, but as usual, his face was impassive, telling me nothing.

My mouth suddenly felt dry, and I licked my lips when Dominic took a small key from his pocket.

It looked nothing like my own key, which probably made sense because the door in front of me wasn't my apartment door.

It was my apartment, with my apartment number hooked in front, but the door was different. The color teal was wrong. It was about a shade or two different from the original and from all the other doors around. Even the doorknob was different.

I had a bad feeling about this.

Dominic unlocked the door, but he didn't push it open.

"What's, uh, what's going on?"

"I need you to brace yourself for what you're about to see, okay? And just know my men have already checked this place out, so we'll be safe inside. Okay?"

"Dominic. What are you talking…" I cleared my throat.

Slowly, he pushed the door open and ushered us inside. The place was dark, and there was a distinct musty scent from being empty for a few days.

I couldn't see anything in the dark, but something felt different, and I wasn't sure I wanted to see it.

It was probably the energy Dominic gave out that clued me in. Though he was quiet, something about him made me think of a bomb near detonation.

Dominic didn't give me a choice when he reached over to the side and turned on the light.

I flinched, my brain taking a moment to understand what I was seeing.

My breath caught.

What the fuck?

I stared at him, and he returned my stare with unemotional blue eyes. There was no pity in them, which was good, because I thought that might just be the thing to throw me off.

"W-what happened to my place?"

"This apartment was broken into the night I rescued you and Braxton."

The word *rescue* was up for debate, especially when it came to me with him, but that was the least of my concerns right now.

Everything, and I mean everything, in my place was ruined.

They didn't spare a single item, including the couch I had saved up for and painstakingly picked out for my place. The fabric on the cushions was torn—or slashed with a knife—and the cotton spilled out and over the floor.

Tears burned my eyes, and I blinked them away, clearing my vision.

My lips trembled as my gaze roamed about, from the thrown-open cabinets to the smashed ceramic dishes on the floor to the—

I let out a small cry and ran over to my keyboard.

I was vaguely aware of Dominic following me, but I couldn't bring myself to care at this point.

The keyboard was—

I closed my eyes.

It was broken.

It didn't matter that I couldn't play as well as I used to. It didn't even matter that I rarely touched it anymore. It was the only thing I'd brought from Nevada with me to California, and now it was on the floor, destroyed.

The cords were cut, most of the keys were detached, and there was a crack down the middle, as if someone had stomped on it.

"I'm sorry, wildcat," Dominic said softly.

I shook my head but didn't know what I was saying no to.

To his pity? Or that I was fucking lucky Dominic decided to take me because I would have come home to this—or, worse, come home to whoever did this, waiting for me and wanting to know where Braxton was.

He wrapped his arms around me and pulled me close, leading me out the door.

I didn't fight him.

"Come on. It's time to get back."

Back home with him, he meant.

Why did he even take me out here tonight?

I had thought he was letting me go.

My mind remained in a sort of daze as we left the apartment. I watched wordlessly as Dominic locked up the apartment, and we returned to his bike.

I barely remembered the trip home or when he parked in front of his house, and we walked inside.

It never even crossed my mind to fight him.

All I could think of was that those men knew who I was and where I lived. They had broken into my apartment and touched my things, and had Dominic not taken me—against my will or not—I might have been there when they broke in.

They would have done more than ruin my things.

They would have brought me in as collateral in a fight that wasn't my own.

I shuddered at the thought.

I didn't have any more energy.

Dominic directed me into the kitchen and sat me down on the barstool we had sat on, what seemed like so long ago.

I didn't even go into my bedroom back at the apartment, but I was sure the state of it would be worse than out in the living room.

My skin crawled at the thought of them touching all my personal things—my clothes, my makeup, my bedding…

I shivered.

They were just things.

I should be thankful it was just my things they ruined, but it didn't make me feel any better.

Dominic placed a steaming cup of tea in front of me. I looked at him in surprise. I didn't even hear him move around the kitchen to prepare it.

"Thank you," I said, my voice soft.

He nodded and leaned his weight against the island, watching me with that unreadable expression again.

I watched the steam billowing to the top of the mug.

"Is that why you had Lucy take me shopping?"

"You need clothes for while you're here. As much as I love the sight of you in my clothes, I'm sure you'll be more comfortable with your own things."

"I don't have any things," I said, trying hard not to lose it.

"Then we'll buy you more," he said gruffly.

I looked up at him, trying to ascertain his emotion. His blue eyes seemed vivid at this time of night. Dominic obviously functioned on less sleep than I did. He didn't even look tired, while I just felt exhausted.

"Why?" I croaked.

"Why what, wildcat?"

"Why are you doing all of this?"

He shrugged. "Drink up and go to sleep. You look tired."

I shot him a glare at the topic change.

"Where's Braxton?" I asked.

He hesitated before he answered, and I wondered if it was because he didn't trust me with that information. I assumed Braxton lived in this house, but I hadn't seen him around. No doubt Dominic had him hidden somewhere because of the danger.

"He's in New Zealand with my little sister."

I didn't know why, but of all the things he told me, I was most surprised by the fact that he had a little sister.

I nodded, taking a sip of my tea before I pushed the mug away.

He stepped closer to me. "All done?"

I could only nod.

Without a word, he reached down and picked me up in his arms.

I wrapped myself around him, my arms going around his neck and clinging to him in surprise.

Our eyes met, and we didn't say anything as he ascended the stairs.

He brought me back to his bedroom and set me down in the middle of his king-sized bed. He stood in front of me, taking me in for a beat before he reached over and pulled off the sweater he had put me in just hours before.

He carelessly threw it on the floor before reaching for the sweatpants and sliding them off.

Goosebumps rose on my skin, and I was sure he could see them, though he didn't comment on it.

I was now back in the same clothes I had been in before he'd decided to take me on this little adventure.

His shirt and boxer briefs.

The light in his eyes told me he liked the sight of me in his clothes a little too much, and while I had been comfortable when I went to sleep the first time, now I felt... naked.

I swallowed, and he pushed me back down on the bed, tucking me in and surprising the hell out of me.

Dominic did not seem to be the type to tuck anyone in.

"Try to sleep, yeah?"

"What about you?" I asked before I thought better of it. I didn't know why I asked. I just... I didn't want to be alone. Not after that. Not when I was still reeling and feeling like those men who had chased down Braxton with a gun were waiting for me, and the only way I could be safe was with him close by.

What a dangerous line of thought to be on.

I should be trying to get away from Dominic.

Not get closer to him.

Dominic watched me with those inquisitive eyes of his.

"Give me a few minutes," he answered, his voice rough.

I nodded.

He made his way to the bathroom, and it wasn't long before I heard the water running, and I took comfort in the sound of him doing something as mundane as getting ready for bed.

Soon he walked out in nothing but a pair of black boxer briefs that molded perfectly around his powerful thighs.

I took in his naked chest, from the colorful ink I had been fascinated with since day one, to his hard abs, trim waist, and the appealing V-shaped muscle on his abdomen that was so prominent on him. In fact, I had thought it was a myth before I'd seen it on Dominic, considering I had never actually seen it on another man in real life.

I swallowed.

This was the worst time to be getting turned on, and I twisted away, showing him my back, when I realized my thoughts were heading toward a more dangerous, *dirty* territory that I had no business being in.

The bed shifted as he climbed in, then the lamp clicked off, bathing the room in a lighter shade of darkness, considering the streetlamp a short distance away.

I tensed when I felt his arms go around me, and then he pulled me into the warmth of his body and buried his face in the back of my neck.

He breathed me in.

I should be repulsed.

But that was the last thing I was feeling right now.

I closed my eyes, trying to calm my racing heart.

"Goodnight, wildcat," he said.

My breath caught as I looked straight ahead. I opened my mouth and spoke softly when I replied, "Goodnight, Monster."

12

EMMY

I WOKE UP FEELING... RESTLESS.

My legs shifted, and I pressed my thighs together, unsure why I was feeling like this.

It took a moment for my brain to shift from sleep to awareness and realized Dominic was cupping one of my breasts under my shirt, his fingers clutching a nipple, making it hard.

There was a noticeable wetness between my legs.

How did we end up in this position?

I gasped and turned around to a sleeping Dominic, though he didn't let go of me.

Fuck.

I took a deep breath, but that only made the fact that his hand was right there much more noticeable.

I bit my lip to keep from making any noise. His face was relaxed in a deep sleep. He made a small noise between his lips that I should not have found adorable before settling down once more.

I didn't want him to wake up.

Not only because I was still working out why I wasn't

feeling as disgusted with his hands on me as I should—or at all, really—but because, for once, he seemed so relaxed.

So different from the man he was when he was awake, always calculating and trying to stay one step ahead of everyone else.

I supposed he had to if he wanted to stay alive, but I thought that had to be… stressful.

If Dominic could go back to his younger self, would he make the same decisions that led him to the life he had now?

That was a question I thought about a lot.

If I could go back, which decisions would I change?

I knew the big one I would change.

My eyes moved down to my hand. The one I had splayed across his chest. The scars, though not as noticeable unless you knew where to look, seemed even more obvious in the sunlight of this room.

I looked away from it and at his face once more.

Slowly, I moved my hand up, my fingers exploring all the warmth and hardness of the male body next to me. I traced the outline of the kneeling angel tattoo on his right pec. I remembered he had another tattoo on his rib, one of a skull wearing a crown—the symbol of the King's Men MC.

My fingers moved up to his throat, feeling my own clog up a bit at the sight of the size of it.

It would be impossible for me to choke him, but—but…

One of his large hands could wrap comfortably around my neck. I should be scared of that thought alone. Instead, I was restless at the image of him choking me slightly as he moved inside me.

I swallowed.

I didn't think I had a choking kink.

Though what would I know?

A mere two bed partners didn't make me an expert, and the first man had turned out to be an abusive asshole.

I let my fingers come up to the rough stubble along his jaw.

Dominic didn't keep a beard the way I had thought men in a motorcycle club did, but he wasn't clean-shaven either.

I didn't think I had ever seen him clean-shaven, and I didn't mind that too much.

I loved the roughness on him. It was so different from all the men I'd known back home, including my own father.

I touched his strong nose, moving a finger up the prominent bridge and between his dark, perfectly shaped eyebrows. A small scar cut through his left eyebrow. It looked like it had happened from a fight.

A man like Dominic wouldn't be without scars. Yet, somehow, those scars seemed to only make him more of a man, while the scars that I had…

They brought nothing but shame.

My eyes roamed over his short hair, cut into a buzz cut that only added to the roughness of the man.

My fingers moved down to his lips.

I traced the edges, surprised by the softness of them, though I shouldn't be.

They were soft when I kissed him.

My lips tingled from the memory, and—

His eyes sprang open.

My own eyes widened, and I quickly took my hand away. His blue eyes, soft from sleep, moved over me, and his lips slowly curved into a smile that had me blushing.

I opened my mouth to say—what, I didn't know, when the hand that had been cupping my breast came to life, and he squeezed me. The first time could have been an accident. The second time, I didn't think so.

I should stop him. Or pull away.

Instead, I lay there and looked at him when he used his fingers and pulled on my nipple roughly.

My chest pushed in and out harshly, and I bit my bottom lip when he did it again, and again, and fuck…

Again.

"Fuck," he said, his voice gruff. "Look at how you fucking respond to me. Are you wet for me, wildcat?"

I opened my mouth, but nothing came out, save for a few sputters that had his eyes glinting mischievously.

He rolled my nipple, and I swallowed back a whimper. If he touched my pussy, he would find me wet—and the look in his eyes told me he knew that too.

I couldn't seem to find my voice to stop him. I didn't want to. I didn't think I had ever craved another man's touch as I did with him, and a part of me wanted to see how far he would take this if I didn't stop him.

He pulled my shirt up, not saying anything. He rested it against my collarbones, baring me to his gaze under the morning light.

My breath caught. My brain was fuzzy, addled with lust and wariness, making it hard for me to think straight.

He kept eye contact as he leaned forward, took the other nipple between his lips, and suckled on it.

I felt it all the way down to my pussy, and wetness gushed out of me.

He hummed around me, as if he loved the very taste of me, and he sucked on my nipple harder, his finger on the other one turning just a little rougher until I didn't know what to focus on.

My chest arched up slightly, and I closed my eyes, rubbing my thighs together. I grasped his large bicep, holding him there. His muscles tensed every time he moved.

How could I possibly be affected by him so badly? I didn't know, and I didn't want to allow myself the time to really think clearly. For the first time in my life, I wanted to act impulsively and not worry about the consequences of my actions. Would it really be so bad?

His hand moved, sliding down my body and reaching for the hem of his boxer briefs.

A slight panic entered me when he moved his fingers under the thin piece of fabric and the panties I had on.

His warm hand covered my mound.

My back arched, and reality tried to penetrate.

"Dominic, wait—"

I gasped when he plunged one finger inside me.

I squeezed around him instinctively, letting out a small whimper when he began to move that finger.

Tremors wracked around the small of my back, and Dominic never looked away as he finger-fucked me.

He pulled away from my nipple with a pop of his mouth, leaving behind a wet spot.

"Fuck, you're tight," he gritted out.

I couldn't say anything. I was robbed of speech, and I was so close to coming. I didn't even know how it was possible so soon.

He quickened his pace, his palm brushing against my clit every time he pushed back inside me, and I could do nothing more than lie there and take all he was giving.

"Dominic," I uttered.

It didn't sound like a fucking protest to me.

No, it sounded like a plea.

A plea for more, and more, and more.

I needed more.

"I knew you would be like this," he said, his voice dark with his desire, taking his finger out to play with my clit. My eyes closed at his words. A little more like this, and I would be pushed off the cliff.

Oh, God.

"I knew you would be tight. So fucking perfect for me, and I'm fucking keeping you," he said.

My eyes opened at his words, and I shook my head.

I wasn't thinking straight after he took me to my apartment last night, and that was probably why I didn't fight him, and let him bring me back to his place.

But for him to say he was keeping me?

"Yes," he said. "I'm keeping you."

"You can't keep me," I protested.

"Why not?" he asked as he withdrew his hand. I would have felt the loss of him if he wasn't pulling off my shirt.

I let out a small squeak when he threw it to the floor on the side of the bed, my arms crossing to cover myself from him.

He shot me an amused look, as if he found my sense of modesty around him funny.

I would have said something if he hadn't dragged the boxer briefs down my legs next, along with my panties.

I struggled against him, but it was too late.

I was now lying naked in bed with him, and Dominic was staring at every inch of me with dark eyes, as if he wanted to devour me whole.

The dark, possessive look in his eyes almost had me coming undone. I shivered, and he licked his lips, looking so much like the monster I had accused him of being so many times before.

He moved between my legs, spreading them.

"Don't," I said.

I wasn't sure what I was saying "don't" to.

To this?

He ignored me.

"So fucking pretty," he said, his finger moving in circles around one nipple.

My breath caught.

"You're mine."

He cupped me fully in one large hand and squeezed the supple flesh roughly, so much so that when he pulled away, I could see the red imprints he left behind on my pale skin.

Dominic seemed fascinated by the sight, and he did it again… and again… and again…

I closed my eyes.

He slapped the side of my breast, and I gasped, my eyes opening in surprise.

"Mine," he growled, looking more like an animal than a man.

"I'm not yours," I said, panic in my voice. "I can't be yours."

I couldn't be anyone's, even if the idea of being his sounded both appealing and so, so terrifying. How would it feel to let a man as big, as scary, and as capable as Dominic carry all my weight?

But no. I couldn't handle a man like him. I wouldn't know how.

He leaned down and buried his face in my neck, his cock pressing up against me.

I gasped and pushed out from under him, but that only added friction between us, making it hard for me to think, to breathe.

My hips ground against him of their own accord. I moved instinctively now, and I didn't know how to tell myself to stop.

I couldn't stop.

I whimpered when I felt him press against me just the right way.

"Why not?" he asked, pulling away from me and looking into my eyes. His blue eyes were nearly dark right.

It took me a moment to remember what we were talking about in the first place.

"I'm a human being," I said. "I don't belong to you. I don't belong to anyone but myself."

Even if it felt like I hadn't belonged to myself in seven long years.

He tugged my hair roughly, tilting my head to the side and giving him better access to my neck. He suckled the skin there, making the ache pounding in my pussy even more noticeable.

I closed my eyes.

"You can belong to me," he said, pushing his hip against me.

I gasped. "No."

"Yes."

He continued his movement. The only thing stopping him from entering me was the thin fabric of the boxer briefs he had on, but it offered little protection. I could feel *everything.*

I closed my eyes and wrapped my arms around his neck as he drove against me, over and over. His muscles grew taut with every hard, brutal thrust.

The bed shook with him, and my pussy quivered from the slight pain. Tremors worked their way around the small of my back, moving across my skin like electricity. It wouldn't be long before I came.

Something about the thought both frightened and exhilarated me.

"Dominic," I gasped.

He groaned. "Fuck. Do you know what it does to me when you say my name?"

He reached his hand between us and grasped my nipple again, twirling it with two fingers and plucking at it.

I was disoriented, which was probably why I didn't notice when he started to move, bringing us to a different position, with him holding me close on my side, my back pressed against his chest, and spreading my legs until one rested on his hip, exposing me even more to his touch.

My fists wrapped around the sheets as I felt his hand skim down my skin from my shoulder to my breast, where he squeezed and fondled roughly before continuing his path down to my stomach. His calloused hand rubbed around it in circles just before he cupped my pussy.

I looked over and met his eyes as he quickly, viciously, moved his fingers from side to side against my pussy lips, drawing out more arousal from me.

He brought his other hand up to my neck, curving around it and squeezing lightly. My back arched, and I let out a small groan.

My muscles grew tense and spasmed. I was close.

"Dominic," I said, and I didn't know why I said it or what I was asking for. This was too much for me to handle, and I was afraid of falling apart in his arms.

I felt him kiss my cheek softly before he said, "Be a good girl and come for me, wildcat."

Perhaps it was the nickname, or the fact that he was touching me so intimately, or even his scent. Whatever it was, it triggered my response, and I exploded in a shot.

"Fuck," I vaguely heard him utter, but I was too lost in the ecstasy of it all to really notice or care.

He stopped his movements and cupped my pussy, squeezing me to him and making me aware of his fiery touch.

I turned my head and buried as much of my face in his neck as I could, given our position. I was afraid to come back down. Afraid to look at him after that.

Not when I was still naked and lying in his arms, and not when he was still touching me so intimately. Not when he knew how I looked naked, and not when I…

I wanted him to touch me like this again.

My breath finally evened out a bit before I dared peek open my eyes at him, only to find those cerulean blues already on me.

Wordlessly, he leaned forward and kissed me. I didn't turn away from him like I should. I kept my eyes open and held still as he explored my lips gently. Almost as if this was the first time he had ever kissed a woman, and he wanted to take his time. To savor the taste.

His tongue pressed lazily against mine. Only a hum of desperation was evident between us, but it was enough for me to feel it… to crave it.

"You taste like heaven," he said, the hand that was cupping my pussy moving languidly against me. His thumb found my clit, and he pressed on it, causing a small whimper to escape my lips.

"Mine," he snapped, his lips only a millimeter from my own.

I stubbornly shook my head.

He slapped my pussy. "Mine."

I gasped and arched from the pain and the sudden sharp arousal that followed. "No," I cried, struggling in his arms. I couldn't belong to him. I couldn't.

He slapped my pussy again. "Yes," he growled. "Mine."

My pussy lips quivered, and I felt a tingly sensation there that wasn't unfamiliar.

"No," I said stubbornly, trying to close my legs.

He slapped me three more times before he rubbed his fingers in circles over my clit.

I shot off again.

"Oh, God," I said when I felt him squeeze me.

He leaned down until his lips grazed my skin. "You can deny all you want, but your pussy knows who owns it, and pretty soon, my sweet girl, you will, too."

I felt him smile against me, and he pressed another quick

kiss against my lips. He pulled both his hands and mouth from me.

I missed his heat instantly. Not that I would tell him that. Something about not having him pressed against me suddenly made me feel vulnerable. And I hated the feeling so much at that moment that I didn't know what to do with myself.

He climbed off the bed and looked over at me. I resisted the urge to cover my naked body from his view, though it was probably a moot point by now.

I swallowed when he licked his lips.

He held out his hand to me, and I stared at it for a moment, confused, before I realized what he wanted.

Slowly, I placed my hand in his large, warm one and let him help me up from the bed.

He brought me to the bathroom and placed a toothbrush in my hand.

He kissed my temple affectionately, confusing me further, as he said, "Get ready for the day."

"Wait," I said, avoiding my reflection in the mirror. "I'm naked."

His eyes twinkled. "So you are."

I shifted on my feet. "I need clothes."

"Brush your teeth first."

I shook my head, a tinge of annoyance making its way through me. I glared up at him. "I need clothes."

"Brush your teeth," he answered calmly, and, if I wasn't mistaken, with a bit of mirth, pissing me off further.

Any shyness I might have over my own nakedness was pushed back and replaced with my anger.

"I can't just brush my teeth like this."

I tried to shove past him, but he stood immobile in the doorway. He wrapped my hair in his fist and tugged slightly, so I looked up at him. My anger, though still very much present, moved to make room for the wariness I was suddenly feeling from the dark look in his eyes.

"Perhaps you've forgotten you're not in charge here, wildcat. I am. And if you leave this bathroom without getting ready first, I have no problem reminding you."

His hungry gaze moved up and down my body, telling me exactly what he meant when he said he would remind me.

I took a step back, and he let me.

I didn't need a reminder.

He shot me a vicious smile, baring sharp teeth, and walked out.

I stood there for a beat before I turned and looked at myself in the mirror, taking in my flushed skin.

I quickly glanced away.

If he was trying to keep me compliant by confusing and scaring the ever-living hell out of me, he was succeeding. I was fucking confused. And fucking terrified.

It wasn't that I had forgotten who Dominic was. It was just easier to forget when he was touching me so intimately. When he was kissing me.

I kept my gaze downcast as I quickly brushed my teeth and washed my face. A jar of the moisturizer I used was brought yesterday and stored in the bathroom, and I slathered it on my skin. I tried to be quick about it, not wanting to stand in the bathroom naked.

I wasn't exactly shy, but that didn't mean I felt comfortable standing around like this.

Still, it was the longest ten minutes of my life, and when I walked out, Dominic was dressed and ready for his day in his signature fitted T-shirt and dark jeans. The shirt today was a navy blue that brought out the color of his eyes and stood out nicely against his naturally tan skin.

I bit my lip and looked away, not wanting him to see the expression on my face.

The fact that he was fully dressed for the day only highlighted my nakedness.

He grabbed my hand and led me to his walk-in closet, showing me all the clothes I had bought the day before.

I was quiet, still reeling.

Dominic was the same man he was before. Still as confident as ever—arrogantly so. But there was something different about him this morning that I couldn't quite put my finger on.

Something much more potent... more *possessive.*

I did not want to be in the possession of a monster.

Yet I didn't know *why* he was different this morning or why he decided to say all that shit about keeping me.

He wasn't keeping me.

He couldn't.

Could he?

Dominic might rule the city, but even he couldn't get away with abduction, right?

My thoughts sounded naïve, even to me.

I watched him shift through all the colorful clothing, a stark contrast against the side of the closet where he kept his clothes, all of which were dark and neutral. He settled on a soft pink summer dress and took it off the hanger.

Then he walked over to me, a slight twinkle in his eyes as he dressed me in it, pulling the soft fabric down my body where it ended at my knees.

His blue eyes were satisfied, as if he was truly happy about dressing me up.

I shook my head. The sick fuck probably was, and I was playing right into his hands by being compliant.

It didn't escape me that he forgot the panties, and judging by the look in his eyes—he hadn't forgotten.

"If you take this off, you'll spend the entire day tomorrow naked. Got it?"

I narrowed my eyes at him.

He grasped my chin with his finger. "Say it, wildcat. Say you got it."

I would have stayed quiet had I missed the daring look in his eyes. I bet a part of him wished I would challenge him. Push him.

"Got it," I said through gritted teeth.

He kissed my lips quickly before I could say anything.

"Be a good girl for me today."

Then he smacked my ass and walked out of there.

I could only stare after him.

13

DOMINIC

I WENT TO THE BAR AND SAT AT MY USUAL TABLE IN THE BACK, looking out at my kingdom, my mind completely fucked over the little innocent I had inside my house.

The right thing to do would be to let her go. Give her some money and tell her to get out of the city while I worked to find the bastards who targeted my son.

I was never a man with a moral compass—not at all surprising, considering where my life had led to now.

I was fucked trying to find the exact reasoning for why I had taken her home with me.

I gave myself excuse after excuse, yet none of them seemed to fit.

First, I'd told myself it was to keep her safe. A fucking service I was doing for the girl who had saved Braxton's life. And who could better protect her in this city than the monster who ruled it?

Then I'd told myself it was fucking entertaining, watching the itty-bitty thing fight me as if she were a match for me.

Then, when that didn't sound true, I'd told myself it was because I suspected she might be working with the traitor, "saving" Braxton to get on my good side and infiltrate the club, so I should probably keep her close—for safety measures.

It wasn't even a day before I realized just how flimsy that excuse was.

But I fucking knew now.

I was keeping her.

She didn't fucking believe me when I told her this morning. She would soon.

I would make sure of that.

That was all there was to it, and I didn't want to consider the reasons why that was.

I shifted in my seat at the memory of her coming apart in my arms. Never had it felt that fucking good just to make a girl come, to feel her trembling in my arms as she cried out and know I was responsible for that.

It had only been a mere hour since I left the house, and already I wanted to go back to her and lose myself inside her.

The chair across from me suddenly scraped the floor, and though I didn't react, I was still fucking surprised to see Roman plopping down on the seat, his brown eyes glinting.

"You okay, prez? You seem out of it this morning."

I raised one eyebrow at him and smirked. "Do I? You must not be paying attention. I'm as fucking focused as I can be."

"Sure?" he asked, grinning. I had the sudden urge to punch his stupid face. I didn't show any reaction, though. I wasn't the hothead I'd once been in my teen years. My expression didn't change, but his face did, the smugness even more unbearable. "You sure it's not a certain girl you're keeping locked up?"

I was sure this was payback for all the shit I'd given him with Ryleigh.

"Pretty sure," I answered casually.

The fucker laughed.

He was damned lucky he was a good VP whose loyalty I would never have to question, because I would have handed his ass to him before now.

I turned to him, my face serious, and it wiped all the playfulness off his face.

"I've been thinking," I began. "We've known there's a fucking traitor in the ranks."

He nodded, glancing around the room. We were hours away from the bar opening, and most of the brothers were in their own homes. They wouldn't be getting up until at least noon. The MC always worked better at night.

That was when we really got shit done.

I was an early riser by nature. Raising two boys by myself didn't leave any room for me to slack off, and Roman—

Well, I didn't know why this fucker got up so early.

"I'm gonna separate the bastards most likely to betray us into groups. We're gonna lure them, and I need you to compile a list of the most likely contenders."

"You think it'll work? How did they even infiltrate us in the first place?"

"Fucking carelessness on my part. I won't let it happen a second time," I said darkly, my fists clenched by my sides.

The door to the bar opened, and we looked over to see who would come in this early.

Trent paused when he realized we were watching him, and bowed slightly to me in greeting.

"I think I know the name that's going on the top of the list," Roman said quietly.

I nodded in agreement. Trent had always been a slippery little fucker. I'd let him in 'cause his old man vouched for him.

Jacob Henderson had been the VP for the King's Men long before I joined. He was also one of the first men to join me when I started the insurgent group against the first president, and he continued to be my VP for a few years before Roman joined.

A shootout gone wrong injured his hip permanently, and he stepped down from the VP position around the time Roman killed a traitor put in by the Mansen Brotherhood, a small local gang that had ruled Sacramento before I took over.

The gang was destroyed by us several years after Roman took over the position of VP.

Jacob died from lung cancer shortly after he stepped down, twenty years of heavy smoking catching up with him. He had two kids.

His daughter Tammy was a fixture around the club, and Trent pledged to become a member.

I had promised Jacob I would look after his kids, and Tammy was all right, but Trent…

I had my suspicions about him for a while now, but he had given me no reason to kick him out of the club—or kill him.

But I wouldn't—couldn't—look the other way just because of who his dad was.

I was gonna find out if Trent was the traitor working against the club, and if so, I would deal with him accordingly.

We were quiet as we watched the younger man take his place behind the bar.

He had worked as a bartender for a few months now, and though there had been complaints about him slacking off, he'd done nothing damaging.

"Do it. One way or another, we're gonna figure this shit out," I said to Roman.

I'd worked too hard to build the club up to what it was today, and I wasn't gonna watch it all go down in flames.

I GOT HOME a little before seven o'clock and, according to Lucy, my little wildcat hadn't had her dinner yet.

Perfect.

Shit would be going down at the club in the next few weeks as we actively hunted for the rats in the ranks, but for now, everything was quiet.

A calm before the shit storm, and I would take advantage of that and spend as much time with Emmy as possible.

I was gonna get her used to my presence, my touch… my kiss. Get her used to me, and to the idea of being kept by a monster.

I hopped off my bike and made my way into the house.

Lucy stood in the foyer, her purse hanging off one shoulder, and Colt standing beside her.

They tied the knot five years ago when Colt finally got his head out of his ass and asked Lucy to marry him. He was younger than her by about ten years, but anyone with eyes could see how much he adored her.

If anyone deserved happiness, it was Lucy. I had known the woman since before I'd moved to California.

She had come to the bar where the King's Men's brothers hung out, beaten and scared out of her fucking mind.

Most of the brothers had ignored her, not wanting to get into anyone's business. We all had shit going on in our lives, but hell, I couldn't turn her away.

I always had a soft spot for women, and I fucking hated to think about what she had been through to have come in with a chunk of her hair missing, a broken nose, and a black eye.

I took her home, and she lived with me to help care for Kai and Braxton until about seven years ago when Colt asked her to move in with him.

She smiled at me now as our eyes met, and wrapped her arms around my middle.

I held her gently because even though she was no longer than the battered woman I found in the bar, there was always something so fucking fragile about her. I didn't want to hurt her unintentionally.

Lucy wasn't that much older than me. She'd celebrated her forty-fifth birthday recently with her husband, my boys, and me.

"Everything smells good," I said when she pulled away. "Thank you."

She patted my chest affectionately. "I think Emmy is experiencing some cabin fever. She barely touched her lunch today, and she's been quiet."

I nodded, noticing the worry in her warm brown eyes. Lucy had a soft spot for Emmy.

Not surprising. Emmy seemed to bring that out in people, including me. Unlike other people, though, she also brought out all my possessive and protective instincts.

Or, at least, I hoped not.

I would kill any fucker who dared become possessive of her.

Now that I'd decided the little wildcat was mine, she was going to stay mine and no one else's.

I stepped aside and let Lucy and Colt go home. They probably wanted to eat their own dinner and rest for the night. I stayed in the foyer after the front door closed behind them.

It was just me and the little wildcat, and for the first time in my thirty-eight years of life, I didn't know what the next step would be.

As terrified of me as she was, she was also fascinated.

She couldn't hide her response to my touch, no matter

how much she wished to, and I wasn't above using that to my advantage.

But everything else...

I didn't know.

I made my way up the stairs. The door to my room was open slightly, and I caught sight of her sitting on the recliner and looking out the window. I paused for a moment, trying to regain control over myself, and pushed the door open.

She turned toward me but didn't react.

We stared at each other for a beat, neither one of us in a hurry to ruin the silence with words.

There was an open book on her lap. I didn't know where she had gotten the book from, but I was sure Lucy might have something to do with it.

She was still in the same dress I had put her in this morning, and something akin to satisfaction settled lightly on my chest at the sight of her.

Fuck, but what did I think I would do with this girl once I found the men responsible for hunting Braxton and trashing her apartment?

Let her go?

Like hell.

She frowned at me. "Why are you scowling at me? I didn't do anything today."

My face relaxed, fighting off a grin at the surliness in her voice. I hadn't realized I was scowling until she said it. I stepped into the room and kept going until I stood in front of her. She tilted her head back to look at me.

Leaning down, I reached for the book on her lap and turned it around to see the cover, taking in the picture of a man standing on the balcony, his back toward the camera.

She said nothing as I set the book down on the nightstand before reaching for her.

She didn't fight me when I helped her up, her hands

running down the fabric of the dress and smoothing away any wrinkles that might have formed.

She was aware of my eyes on her.

She kept her gaze downcast, and I took a moment to savor her scent and the way her dark brown hair fell in waves and ended near the bottom of her perky tits.

The image of her on my bed, naked, her hair spreading over the pillow, had fucking haunted me all day, and I had to stop myself several times from coming back home—coming back to her.

Jesus, but since when was I without self-restraint? Since when did I let someone get to me this way?

Slowly, she looked up at me, her hazel eyes lighter this evening than they had been in the morning.

More green than brown, and just as fucking beautiful.

My heart constricted, and I reacted without thinking.

I picked her up in my arms. She let out a surprised squeak and wrapped herself around me, her arms around my neck and her legs around my waist. Clinging to me like a baby monkey to its mother.

I cupped her ass cheeks with my hands and carried her out of the room and down to the kitchen.

"What are you doing?" she asked, sounding breathless.

"Feeding you."

She didn't say anything for a moment, and since she was facing over my shoulder, I couldn't tell what she was thinking.

Then, "Why?"

I didn't answer her.

I fucking loved feeding her and clothing her and holding her. I fucking loved doing all these things for this small girl who brought out all these unfamiliar feelings inside me.

I didn't answer her. I placed her on the chair by the dining table and went to see what Lucy had cooked up for the night. My stomach growled at the chicken pasta set by the stove on top of a warming plate.

Lucy was a fucking godsend. Whenever I felt lost because I didn't know what the fuck I was doing when it came to my kids, she had been like a guardian angel.

The only woman I hadn't been able to live without, although—

My gaze shifted to Emmy, and she looked back at me with narrowed eyes.

She seemed moments away from bolting from her seat.

I pointed at her.

"You run, and I'll chase you."

I grinned when she gasped.

"I'm in the mood to play," I added, "but I'm not sure you're up for the kind of games I have in mind, are you, wildcat?"

She stared at me with her mouth agape, and I turned back to the food, my smile widening.

A part of me hoped she would call me out on it and run.

Wouldn't it be fucking fun to chase her around the house?

My dick stirred at the thought of what I would do to her once I caught her.

Fuck, but I really hoped she'd run.

I prepared the food on one plate, piling on enough for the both of us.

Her brows lowered when I turned around with the plate, probably guessing what I was planning on doing.

She didn't fight me when I set the plate down in front of her and pulled her off the chair.

Like the last time, I sat on the chair and took her into my lap. She wiggled, rubbing her ass against my dick in the best way possible. I grunted, trying to hold on to what little control I had whenever I was with her, and she turned to me.

"Is this a kink for you or something?"

I laughed.

I had never even helped feed anyone in my life, save for my boys and baby sister, and that had been when they were all little.

And I hadn't fed my sister because I wanted to, but because our parents were pieces of shit, and if I didn't, no one would.

The other women in my life had been temporary and served one purpose and one purpose alone.

To get me off.

My one long-term relationship had been with Veronica, the boys' mom. I could only imagine how that Medusa incarnate would have reacted if I'd tried to place her onto my lap and feed her.

I shook my head and looked down at Emmy, tugging on a long strand of her hair playfully, and grabbed the fork.

I twirled the pasta around and brought it to her lips.

"Open."

She looked at the food before returning her eyes to me. I waited for her to refuse, and fuck me, but I could think of some things I could do to help persuade her.

All of them would be so fucking *pleasurable*.

I was almost disappointed when she opened her mouth and let me feed her.

I hummed in satisfaction, watching her chew, and took a bite myself.

"Weird fuck," she muttered.

She grabbed onto my bicep when my chest shook from laughing, trying to keep her balance. She glared up at me once she was sure she wouldn't fall off.

I fed her another bite of pasta and chicken.

I watched her chew her food, her thoughts running a million miles an hour behind her eyes as she looked at anywhere else but directly at me.

"Did you always want to be a criminal?" she asked bluntly, surprising the hell out of me.

I shook my head, trying to hide my amusement. "What makes you think I'm a criminal?"

She scoffed. "Please. You're infamous in this city. The King's Men's club gets on the local news from time to time. Aren't you scared the notoriety will catch up to you someday?"

I shrugged. "I don't know what you're talking about. I'm just a businessman."

A very successful one, at that.

The look she shot me told me she didn't believe me.

Good. She shouldn't, and had she, I would have wondered just how innocent this girl was.

There wasn't a person in California who didn't know the kind of men the brothers of the King's Men were.

They might not know the extent of our business dealings and with whom we did those dealings, but they probably guessed that owning local businesses was just a small portion of what I did.

"What if it does?"

"Then I'll cross that bridge when I get there."

She shook her head. I fed her another bite and took one for myself.

"You're so arrogant," she said once she swallowed the food.

"Don't you find my arrogance charming, wildcat?" I asked, holding up the fork.

She looked at me as she took the chicken.

"No," she said.

For a moment, I almost forgot what we were talking about.

I forked up some food for myself without saying anything.

We ate in silence for a moment before she broke it. "Don't you ever want to have a normal life? Get married?"

I had only entertained the idea of marriage once, with Veronica, and that hadn't been about love. It had been about ensuring my boys grew up in as much of a normal household as I could provide. It was fucking stupid because there was nothing normal or sane about my relationship with Veronica. And it wouldn't have worked, not only because I didn't love her, but because I didn't fucking trust her either.

I wasn't possessive with her.

Not like I was with Emmy, and I wondered how Emmy would feel being my old lady.

She would fucking wear my patch, my mark. She would be mine, and I had a feeling, unlike with Veronica, that I would never let Emmy go.

I didn't say any of that to her, though, so I fed her another bite.

She turned her head away and rubbed her stomach. "Full."

Fuck, but it wouldn't surprise me if she started cuddling in my chest and purring like a little kitten.

How fucking adorable.

I finished eating, feeling her eyes on me the entire time.

"Do Kai and Braxton have the same mom?" she asked.

I looked over at her, one eyebrow raised. She didn't shy away from the intrusive question. Seemed only fair, I supposed, since I was keeping her here against her will.

"Yeah," I answered.

"Where is she now?"

"The last I checked, she was stripping in Las Vegas," I said casually.

Her eyes widened. "Why would you make your kids' mom strip for a living? Surely you could take care of her with all the money you have, even if you're not together."

I nodded. "I would have married the woman. For my

boys. But the bitch didn't want that. She didn't want kids to tie her down. She fucking abandoned them, and I told her that if she left, she wouldn't have access to any of my money. That didn't go over well with her, and she would have used Braxton to get to me."

"Not Kai?" she asked quietly, her eyes directed at my chest.

"Kai was a wild teenager. Things were bad with him because… well, because of shit that happened. He wasn't someone anyone could use. And he hates his mom. Not that I blame him. Hard for him to love the woman when she brought strange men back to my house to fuck in front of him."

Her eyes widened at that. "And you didn't do anything about it?"

"What would you have me do?" I asked. "Hurt my kids' mom?"

Her expression told me that was exactly what she thought I would do.

I shook my head. I didn't get off on hurting women. They were inconsequential in my world. Tight pussies to get my dick wet, and that was all.

But if there were someone who could drive me to anger, it would be Veronica. Being my boys' mom offered her some protection.

I would never put my kids through what I'd been through growing up, watching my old man come back home in a bad fucking mood and taking it out on everyone in the house, including his wife.

That wasn't the kind of shit anyone could get out of their mind.

I might be a terrible man, but fuck, I hoped I wasn't a terrible dad.

"My boys are very different from each other. Braxton is

softer than Kai, and he loves his mom. Which made it harder when the bitch looked at him and saw a fucking piggy bank. When she decided to abandon her kids, I kicked her out of California so she wouldn't have any hold on them any longer. I told them she left the state because sometimes shit got too hard. Kai probably knew I was lying, and Braxton… well, I hope this won't affect him later on in life, but he's very close-lipped about anything that has to do with Veronica."

She nodded, and I wished I hadn't said so much.

Jesus, but since when was I so fucking talkative?

It wasn't like Emmy could possibly use my kids against me, but I didn't like showing this part of me.

Carefully, I shifted her off my lap. She stood in front of me, her beautiful two-colored hazel eyes set in confusion as she watched me.

I got up, took the plate to the sink, and quickly washed it.

There wasn't a lot that needed to be done. Lucy ran a tight ship when it came to the kitchen, and she would no doubt do more cleaning once she got here tomorrow morning.

I could feel Emmy's eyes on me the whole time. She hadn't left like I'd expected.

Once I was done, I turned around and leaned against the sink.

I was usually good at reading the expression on her face, but I didn't know what she was thinking after I'd told her so much about a significant part of my life.

Veronica wasn't someone I liked to think about.

I was fucking grateful for her, sure. She had a hand in giving me the two greatest gifts in my life, but sometimes, I thought it would have been better if the bitch just dropped dead.

Emmy swallowed, and I watched her throat bob before

she opened her mouth and said, "What's going on with the investigation?"

"Investigation?" I asked, pushing away from the sink and walking over to her.

She tracked me warily, taking a small step back before she seemed to think better of it, and stood still.

She tilted her chin up stubbornly, her hazel eyes flashing. It might be a trick of the light, but I swore her eye color changed along with her moods. Right now, they were a burning green that I was so fucking fascinated by. The left one was more green than the right one.

Fuck me, but I wanted to lose myself in them.

I tried not to show any expression, not letting her see just how badly she affected me just from standing there.

"You know," she said, shifting slightly on her feet. "The investigation on who was chasing Braxton. You're still looking into that, right?"

"You think I would stop looking into that?"

She shook her head. "Where are you on that?"

I took another step toward her. We were so close now, all it would take was a small move from either one of us and we would touch.

She let out a small breath of air.

I kept my hands to myself. "Why do you want to know about that, wildcat?"

She shot me an incredulous look. I bit back a grin.

"Because they're after me, too!" she said.

That took away all my amusement. "You don't think I can protect you?"

I cupped both hands around the balls of her shoulders.

She felt so fucking delicate in my hands.

Emmy blinked up at me. "That's not it."

"Are you hoping I will soon find those bastards and you can leave the safety of my house?"

She said nothing to that, confirming I'd guessed right. I also realized that after I found them, after I made sure they wouldn't ever again pose a threat—not only to Braxton, but to her—I couldn't let her go.

It was her fucking bad luck to catch the attention of a monster.

Because when something was mine, it stayed mine.

I shook my head and said darkly, "Don't worry about the investigation."

Not only because I didn't involve women in club business —and this was fucking club business, no matter how personal it was—I wasn't going to give her any more reasons to fight me.

I wasn't fucking stupid.

Most of the fight had left her once I'd shown her the apartment. Once I showed her I was fucking protecting her. But when she felt it was safe enough to leave, she would fucking try.

I needed to make sure when that time came, she wouldn't want to.

I needed to make sure she became as obsessive with me, as lost to me as I was to her.

I needed to make sure she fucking loved me.

I didn't know about love. Didn't know if there was enough of my heart to give to her that wasn't already given to my boys, but I would make sure she'd want for nothing.

She would flourish as mine.

She would be my old lady.

Emmy shuddered, bringing me out of my thoughts.

"Why do you look like that?" she asked, her voice set in whispers.

"Like what?" I asked, wondering what expression I was making to put that wary look in her eyes.

"Like you're thinking about something… dark, and you like it."

I threw my head back and laughed. Fuck, but she was cute.

I pulled her into my arms.

She fought against me. "Dominic, wait. We're still talking about the investigation—"

I silenced her with a kiss, eating away whatever protest she might have offered. I didn't want to talk about the investigation. Didn't want to talk about why she might be so fucking eager to leave me.

I would have to show her why staying here with me forever would be best, and nothing showed her more than when I was kissing her… touching her.

I molded my lips around hers, letting my hands drift down her body, exploring those fucking curves that were on a long list of my new obsessions, and settling on her waist.

I drew her closer to me, letting her feel my hard-on and eliciting a gasp from her lips.

I wasted no time and pushed my tongue inside of her.

She made a small noise in the back of her throat, a cross between a whimper and a moan.

Fuck.

Electricity shot up and down my arms, driving my actions. I steered her toward the kitchen island and lifted her, setting her on the flat surface.

She tensed around me, but I didn't give her a chance to think.

I pushed up the pink fabric of her dress. My fingers skimmed the outline of her panties—the ones I didn't put on her—and pushed her down so she was lying on her back on the flat surface.

She looked up at me with swollen lips, dark eyes, and flushed cheeks.

She licked her lips, and I had to stop the groan that wanted to escape from the sight alone. Like fucking Aphrodite.

I shot the white panties a disgusted look and slid them down her legs, letting them fall to the kitchen floor.

She let out a small squeak when I brought her legs up to my shoulders, but she didn't stop me when I leaned down and licked her slick pussy with the flat of my tongue.

Her back lifted off the granite, her fingers tangling in my hair, and her legs clenched around me, as if she was afraid I would move away.

Not fucking happening.

Not until I wrenched an orgasm from her greedy pussy, and maybe not even then.

"Fuck, you taste good," I said, making her leg muscles clench. I pressed my mouth to her center, pulling on the outer lips with my teeth and watching the way she shuddered against me.

As much as Emmy tried to deny it, she couldn't hide her body's reaction to me.

She fucking loved it when I touched her.

"Dominic, please," she sobbed.

I took in more of her juices, feeling myself becoming more fucking addicted to her, the more I tasted her.

I didn't think I would ever tire of this.

Tire of her.

What a fucking scary thought.

I shook away the thoughts and the powerful emotions I couldn't comprehend that came with them, and took more of her into my mouth.

She tried to jump back when I dipped my tongue inside her tight pussy, groaning at the taste.

Fuck me.

I reached up and slipped the straps of her dress down,

along with the neckline. The straps settled on her elbows and restricted her movements a bit.

I stood back and took her in.

Emmy watched me with dark eyes as her bare chest heaved up and down with every hard pant. My eyes zeroed in on her nipples, puckering from the cool air and my heated gaze.

I licked my lips, and she bit her bottom one. Without saying anything, I went back to eating her out, my hand moving up and cupping both tits fully, squeezing her in the rhythm of my tongue.

"Fuck! Dominic," she said, driving me on.

I fucking loved it when she lost control.

I ate her out more vigorously.

She squirmed, trying to get away from me and pushing back against my lips in the next breath, as if she didn't know what to do with herself.

I let one hand glide down and grabbed hold of her hip, keeping her still.

"You taste so fucking sweet," I muttered, lapping her swollen clit.

She cried out.

"Spread your legs wide for me, wildcat," I said, making sure she could hear the command in my voice.

"Dominic," she whined.

I squeezed her hip. "Do it. Spread them wide and show me what belongs to me. Show me your weeping cunt. Show me just how much you fucking love it when I eat you out."

Another whimper escaped, and she did as I asked, moving her legs off my shoulders and spreading them open.

I grinned against her and sucked more of her into my mouth.

When she was good and wet, I slid the hand that was holding her tit down her body, tracing her curve before I found her center. I pushed two fingers inside her, feeling her quivering around me.

"Please," she said.

"Oh, I know exactly what you need, baby," I said, slowly fucking her with my fingers before I built up the momentum.

I quickened, reveling in the sight of her squirming on the kitchen island, leaving a wet mess behind.

"Come for me," I said.

She shook her head and sobbed.

"Yes," I said, fucking her harder.

"Dominic."

"Come for me, baby."

She came on a cry, tears falling down her cheeks.

I watched her. The sight of her like this was something I wouldn't soon forget. I would visit it over and over and fucking over for *decades* to come.

I would fucking keep her for *decades* to come.

I couldn't offer love, but I could offer protection. I could offer security. I could offer her the fucking world.

Wordlessly, I pulled her into my arms.

Like a trusting little kitten, she buried her face into my neck right away.

I walked us up the stairs and into my room, bouncing her down on the bed.

She flopped, and I grinned at the sight of her as she turned and shot a glare my way.

I yanked off her dress before she could so much as protest, letting it fall to the floor and staring at her naked body.

She swallowed noticeably and tried to move further away from me on the bed.

I grabbed hold of her before she could get too far and turned her around, positioning her on all fours and presenting me with the sight of her back, the rows of her spine, and the most amazing ass I had ever seen in my entire fucking life.

I cupped an ass cheek, and she squeaked.

My dick twitched in the confines of my jeans, and if it didn't think it would fucking scare her if I pulled out my dick and fucked her hard, I would have done it days before, losing myself inside her…

Watching her pussy fill with my cum and getting her pregnant with my kid.

That would be one way to keep her with me for-fucking-ever.

I already had two kids.

It would be nothing to add a third kid to the mix.

I would fucking love and protect the child with everything in me.

And the little wildcat would be stuck with me.

The more I thought about it, the more I fucking wanted it.

She turned her head around.

"What are you doing?" she asked, her voice breathless.

"Making you feel good," I said, moving my hand in her crease and pressing my thumb against her tight little asshole.

She tensed and when I felt her trying to get away, I wrapped my hand around her, letting it settle between her tits, and hauling her up so she was kneeling on the bed with her back pressed tightly against me.

"Dominic," she said, and I couldn't tell if it was a protest or a plea.

It didn't fucking matter.

I slowly finger-fucked her, feeling wetness gathering between her legs and coating my hand.

"Fuck," I whispered against her ear.

I took the earlobe between my teeth, and she moved toward me, seeking more of my touch.

My hand roamed down from her tits and settled on her clit.

I rubbed my fingers over it in circles, drawing out another orgasm as I continued to finger-fuck her asshole.

It didn't take long for her to come completely undone in my arms, her screams so loud, it wouldn't have been surprising if they shook this entire house on its foundation.

Fuck.

Once she finished, she went lax in my arms, falling forward.

I stood there and watched her for a bit, taking in the sight of her arousal covering the skin on her inner thighs, her dark messy hair against the sheets, and the flush on her skin.

"How fucking pretty," I said.

She turned and looked over at me. "What was that?" she asked, her voice soft.

I grinned. "Gaining your compliance."

Now she wasn't thinking about the fucking investigation.

That was the way I needed it. I didn't need her to get up in all the fucking business that I did.

It took her a moment to comprehend my words, and when she did, she sat up, fire blazing in her eyes.

"What?" she asked quietly.

That should have been my first warning sign.

I opened my mouth to answer her when a pillow hit my face.

I watched her as it fell to the ground, but if she was scared by the dark look in my eyes, she didn't show it.

"Get. Out."

I frowned. "Emmy—"

"Get out!" she screamed, throwing another pillow at me. I dodged that one easily enough, but couldn't when a third one hit my face.

Jesus. Since when did I have so many fucking pillows on the bed?

It took a moment for me to realize half of these weren't here before I'd had Lucy take her shopping. Did she buy out the whole store?

"Get out, get out, get out! I'll show you compliance, you piece of shit. Get out!"

I frowned. If there was one thing I recognized, it was a woman in hysterics, and Emmy was it. It wouldn't be long before she did something drastic like try to hurt me—or, worse, hurt herself in the process.

She sat on the bed and pulled the covers over her body, breathing hard. I waited for a beat before I turned and walked out of there.

Getting kicked out of my own room.

Fuck.

14

EMMY

DESPITE HAVING GONE TO BED ALONE LAST NIGHT, I WOKE UP with Dominic close behind me on the bed in a similar position we had been in before, his one arm between my breasts and with his hand gently over the curve of my neck, and the other hand wrapped tightly around my middle.

I let out a small sigh.

So much for thinking he respected my personal boundaries.

The fucker only waited until I was asleep before he crawled his way back into bed.

I turned around, only to find bright blue eyes on me.

He smiled.

My expression didn't change.

I might have gone to bed angry, but I was past that now, and I didn't feel like fighting him, or drawing attention to the fact that one of his hands was so close to my nipples.

I blinked and slowly pulled away.

Surprisingly, he let me go without a fight, and I sat up on the bed, pushing my feet out from under the blanket and onto the rug beneath the bed.

I could feel his eyes on me the entire time. I stood up without saying anything, moving to the bathroom.

I looked at myself in the mirror, wondering if I looked as different as I felt, or if it was my own biased perception staring back at me.

I reached over and locked the door, and I couldn't be sure, but I thought I heard him let out a soft chuckle from the click.

Shaking my head, I stripped out of my clothes—one of Dominic's shirts and boxer briefs. I was going to convince Lucy to take me out today so I could purchase some sleep clothes of my own. I hopped into the shower.

The water was icy when I first turned it on, but it soon warmed up, and my shoulders relaxed.

I closed my eyes and ducked my face under the spray.

If I stayed in the shower long enough, would Dominic leave soon for his day?

I didn't know which I wanted more, for him to still be here when I got out of the shower, or for him to leave without saying anything to me.

I hated how conflicted my feelings were for this man.

What should have been straightforward—my disgust, anger, and hatred for this monster—was muddled by my lust, loneliness, and feeling of safety.

He was keeping me here against my will, but right now, this house was the safest place I could be.

I had no doubt those men after Braxton were also now after me.

They didn't like that I'd interfered and prevented them from taking him.

Cool air blew into the shower, and I opened my eyes in surprise to see Dominic standing there, naked.

His blue eyes glinted in amusement and lust as he forced

his way into the shower, and I had to move back to make room for him, not wanting to touch him.

I didn't know where to look.

This was the first time I had seen him naked, and he was everything I had expected him to be.

I turned away and closed my eyes, eliciting a small laugh from his lips.

"What are you doing?" I asked.

"Saving water. Don't you know California is going through a bit of a drought right now? We're supposed to conserve water."

I turned my head back and shot him a scathing look. "Then don't shower."

He laughed, his large hand drifting down his hard stomach and lower down—

I quickly turned back around.

"Are you getting shy with me now?" he asked, a hint of mockery in his voice.

I gritted my teeth. "I am not."

"Then why don't you look at me, wildcat?" he asked, his voice a hell of a lot closer than it was before.

I took a deep breath and turned around, keeping my gaze leveled on his chest.

I didn't want to look up to see his eyes, but I didn't want to look down and look at his—I swallowed—his *dick*.

Dominic reached over and grabbed a shampoo bottle, squirted a good amount in his hand, and slowly massaged it into my hair. I could only stand there, a part of me wanting to pull away, to protest and tell him I could do this myself. The other part...

I liked the feel of his hands on my scalp.

My eyes tracked up his body, from soft lips surrounded by day-old stubble to his strong nose, and eyes that were no longer looking at me—

Until he was.

My breath caught.

He didn't look away as he continued to clean me, and I wondered what he was thinking when he did these sorts of things for me.

Feeding me, cleaning me—taking care of me.

I should resent all of that.

I was…

Feeling so goddamned emotional, I didn't know what to think anymore.

He directed my head under the water, meticulously washing away the shampoo.

We were silent as he continued to wash me, then himself, before we both got out of the shower. We toweled dry and got ready for the morning.

I secured the towel around myself, looking down at the floor. I had resisted all morning to not see him naked, then I got mad, thinking he didn't give me the same consideration. At this point, he probably knew my body more intimately than I knew myself.

I looked at his cock.

Then quickly looked away when it twitched, causing Dominic to laugh and me to blush so red, I could be mistaken for an Airhead candy balloon.

He wrapped a towel around his hips, his muscles straining every time he moved and his upper body tattoo on full display.

I peeked over at him at the other sink while we brushed our teeth, but he seemed content not to say anything.

The kneeling angel on his right pec caught my attention, the same way it always did, and I wondered why he had gotten it in the first place. It was easily one of the most detailed tattoos on his body, though the rest were beautiful too.

There was just something about this one...

He looked over at me.

I quickly averted my eyes and spat out the toothpaste.

Finally, after he dressed me as he had done yesterday morning, he led me down to the kitchen.

Lucy was already here, and she looked up from where she was cleaning when she heard us, smiling.

"Oh, good. You're up. Have some breakfast, okay?"

I didn't know who she was talking to, me or him. It seemed like both of us, but it was Dominic who answered her.

"Thank you. It smells great. Will you be joining us?"

She shook her head. "Already ate with Colt. You two enjoy."

She left us alone in the kitchen.

Dominic piled a plate with food.

I shouldn't have been surprised when he only grabbed one plate, but I was. Already expecting it, I didn't react when he sat down at the dining room table and brought me onto his lap.

I sighed and let him satisfy his little feeding fetish, shaking my head.

His lips twitched, and I could tell he was amused by my response.

Once he was done feeding us, he stood, planted a hard kiss on my lips, and said, "Be a good girl today."

Then he was gone.

Off to rule the world, like one does when one owns it and everyone in it.

I could only stare after him for a while, unsure of how I was feeling.

I WAS FEELING TRAPPED, was what I was feeling.

Since Lucy didn't have permission to take me out of the house today, she couldn't.

She tried to call Dominic, but wherever the hell he went off to for the day kept him busy. He didn't answer any of her calls, and if he called her back, she didn't tell me.

Pretty soon, six o'clock came, and Lucy left for the day with the man who I had learned was her husband.

Lucy, this sweet lady, was married to a tough biker guy with more tattoos than Dominic, whose face would probably crack if he ever put a smile on it.

It was pretty late now. Ten o'clock, the last time I checked. I didn't want to look at the clock again.

I walked around the house, feeling a sense of déjà vu.

Unlike the last time, I didn't have any weapons.

Those were now locked away by Lucy whenever she left for the day.

It was as if Dominic was afraid I would attempt a second attack on him.

I wasn't that stupid.

The front door clicked open, and I froze on the spot in the hallway.

I didn't know why my heart was pounding so hard in my chest, why it felt like something akin to relief that he was home.

I shouldn't want him here.

I should want him to stay as far away from me as possible, yet I was—

I was lonely.

And it was all his fucking fault.

I dreaded the silence this house took on the moment Lucy left for her house and before Dominic got home.

I wasn't someone who craved or needed company, but with him, I was beginning to hate the solitude.

"Where the hell have you been?" I asked once the front door closed behind him.

He paused at the threshold and looked at me, frowning. "Excuse me?"

I should probably heed the warning in his voice. I didn't.

"It's late."

"Not really."

"It is late when you're fucking trapped!" I screamed.

He narrowed his eyes at me before he took slow, steady steps toward me.

I backed away a little, but I didn't want to show him I was intimidated, even if I was.

I stopped when I came to the kitchen. The small of my back pressed against the dull edge of the kitchen island, the same island on which he had laid me down like a fucking buffet and ate me out until I screamed my release.

I glanced back at it, heat moving through my body from the memory, before I turned back to him.

He was about half a foot away from me now, the heat of him coming out in waves and causing a slight shiver to overtake my body.

He cupped my cheeks with both large hands, and I could only look up at him.

"Okay?"

I shrugged off his touch, glaring at him. "No, I'm not okay."

His calm demeanor was fucking me up a little more than it would have had he exploded and showed me all his ugly sides.

"What's going on with the investigation? When can I leave?"

His eyes flashed with some unnamed emotion. Something I didn't like very much. I almost wanted to take the words back, but no. I had the right to know, didn't I?

I had the right to know when I would be getting out of here.

He took a step forward, closing the small six inches of space between us, and I leaned back, trying to put as much distance between us as possible. That only worked to make the lower halves of our bodies press against each other in the worst way possible.

"Dominic. Give me space."

I tried to sound commanding.

It just sounded soft and unsure.

I pushed my hands against his chest and tried to shove him off. He didn't budge.

He wrapped his arm around the small of my back and pulled me back to him.

"Don't ask questions that are none of your concern," he said, right before he slammed his lips against mine, swallowing my gasp.

Fuck.

He pushed against me, moving his lips over mine in a brutal kiss that had me seeing stars. The hands I had splayed on his chest were no longer pushing him away. No, now I had them bunched in his shirt.

Would it always be like this?

Would I always be so affected by a simple kiss?

He pushed his tongue between my lips, and I realized there was nothing simple about the way he kissed me.

Not at all.

Not even a little bit.

He pulled away and bit my lip, the sharp sting causing nerve endings to shoot all the way down to my clit.

"Dominic," I moaned.

"Fuck. It always feels good with you." He pressed his lips harder against mine, deepening the kiss once more.

I wrapped my arms around his neck, and I kissed him back.

Lord helped me, but I kissed him back as passionately and as frantically as he was kissing me.

It was as he said. It always felt good with him, and I didn't want this kiss to end.

Then I remembered his compliance comment.

He did this before.

Last night, when I asked him about the investigation. This was his way of getting me to shut up about it.

I shoved him.

I did it three times before he realized I was trying to push him away.

He stepped back, his blue eyes hungry with his arousal. Arousal that I could feel pressed up against me.

I shook my head. "You can't just use sex to get what you want."

"Technically, we haven't had sex *yet*."

I narrowed my eyes at the "yet."

"And we're not going to," I said.

He shot me an arrogant smirk, bringing my gaze back to his swollen lips. I didn't know whether to slap him or kiss him again.

"Wanna bet, wildcat?"

I said nothing to that. The problem was, I didn't want to bet with him, because I wasn't sure if by the end of this, I would be strong enough to resist him.

The look he shot my way told me he knew exactly what I was thinking.

I didn't do anything, my hand resting on his chest.

I squirmed away from him and dashed up the stairs, running to his bedroom and slamming the door behind me. I clicked the lock, though it was probably useless. He had the key, but this way, I would hear him come in.

Wouldn't I?

Something told me that wouldn't be the case.

I WOKE up in the same position as before, with Dominic lying close to my back.

I felt warm and comfortable and I didn't know what to make of it. A part of me wanted to hug him close while the other part wanted to get as far away from him as possible.

Not that it would have done me any good.

Getting as far away from him as possible would still be in this house.

I turned, and his arms shifted around me a bit. I looked up at him, wondering why my heart hurt so badly.

I never thought I could be fascinated with a man's face while he slept, but I was with Dominic's.

There was no pretense and lying here in his arms felt… nice.

Even when I was mad at him, like yesterday morning, all that anger just went away.

I took a deep breath.

"I wish I could hate you," I whispered.

He didn't even stir.

Perhaps there was something wrong with me. I shouldn't crave a man like him, and at this point, I might have wanted him more than I needed him, and given my situation, I needed him.

As much as I hated admitting to such, I needed him.

Slowly, I peeled his arms away from me and walked to the bathroom. I closed the door silently behind me, not wanting to ruin the atmosphere around such a peaceful morning, and if Dominic woke up, it would be anything but.

Perhaps that wouldn't be such a bad idea. Perhaps that was what I needed. Excitement.

I shook away the thought and quickly got ready for my day, dressing and sneaking down to the kitchen.

Lucy was by the stove, cooking breakfast.

I wondered if she ever got tired of the same routine. Like I had before I met Dominic Madden.

"I can feel your eyes on me, girl," she said, her voice light. "What are you thinking so hard about?"

I smiled and walked further into the kitchen. "Thinking about your life."

She turned around and looked at me, a spatula in hand. "My life? My life's boring."

I shrugged. I didn't really know anything about her, other than that she was married to a rough biker and worked for Dominic, whom she had known for over a decade.

I sat down at the kitchen island, and she placed a mug of coffee in front of me. Black, just the way I liked it.

I smiled my thanks, taking a sip and savoring the taste. I could feel her watching me the entire time.

"Don't you ever get tired of the same routine?" I asked, taking another sip.

"In my boring life?"

I shrugged. She said it, not me.

Before my hand got smashed, I used to dream about traveling around the world and doing shows. In my fantasies, all my shows would be sold out, and I would end almost each night to the sound of the crowd applauding me.

I wasn't completely lost in fantasyland, though.

I knew composers and pianists didn't make all that much, especially in the United States.

People here didn't exactly get into classical music anymore—if they ever had.

My dream had been to play at Carnegie Hall.

"Did Dominic ever tell you how he and I met?" Lucy asked.

I shook my head. A dark shadow passed over her brown eyes, and I wondered what had brought that look on. I set my coffee mug down and paid attention to her.

"I stumbled into a biker bar in Las Vegas, looking for help after my ex-husband beat me within an inch of my life. Dominic was the only one who helped."

I blinked. "Lucy… I'm so sorry. I didn't know."

She offered me a kind smile and placed the spatula on the counter before walking over to me. She grabbed my hands.

I looked down at them, noticing the difference between us. Her skin was a shade or two darker than my own, her hands a little wider than mine. Her palms were warm and comforting, reminding me of the way it had felt when I was little, when I had held my mom's hand.

Though a decade or so older than me, her hands were nice, free of any imperfections, while mine were deformed—scarred and so ugly.

I kept my gaze there. I shouldn't have said anything or made any assumptions. I wouldn't have blamed her if she had been angry at me.

"Silly girl," she said softly. "How could you know?"

I shook my head. "I shouldn't have made any assumptions."

I looked up to see her smiling at me. I felt like crying, imagining her face covered in bruises and scars.

"I'm okay now. But to answer your question, dear girl, I don't get tired of the same routine. This life—the life Dominic has given me and all he has done—I can never repay him. I love my life now. I am married to a good man, and I have the protection of the King's Men MC. It's a good life."

I offered her a small smile.

"There is nothing you need to repay me for," came a gruff reply by the kitchen's doorway.

I stiffened and looked over to see a disheveled Dominic standing there, watching us. His blue eyes were soft and light this morning.

He made disheveled look good.

I felt like I had swallowed my own tongue as he walked further into the kitchen. Lucy shot a smile my way, and patted Dominic's chest in a way that sent a small tinge spreading across my chest that felt a hell a lot like jealousy before she went back to the stove.

I didn't say anything as he walked up to me, his eyes heating a blazing trail across my skin.

He held out his hand.

"I'm guessing you haven't made it out to the living room yet?" he asked when I placed my hand in his.

I shook my head as he led me out of there, feeling a small frown forming between my eyebrows.

"Why?" I asked when we got there.

He nudged me with his shoulder and nodded in its direction. I followed his gaze and paused, my breath catching at the sight and tears forming in my eyes.

"W-why?" I croaked, my breath catching.

My hands shook, and I pulled away from him, not wanting to know. Though it was probably too late, because in front of us, in the middle of the living room and taking center stage, was a gorgeous grand piano in a traditional mahogany coat.

I found the brand name right away. It was worth nearly six figures.

I shook my head.

He cupped my cheek just as the tears fell from my eyes and hit his thumb.

"This is for you. You probably miss playing, and after

what those bastards did to your keyboard, I thought you would like it." He frowned. "It wasn't supposed to make you cry."

"It's beautiful," I said. "But it's too much."

He relaxed and shot me his signature arrogant smile. "Not at all, wildcat."

Again, I shook my head. "No. You don't understand. This is wasted money on me."

He scoffed at that. "No. It's not. It's worth every penny."

Did he really not know?

Dominic didn't seem like the kind of man to miss anything, but did he not really notice all the scars?

I looked down at my hands. He did, too.

His fingers gently moved over the biggest and ugliest one of all, on the outer side of my right palm.

I flinched, even though his touch didn't hurt at all.

"You can still play," he said matter-of-factly.

So he had noticed.

I swallowed. "Not as well. After my hands got… like this, I can't play for long. Or smoothly."

"What happened?" he asked darkly.

I was surprised he'd waited until now to ask me, the man who had no personal boundaries.

"Do I have to tell you now?"

He seemed to think about it, and something about my face must have told him to back off, because he shook his head. "Not now, but soon."

I mutely nodded. I would take that. I didn't want to spend such a wonderful morning talking about my ex.

I turned my gaze back to the piano.

"Is it really for me?" I whispered.

"I can't play for shit, wildcat," he said, making me laugh. "If not you, then who?"

My bottom lip trembled. "Thank you. It's the nicest thing anyone has ever done for me."

I felt him pause. Then his shoulders relaxed, and he wrapped his arms around me. "Well, that's just sad, wildcat. We're gonna have to change that, aren't we?"

I didn't say anything to that, but I wondered the entire day if he really meant what he said.

15

EMMY

I SPENT AN ENTIRE TWO DAYS STARING AT THE PIANO.

I hadn't tested it out, and I didn't know why. I couldn't even bring myself to play a simple rendition of "Twinkle, Twinkle Little Star," one of the first songs I had ever learned on the piano.

But I spent a good amount of my time *near* the piano.

If I wasn't spending time with Lucy, then I was either reading on the bench, letting my hands run down the smooth wood, or I was watching TV on the iPad Dominic had gotten me—with restrictions placed on the internet, of course—or I was drinking coffee close to the piano, admiring the beauty.

Never had I been so close to such a beautiful instrument, and if my being near it and unable to play wasn't so sad, I might have come across as weird.

It didn't matter.

Something was pulling me toward it.

Yesterday morning, Dominic had woken up to find me sitting on the bench and going over music sheets for some of the most famous classical pieces, including "Moonlight Sonata."

He had said nothing, and if he found it strange, he didn't show it.

All he did was lift me up into his arms, do his weird feeding fetish, then head off to work.

All of this only further confused my feelings for this rough, mean-looking biker.

I spent most of my time either defending him or cursing him in my head.

Today I was leaning toward the former, but I was sure he would do something to piss me off later in the day that would change my mood completely.

I let out a small sigh and looked out the window.

I was still stuck in this house, no matter how I looked at it, even if I wasn't spending most of my time in fear any longer.

The sound of the engine rumbling had me perking up a little. The sun was still bright, and the last time I checked, it was a little after noon. He usually wasn't home at this time, and part of me expected him to walk through that door bearing some injuries from *club business.*

Sure enough, the front door clicked open moments later, and Dominic's enormous frame filled the doorway.

His eyes found mine automatically, and he didn't seem surprised to find me sitting there.

We didn't say anything for a beat.

Then he walked inside, making this enormous house seem that much smaller.

It was his special ability, I decided. Sucking up all the energy in the room and making any space he came into smaller.

"Have you eaten yet?" he asked.

I shook my head.

One corner of his lips tilted up in a slight smirk.

"Are you hungry?"

I shrugged.

The smile grew.

"Cat got your tongue, wildcat?"

I narrowed my eyes at him. I wasn't really mad at his teasing, but I wasn't amused either. Perhaps that was what drove my next words.

"How's the investigation going?"

I didn't know why I asked, considering the last two times I had asked had led to him finding a way to distract me—or making me *compliant*—his word.

I shivered, thinking about it.

I didn't want that... did I?

We didn't speak for the space of one small exhale. And I realized I'd probably made a mistake when his blue eyes took on a *scary* but playful light.

I pushed off the bench, but it was too late.

He wrapped his arms around my middle, took a seat on the piano bench, and before I knew what was happening, he had positioned me facedown over his lap.

I squirmed, trying to get away, but he only tightened his hold on me. His hand molded around one ass cheek through the thin black leggings he had dressed me in this morning.

"Dominic—"

"It hasn't been that long since I've distracted you. Touched you. Do you need a reminder to not ask shit that's none of your business, wildcat?"

"None of my business?" I asked slowly. I pushed my hands down on the floor to keep balanced, though it was almost laughable to think Dominic would let me fall.

Not when he now had me exactly where he wanted me.

That hand cupping my ass began to move in circles, making it hard for me to think. "This *whole thing* is my business. I got dragged into this because I was trying my darnedest to save a little boy who didn't deserve to be hunted down. This *is* my business!"

"Not anymore," he said quietly. "The moment I decided to take you home and keep you, you were no longer involved in that. All you need to focus on is being my good girl."

"*Your* good girl?" I asked.

"Yes. I said what I said. You don't have to repeat my words back to me," he said, infuriating me further.

I tried to slide off him. He spanked me. I let out a small squeal—of surprise more than pain.

It hadn't hurt at all, but the bastard actually *spanked* me.

I couldn't believe he had spanked me. I had never been spanked in my entire life.

"Dominic!"

He rubbed his hand over the sting, and I could feel his erection pressing against my side. He was turned on by this.

God.

I didn't know if I was more turned on or outraged.

There was something seriously wrong with me.

"If you keep asking about the investigation," he said, his voice filled with dark promise, "you're gonna end up with a sore ass."

"You can't do that!"

He chuckled. "Can't do what? Spank you?"

He raised his hand and spanked me once more.

I let out a small groan, a part of it from pain and the other part…

I didn't want to think about it because I could feel a slight wetness against the fabric of my panties.

I turned around and glared at him. He was full-on smiling at me, and I didn't know what to do when he looked like this.

"Let me off," I said.

He didn't say anything for a moment, and I really thought

he was going to keep me in this position for a while, risking Lucy walking in and seeing us, but he relaxed his hold on me, then helped me up so I was standing between his thighs.

Even like this, with him sitting in front of me, I wasn't that much taller than him.

I had almost forgotten how big he was.

Today, he wore dark jeans, a white T-shirt, and a leather vest with the King's Men logo. The vest was what people usually referred to as a biker's cut, and, like everything he wore, he made it look good.

I could feel my lips going dry at the sight of him, and when I finally met his eyes, I stilled.

He was staring right at me.

Not for the first time, I found myself wondering what he really thought when he looked at me like that. What was it about me that he was so interested in? He spent most of his nights with me, so unless he had some godlike stamina and all the time in the world, I doubted he was also getting some with someone else. Though the thought made me feel a little... murderous.

I blinked, and that must have broken the spell because Dominic suddenly stood and grabbed my hand.

"Go put on some shoes, wildcat. I'm taking you out for lunch."

"Really?" I asked, surprised and excited. The prospect of having lunch somewhere that wasn't here was enough to get me moving without any hesitation or questions.

"Really," he said. I ran up the stairs and into the closet. I looked around and finally picked out some black leather boots that would go well with my black leggings and white shirt, then hurried back down to where Dominic was waiting by the front door.

I smiled. "Ready."

"Not yet," he said, plopping the helmet on my head. I held

still as he buckled it, then he held out a pair of sunglasses I hadn't even noticed and put them on me.

"Perfect," he replied, donning a pair of his own.

Without waiting for me to say anything, he grabbed my hand and led me out into the blazing sunshine. His bike was parked in front of the house, and though I had been on it twice before, there was something intimidating about seeing it in the light of day.

I tugged on Dominic's hand, and he looked back at me.

"All right, wildcat?"

It was on the tip of my tongue to say no, to ask him if he had other means of transportation. Surely a man with his money would have more than just a motorcycle. At the last moment, I changed my mind. I had been on the bike before. There was no reason to be so nervous.

He squeezed my hand. Like last time, he climbed on first and started the bike before holding out his hand to me. I ignored how loud the engine was and climbed on, sliding close to him until I was pressed against his back, and there wasn't an inch of space separating us.

He wrapped my arms tightly around his middle and took off without warning.

I squealed, and I couldn't be sure, but I thought I heard him chuckle at that.

The wind blew my hair, and I closed my eyes for the first five minutes. Somehow, this ride was much scarier in the daytime than it was at night.

Then he came to a stop at a streetlight, and I peeked my eyes open.

It was still scary but in an exciting kind of way.

Like riding a roller coaster but not as bumpy, and Dominic was close by.

I tightened my arms around him but kept my eyes open.

The sunglasses were a smart idea. They took some of the impact of the wind.

I didn't really care where we went. I was enjoying this little bit of freedom now.

Too soon, he pulled into a bar somewhere close to the mountain near White Horse Hill. He parked the bike and killed the engine. The silence that followed was a little loud.

Dominic reached for my hand, and he helped me keep my balance as I climbed off the bike.

My legs were shaky, but luckily, I didn't fall.

I took off the helmet and watched silently as he climbed off the bike—the confident way he moved, his strong muscles stretching and straining, and even the way his large frame seemed to have made the huge bike appear smaller.

I quickly looked away when I noticed his eyes on me.

He grabbed the helmet out of my hand, but I didn't bother to look back at him.

I wondered why he took me so far out here. It seemed a bit much just to go to a bar for lunch.

As if he could tell what I was thinking, he said, "I'm keeping you hidden. Those bastards have probably guessed that I have you, but they don't know for sure, and we want to keep it that way." One corner of his lips quirked up in a teasing smirk. "You can be my dirty little secret."

I rolled my eyes and walked away. That comment didn't warrant a response.

Dominic quickly caught up to me, though, and wrapped one arm around me. He didn't budge when I tried to push him off.

Grasping my chin between two fingers, he said, "Be good in there. And stick close to me."

I stopped, and he stopped with me. "Is it dangerous? Why are we even here?"

"We're here because I like this bar. It reminds me of

home. And no, it's not dangerous. At least, not for you, but let's not risk it, okay? If you don't want me to beat the shit out of some fucker for looking at what's mine, then behave."

I crossed my arms over my chest and glared at him. "I'm not yours."

"Oh, that's where you're wrong. You're mine. I own every little inch of you, including your greedy little pussy. Don't mistake my ownership of you as anything else just because I've been nice and haven't fucked you yet."

I resisted the urge to show any outward reaction to his words.

"This is you being nice?"

He chucked my chin affectionately, leaned down, and pressed a quick, hard kiss against my lips before he led me inside the bar.

I was still reeling when we finally made it inside.

It wasn't as dark as I expected, but it wasn't light either. There were about two handfuls of people here, including a group of three men loudly laughing in the corner and playing pool.

I stepped closer to Dominic.

He might be a monster, but at least I knew this monster. This was not my scene, and I didn't know why Dominic decided to take me here.

We went to the bar and sat down.

The bartender, a woman in her mid-forties with long, flowing, light-brown hair and two full sleeves of tattoos, came up to us with a smile. Her eyes brightened when she saw Dominic, and I resisted the urge to bristle.

He wasn't mine, and I wasn't his, despite what he had said in the parking lot. I didn't have any claim on him.

I didn't.

"What can I get you, sweetheart?"

I wondered if I had suddenly become invisible. She did see me come in with Dominic, didn't she?

"Two beers and two cheeseburgers with fries."

"No onion on one of them," I added.

Dominic turned to me. It must have been a trick of the light, because I was sure I didn't just see a soft look in his eyes.

"You heard the lady," Dominic said, not looking away from me. "No onion on one."

"Got it," the bartender rasped. I didn't even notice her walking away.

I shifted in my seat.

"Have you been here before?" I asked, trying to get him to stop looking at me like… *that.*

"Once or twice before. I have no reason to come to this place."

"Because you have your own bar, right?" I asked.

He nodded, smiling slightly. "Right. How much do you know about the King's Men MC?"

"Very little," I admitted. I wished I had learned more than just snippets of gossip here and there. But I didn't think I would need to. I didn't know I would catch the attention of their king.

"Would you like to learn more?"

I turned to him. "Would you tell me?"

He seemed amused. "I won't go into details, but yeah, I'll tell you mostly whatever you want to know."

His eyes seemed sincere, but I didn't know if I could trust that or not.

"The chapter started in Las Vegas?" I asked, thinking back to what Lucy had told me. He nodded. "Why did you move here to California?"

"Because after the old president died in a tragic and gruesome *accident* and I took the throne, I thought it would be a good idea to start somewhere new. California seemed ideal. It's not too far from Las Vegas. It's not as corrupt, and there isn't much competition. The Irish mob ruled the casino scene in Vegas, in case you didn't know. And here, we're closer to the ocean."

I nodded, ignoring the emphasis on the old president's death being an accident. I wasn't naïve about the kind of man Dominic was. It shouldn't be surprising that his rise to power had started with violence.

"I heard about the casinos," I said. "I grew up in Nevada, close to Las Vegas."

He nodded as if he already knew. He probably did. I was sure that for a man with his reach, there was very little he didn't know.

"Why the ocean?" I asked.

He didn't answer me right away. The bartender came back with two beers and placed them in front of us. Dominic took a small sip.

"Business reasons. Overseas distribution is where a lot of the money's at."

I opened my mouth—to say what, I didn't know—before I closed it and nodded. He didn't say what kind of distribution, but I was sure I could guess. And that was probably all I would get from him regarding that.

"Do you regret the move?"

"To California?" he asked.

I nodded.

"No. This was a good choice for the club."

"What about the men who didn't want to move?"

"There are men who are loyal to the old club and the old ways. I gave them a way out of the club, which was a mercy, because once you're in the club, there's no getting out. They stayed behind in Las Vegas, and I'm sure some of them joined the Sons of War, the new chapter that started a few years back."

I nodded but didn't know how to respond. It was a lot of information, but I was beginning to see the way Dominic ran things.

There was very little he didn't know, and he seemed to like it that way.

Our food was set in front of us then, and I realized I was famished.

Dominic looked at me and laughed. He tugged on my hair playfully. "Eat up, wildcat."

I smiled and dug in, nearly moaning when I took my first bite.

Turning, I was about to ask him how he liked his food when I realized he hadn't taken a bite. He was too busy looking at me.

I blinked, and he reached out, swiping something away from the corner of my mouth with his thumb.

My breath caught when he sucked on his thumb, never taking his eyes from me. I squirmed in my seat.

"Eat up, baby. Before it gets cold."

I could only nod.

We both ate in silence for about ten minutes before I turned to him. "Are you really not going to let me go?"

There had been some part of me that thought he was joking when he declared he was keeping me and that he owned me. That couldn't possibly be the case, and most sane men wouldn't have uttered those words to begin with, but I was starting to realize there was probably nothing sane about Dominic.

He took another sip of his beer before he turned to me. "I'm keeping you."

"Why?"

He let out a sigh. "Why are you fighting this, wildcat? Can't you see I'm protecting you?"

"I don't think it's wrong to want a choice in the matter."

He shrugged like it wasn't a big deal and went back to eating.

My cheeseburger was already almost gone, along with all my fries. I was full.

I made a move to get off my seat when he placed a hand on my thigh.

"I need the bathroom," I said.

He didn't say anything for a moment. Then, "You'll come straight back to me."

"It's not like I have any other means to get out of here," I grumbled. His lips twitched.

He finally let me go, and I hopped off the stool and left for the bathroom.

I quickly did my business, and, as I was washing my hands, I glanced at my reflection in the cracked mirror.

I'd always felt like something was different about me, and I wasn't sure if that was a good thing or not.

I averted my eyes, turned off the tap, and plucked some paper towels from the dispenser to dry my hands before I used them to open the door in the bathroom. I almost didn't want to touch anything in this place. It wasn't as dingy, but it wasn't a nice place either. And the other people here were questionable, at best.

I was just at the mouth of the hallway leading into the bar's main area when another person stepped in front of me.

"Excuse me," I said, moving aside for the man to pass.

He didn't move.

Slowly, my eyes tracked up his body, from his dirty jeans up to the beer belly, beefy arms filled with tattoos, thick neck, unkempt beard, bumpy red nose, and, finally, dark eyes that looked black from where I was standing.

I backed up a step when he smiled at me, showing off a row of yellow teeth.

"My, what's a pretty little thing like you doing in a dirty place like this? Don't you know there are all sorts of bad men in this bar?"

"And I suppose you're one of them?"

He threw his head back and laughed, and I looked past him to the bar. I could see Dominic from here, but I wasn't sure if he could see me. I tried to shove past the man. I just needed to make it to Dominic, and I would be safe. But he grabbed my arm and pulled me back roughly before I could.

My eyes widened, and I felt the first inkling of fear.

"Let go of me!" I screamed before he covered my mouth with one sweaty hand.

So gross.

My eyes connected with Dominic's, and a dark look passed over his face. But I wasn't scared.

Thank fuck he saw me.

Dominic stood as the man dragged me further into the dark hallway and slammed my body against the wall.

I groaned.

He leaned down. "This is your fault for being so fucking pretty. I can't resist you. Now be a good—"

The man was yanked away from me, and Dominic stood between us. My monster was angry. So angry.

Dominic's back heaved up and down, and he was likely wearing his scary face.

I stayed frozen in place.

"What the fuck, man?" the stupid man said, obviously not picking up on the fact that he was facing someone hell-bent on killing him. "I was just having a bit of fun."

I tried to swallow around the lump forming in my throat. What would I do if Dominic killed the man? In front of me?

"Fun?" Dominic asked quietly.

The other man finally understood the expression on Dominic's face because he froze for half a second, and fear entered his eyes briefly before he backed up, chuckling a little.

"I didn't know she was yours. Otherwise, I wouldn't have touched her."

"You didn't?" Dominic asked, matching the man step by step. "You didn't see her come in with me? You thought someone like her would come into a place like this without some protection? You don't think very bad things are going to happen to you for touching what's mine?"

Dominic turned slightly, giving me a glimpse of him as he took in the man the same way a predator would its prey.

His eyes took in a vicious glint that even I was scared of. He spoke low, calm. I would have thought he was calm if it weren't for his tense shoulders. "Even if she came here alone, what makes you think it would be okay to touch her?"

"I—"

The man didn't get the chance to say anymore. Dominic punched the man in the face, knocking him to the floor.

The whole bar was silent as everyone turned to the noise and saw us. No one moved, not wanting to get involved, and I didn't blame them.

I covered my mouth, my heart thudding so loudly in my chest I didn't know how I stayed standing.

I felt light-headed as Dominic climbed on top of the man's body and pounded his face.

The man sobbed, covering his head with his arms, but it was useless. Dominic was relentless, and I could feel saliva building in my mouth at the sight of all the blood. I didn't know how much the other man had lost, but it wasn't normal for all this blood to be on the floor, was it?

Fuck. What should I do?

I should try to stop Dominic, but I couldn't try to get in

the middle of that. I didn't want to get hurt, but I didn't want Dominic to kill him, either.

A loud gunshot rang out, and I screamed, covering my ears.

My heart pounded crazily inside my chest, and I felt like throwing it up. I swallowed, trying to will away the feeling and calm myself down.

Slowly, I opened my eyes. The bartender stood atop the bar and aimed her shotgun at Dominic—who wasn't throwing punches anymore—and the no-longer-conscious man beneath him.

"Get out of here," she said. "We don't want any trouble, and the last thing I want is cops sniffing around the place because of a body."

Dominic didn't say anything for a moment, probably still in the frenzy of bloodlust.

I took advantage of the stillness and approached him on shaky legs. Cautiously, I placed my hand on his back. He turned to me quickly, and I flinched, but he seemed to calm down when he realized it was just me touching him.

Wordlessly, he stood and reached for me. He picked me up in his arms. I wrapped my legs around his waist and my arms around his neck.

He cupped my butt with both hands as he walked to the bar and slapped a hundred-dollar bill down before walking us out of there.

The entire bar watched us with varying degrees of incredulousness in their eyes.

When we got to his bike, he set me down on my feet. His knuckles were bloody. I wasn't sure whose blood it was, but the sight was making me feel nauseated.

We drove home in a blur.

I buried my face in his back, and Dominic must have

broken every single traffic law on the way because it wasn't long before we were parked in front of his house.

He carried me into the house the way he'd carried me out of the bar, and we went straight to his bedroom. He set me on the floor by the bed and started pulling on my clothes.

"Dominic," I said. "What are you doing?"

"Need you," he said, pushing my shirt off, then my bra. My nipples pebbled, and I crossed my arms over my chest. He took me in for a moment before he took my arms away. "Need you now."

He grabbed my breast with one bloody hand and squeezed.

"Dominic," I said, a slight panic making its way through me from the look in his eyes. "Wait."

He pushed me down on the bed and pulled off my boots. Then he reached up and slid my leggings and panties down.

"Fuck. Look at you."

I shook my head. "There's blood on your hands."

It didn't matter whose blood it was. I didn't want it on me or *in* me. He had already left a brownish-red stain on my breast.

He sat me up and plucked at my nipple, and I grabbed his wrist, stopping him when it hurt.

"Dominic!"

He sighed, as if I was annoying him, before he grabbed my hand and took us to the bathroom. He pushed me inside the shower and turned on the water. I moved to the corner and waited for the water to warm up, watching Dominic quickly remove his clothes.

My eyes moved down to his cock. He shot me a vicious look as he roughly stroked up and down his length before stepping into the shower.

I licked my lips, and his cock twitched.

Fuck, he was a work of art.

Without saying anything, he pushed me against the shower wall and pressed his body against mine. The water ran over us, going brown to red to pink and finally clear, though there was still some blood on his hands.

His eyes were dark as he suckled on the skin of my neck. I felt it all the way down to my clit, and I tilted my head to the side to give him better access. He played with my nipples while he sucked, and I could only stand there.

"Need you so fucking bad," he said, and trepidation entered me.

"Dominic—*God*."

He took one nipple in his mouth, and when he rolled the hardened nub between his teeth, I realized it wouldn't take long for me to come.

"Please."

"I got you," he said.

I didn't tell him that was what I was afraid of. I didn't want a man like him to get me.

He kissed his way down my body, leaving a trail of goosebumps. My legs shook when he dipped his tongue inside my navel before he knelt and pulled one of my legs over his shoulder.

My head leaned back, and I closed my eyes when I felt him press a kiss on my center. My pussy gushed, and I was sure he could feel it, could taste it.

"I'm gonna own every piece of you," he said, his tongue moving to my clit over and over.

He spread me further, causing my leg muscles to strain as he doubled his efforts.

The first tremors of the orgasm came when I felt his tongue enter me. Then his finger. Then another one, and another one.

I whimpered in pain as he stretched me, and I looked

down, pulling on his scalp, trying to get him to ease up. I wished his hair was longer so that I could pull on it.

He didn't ease up on me.

He fucked me roughly with those fingers as he continued to lick and suck on my clit.

I threw my head back, the running water almost drowning out my screams as I fell.

Fuck.

Fuck.

I was aware of him standing, then he had my legs wrapped around his waist.

I opened my eyes when I felt the tip of his dick nudge my entrance.

Our gazes met, and I shook my head.

"No," I said, when I felt him push in another inch. My abdomen muscles clenched from the strain of him stretching me. It had been so long, and there was a slight burning sensation.

He plunged inside me.

God.

Dominic buried his face in my chest, holding still and allowing me to adjust to his size in this position.

I slapped him on the back. I couldn't even think. Not when he was filling me up, and it was so, so good.

He leaned back and looked me in the eye as he grabbed my hips and started pushing me up and down his cock.

My eyes fluttered shut, and he fucked me harder.

"Dominic," I moaned.

Fuck, but it felt so good.

So good.

"I knew you would be like this," he said through clenched teeth. "Knew you would feel like this. You're fucking mine, got it? I own you. And that is the only way it will be for you.

If I have to fucking brand you to get you to understand, I will."

Brand me?

What the hell did that mean?

His hand moved towards my clit, and he rubbed the swollen nub roughly. I was done. I couldn't think anymore.

I shot off with another orgasm.

Dominic kept up his thrusting.

I shifted my legs when it got to be too much, when I was still feeling remnants of the orgasms, and, and, and…

I shook my head.

I couldn't come again. I couldn't.

"Dominic," I sobbed. "Please. This is too much."

"Not at all," he said darkly. "God made you for me. You can take whatever I give you, and you'll be fucking thankful for it."

He hoisted me up by my hips, then slammed against me, the lower part of his stomach slapping against me.

I couldn't take it anymore.

I cried out when I came a third time, and that was all it took for Dominic to come.

He swelled inside me before I felt the wetness between us. His chest pushed against me, and he was breathing hard.

As for me, I felt…

Limbless.

I couldn't do anything anymore.

He pulled out of me, and my legs twitched from the sudden move and from his cum dripping out, then I was standing, leaning against him. If he wasn't holding onto me so tightly, I might have fallen.

Then he washed us.

I didn't know how he could have done it so quickly, but soon we were both clean, and he had the water turned off.

He took me into his arms and carried me to bed without drying us off.

He pushed me down on the mattress, and I watched as he took me in with dark eyes.

My own widened when I realized what that look meant. I saw he was hard again.

Fuck.

I turned and tried to crawl away from him.

He grabbed my legs and dragged me back.

"No more!" I protested as he slid me over to him. He wrapped my legs around him and lay down on top of me, pressing me against the mattress.

"Fuck." He leaned down and nipped at the top of my breast. "Yes."

"Dominic—" I let out a small moan when he entered me fully.

My nails raked down his back.

"I'm sorry you're sore, wildcat. But I can't seem to get away from you. Fuck, but you feel so good."

Slowly, he moved in and out of me.

I closed my eyes and buried my face in his chest, unable to do anything but let him fuck me like this.

Oh, God.

I shuddered against him.

"That's it," he said softly, never losing momentum. "This feels good, doesn't it?"

I nodded on a sob.

I scratched him as he kept fucking me, feeling too much and not enough.

"Please. Please."

"Come for me, wildcat. Be a good girl and come. Let me feel your greedy little cunt tremble around my dick. Let me feel how wet you get because I'm fucking you. Just me. And just you. No one else."

The possessiveness in his voice was what did me in.

I bit the skin on his shoulder as I came, and he soon followed, letting out a low groan that was just about the sexiest sound I'd ever heard.

My back arched, wanting more of him, and when he was finally done, he let his weight relax on top of me.

I closed my eyes and let it comfort me.

I didn't know how long we stayed like that, but it wasn't very long before he pushed himself up and looked at me.

We didn't say anything.

Me, because I was filled with so much emotion, I didn't know which to focus on, and him—well, I didn't exactly know. Dominic's face, as usual, gave nothing away.

I cupped his cheek and let my palm run over the rough stubble that covered a part of his cheek. He burrowed into my touch, almost as if he couldn't help himself, and then kissed me softly.

He moved away much too soon.

I winced when he pulled his cock out of me, and he watched me carefully.

"Are you sore?" he asked, cupping my pussy.

I nodded with a wince.

"Fuck me. I'm supposed to be remorseful about this, but I can't fucking help myself around you. I fucking love the thought that you'll be feeling me throughout the day."

I bit my bottom lip, not knowing what to say to such a deranged statement from him. I might be just as deranged because I also liked the idea of feeling him throughout the day.

My legs twitched when he started to rub his cum over my pussy.

My eyes widened.

"Dominic, we didn't use a condom!"

I tried to sit up, but he pressed his hand down on my

stomach, holding me still and plunging one finger inside me, lazily fucking me with it.

"So we didn't," he said calmly.

He really was crazy. I shook my head.

"I'm clean," he said, as if that was what I was worried about, though that was good to know. "A copy of your medical records tells me you're clean as well."

It took me a moment to realize what he had said. "You have my medical records?"

His eyes briefly went down to my hands. I knew then that he was aware of the surgery I'd gotten for it. However, the reason listed behind *why* I needed the surgery in the first place was ambiguous.

I held my breath and waited for him to ask.

He didn't ask.

Instead, he moved his finger a little faster against me, and I tried to focus on what we were talking about.

"Of course," he answered as if obtaining someone's medical records was such a normal thing.

"You're so fucking neurotic. And I wasn't talking about an STI. What about pregnancy?"

"What about it?"

I dropped my head back and whimpered when he pressed his thumb against my clit.

"Dominic. Be serious."

"I am. Fuck, you look amazing like this, with my cum dripping out of you. What I wouldn't fucking do to make it so for the rest of our lives."

The rest of our lives?

What the fuck?

"You're crazy," I said with a panicked laugh. How could it have taken me this long to realize? Sure, I thought it before, but I never thought the crazy was to *this* extent. I was taken by a crazy man.

"Perhaps so."

His finger quickened.

I moved my hand down to stop him, but it didn't do any good. He continued to finger-fuck me, and all I could do was lie there, letting the lust cloud my mind.

"Dominic!" I screamed when he finally wrenched the orgasm out of me.

He pulled out when my legs twisted, and I stayed where I was, staring up at the ceiling and unable to do anything else.

His face loomed over mine, and there was something light in his expression. He kissed the corner of my mouth before muttering against my skin, "Be good."

Then he was gone.

Fucking hell.

16

DOMINIC

I WALKED TO THE BAR IN A GOOD FUCKING MOOD.

Fuck, but Emmy's pussy had been everything I thought it would fucking be, and so much more. I was already thinking about when I would be inside her again.

I shook my head and schooled my features as I went into the bar.

I wasn't the kind of man to be led by his dick. And if I didn't fucking watch myself, Emmy might just have me wrapped around her little finger.

I spotted Roman and Axel at the back of the bar.

The list Roman compiled of the potential traitors was done, and now we had to wait for someone to take the bait, but until they did, there was fuck all that could be done.

Only Roman, Micah, and Kai were aware of the list.

I might have trusted others to help as I built my empire, but my first instincts still stood. I didn't fully trust anyone, save for those men.

I walked up to them and sat down.

Roman took one look at me and grinned. "Hey, prez. Where did you go in the middle of the day?"

I shook my head and rolled my eyes at the bastard. Once again, I was sure this was payback for all the shit I gave him with Ryleigh.

"Watch it, boy. Before I send you home with your face fucked up."

I must be losing my touch because he didn't seem scared of me.

Fucking bastard.

"Am I missing something?" Axel asked. "Are you talking about the girl who helped Braxton?"

I didn't answer him.

I was feeling fucking possessive when it came to her. I didn't even want to utter her name in front of any other bastards. It was surprising that I'd let the fucker from the bar live after touching what was mine.

My fists clenched at the thought, and Axel must have read the dark look on my face because he smartly let it go.

I flagged down the waitress for a beer and was about to ask Roman about the shipment date we had planned for a month from now, when my phone rang. Micah's name flashed on the screen, and Roman sat up, taking notice.

"Yeah?" I answered.

There was a beat of silence. Then Micah's voice came through, as cold and emotionless as it ever was.

"I have a present for you."

I DROVE to one of the warehouses I had purchased to store the drugs before we got them ready for shipment. Roman followed close behind.

Axel had stayed behind to take stock of the new inventory that came in this morning, which was good because I had a feeling whatever "present" Micah might have for me wouldn't be for anyone but those in my inner circle.

I caught sight of Micah outside the warehouse right away, his huge frame standing out like a sore thumb. Next to him were two people.

One was my son, using Micah's bike seat as a table for his laptop, which had the other man scowling at him, and the other was a man I didn't recognize.

The man was on the ground, tied up and with a gag in his mouth.

My present, I assumed.

I parked my bike and shut off the engine before I slowly walked over to them, examining the man's face. I had never seen the fucker before in my life.

I had a good memory, especially when it came to remembering the faces of men who might be a threat to the club.

I kicked the man. He let out a whimper, and I had to hold back a small groan.

Fucking pathetic.

Did he really think to gain my sympathy by making those kinds of noises? I'd barely touched him. And the fun hadn't even begun yet.

"Where did you find this piece of shit?" I asked Micah.

Kai looked up from his laptop at me, and, like every time I looked at one of my kids, I felt my heart softening a bit.

If there was anyone who could make me feel human, it was Kai and Braxton.

And Emmy.

I reached over and cupped the back of his neck, squeezing affectionately, wondering if I was just imagining things as a parent, but it looked like he wasn't sleeping or eating right. One thing about kids getting older was that it was harder to keep an eye on them and ensure they were taking care of themselves.

Kai was away from home. He had his own apartment near downtown Sacramento, just near the Sacramento River.

But he seemed to be holding up well right now, though, like me, he was good at hiding his emotions and how volatile he felt sometimes.

"Found him loitering around the warehouse, trying to take stock of what we have," Micah said, tapping the bastard with his foot.

Micah took something out from his pocket and threw it on the ground by the fucker's face. He started weeping at the sight of it, and it took me a moment to realize what it was.

A small bomb made out of what looked like a pencil sharpener and a metal lighter.

"Found this on him," Micah said.

"Well, fuck," I said. "What were you doing with a bomb near my property?"

He cried through the gag and made some noises that sounded like he wanted to say something.

I kicked him again.

"Pull the gag from his mouth," I ordered. "I want to hear what he has to say."

Micah dragged the man up to a sitting position and removed the white cloth from his mouth. I laughed when I realized it was the fucker's own sock.

"Please. I'm sorry. Just let me go, and I promise you won't ever see my face again."

I thought about it. "Okay."

The man paused. "Really?"

Roman laughed from behind me. "I hadn't realized the Sons of War recruits such dumbasses to join their ranks."

It wasn't until Roman said it that I noticed the patch on the man's vest. Two swords crossing each other in an X, with the club's name underneath.

"I think you're a little far from Las Vegas, no?" I asked.

Fuck, but how could I not see this coming?

The Sons of War MC was the chapter that took over when I moved the King's Men to Sacramento. Many brothers from the King's Men ruled by Boomer stayed behind and joined them. Those were the men who hated my guts. Who didn't like that I had joined so much later than them and could take the club out from the slimy little bastard.

I should have fucking known they hadn't let go of their grudge.

"Please. I d-don't know anything. I was supposed to mess with your supplies and come back. That's all. He didn't tell me anything."

"He?" Roman asked.

I crossed my arms over my chest and waited.

"Our prez, Sunny McCain."

I already knew who Sunny was. He was Boomer's illegitimate kid. He thought no one would know his connection to the old chapter if he changed his last name. Or perhaps he had used that connection, and that was how he was able to rise to the rank of president so quickly.

The boy was about Kai's age, if not one or two years older than him.

"Did he send men here to go after my youngest?" I asked, my voice low.

The fucker shook his head. "I don't know."

I grabbed a fistful of his hair and pulled until he looked at me. "You sure you don't know anything? I've been known to make men sing like a fucking canary once they've spent twenty minutes with me, tops."

He cried harder, his tears falling down his ugly mug. I shoved him away, disgusted.

I kicked his stomach, and he flinched but didn't make any noise.

"Give me twenty with him. And I want you to send men to Las Vegas," I said to Roman.

"Do you want them to go on the offense?"

I shook my head. "Not yet. I want them to get me intel on those little fuckers. I want to know everything about them, from whether any of the members have a fucking sixth toe to whether they're stupid enough to create an insurgent group to try to take away my fucking empire."

"I'll go," Micah said.

I turned to him, surprised.

Micah had been quieter than usual, and I wondered if it was because his little brother was taken by Ryleigh. Whatever it was, I didn't want him to go down there unless his head was on straight.

I didn't say anything for a moment, but Micah probably sensed my hesitation because he said, "I'm good for it. You know that. I'll go, and I'll find out whether any of those ugly fuckers have a sixth toe, like you ask."

I rolled my eyes, and Kai laughed.

"Fine. Go. Keep in contact at all times." I walked up to him, cupped his neck, and pulled him in until our foreheads touched. "Be careful."

"Always am," he said.

He turned to his bike, pointing at the laptop Kai still had sitting there. Kai took it away and shot Micah a sheepish smile. The three of us watched the bigger man hop on his bike and ride off.

"Is he okay?" I asked Roman.

He let out a sigh. "You know Micah. No one can tell with him."

I nodded. "Fair enough."

I turned to my latest present, anticipation strumming in my veins.

Fuck, but this was where I excelled. I'd scared Emmy today when I lost it at the bar, but I got off on the violence. The blood.

This was why I was good at what I did. I loved what I did too much to quit. I could never really go straight.

Emmy would just have to get used to it and deal with her monster.

THREE HOURS LATER, I finally made it back to the house.

The fucker I played with was dead, and it was as he said. He didn't know shit, which would have felt like a waste of a day, had we now not had something to go on. Micah was probably halfway to Vegas, Roman was probably home with Ryleigh, and Kai was probably back at the bar, doing what he did best—and that was research into any fuckers who might be a potential threat to the club while helping me run my business.

The kid liked to keep busy, and if doing all this shit would keep him out of trouble, I wouldn't stop him.

And I was now back at home, back to Emmy.

It was probably a bad idea.

I had already washed away all the blood and dirt and burned the body, but I was still feeling too strung up. It wasn't much different from when I pummeled the bastard at the bar within an inch of his life earlier today, but this time felt so much more than that.

I didn't think it would be a good idea to be in her presence, but being near her was what *I* needed, even if I wasn't touching her.

I got off my bike and walked into the silent house. Lucy had left early today, something about date night with Colt. I didn't ask for details, but she'd probably cooked something before she left.

It also meant Emmy and I were alone in this house.

I walked in, and when I didn't find her downstairs, I moved upstairs. She was sitting in my room, in her usual place in the recliner, reading a book.

I must have made a noise because she looked up at me.

"You're home," she said.

I didn't say anything.

She was wearing one of those things I was sure was called a romper. It was short on her and showed off shapely legs that had me imagining her wrapping them around me while I drove mercilessly inside her.

I shifted a little from the thought.

"Are you okay?" she asked.

She was probably still sore from this morning. Even if I wasn't a good man, I should probably be considerate of the girl I owned, shouldn't I?

Let her heal a little.

"You look exhausted," she added.

I nodded, then walked away.

I came down to my home office where I used to run some of my more legitimate businesses and fired up a desktop. Perhaps it wouldn't be such a bad idea to try to work off this hard-on.

I probably shouldn't have come home, but things felt easier with her nearby.

It was easier to breathe.

I clicked and opened my email just as movement caught my attention in the doorway.

"Go away, Emmy," I said without looking over at her.

The little innocent wildcat didn't heed my warning. She walked further into the room.

"Why are you like this?" she asked, coming into my line of sight. She was frowning at me.

I let one eyebrow raise from the surly note in her voice.

"You should leave because I am holding onto my self-control by a fucking thread. Unless you want to find out what happens when you provoke the monster, I suggest you go back to reading your book."

She took half a step back, and I thought she finally understood the warning, but then she stood her ground and crossed her arms over her small but perky tits.

Stubborn woman.

I could feel my cock twitching at the thought of ripping that romper away from her body and making her go around the house naked for the rest of the night.

Fuck.

The words on the screen blurred.

She took one step toward me. I subtly tracked her movement. I estimated her about six small steps away before she would be within my reach.

"I don't want to read. I've been reading all day, and I'm bored," she said, a scowl on her face. I was sure she meant for it to look mean.

She just looked like a pissed-off kitten to me.

How cute.

Another step forward.

"Why are you so tired? You are usually so full of energy. Too much, actually."

The last part was said quietly. I was sure I wasn't meant to hear it. My lips twitched. Fuck me, but I could feel my energy level rising.

She took three more steps forward.

So close.

"You don't get to be exhausted," she said. Another step. "Not when you play the monster in my story."

She took that final step.

Thank fuck.

I reached over and pulled her into my lap. She realized the position she put herself in too late. Now that I had her, I wasn't letting her go.

I pulled on the thin straps of her romper until it ripped, and the fabric from the front fell, baring one tit. She wasn't wearing a bra, and my mouth watered at the sight.

"How many times do I have to say this? I might be the monster, but I'm your fucking monster. You need to fucking deal with your monster."

I leaned down and took her nipple in my mouth. Her palm came down to my forehead, and she tried to push me away. I nipped at her, and she screeched, making me wince.

"Fuck. Did you just bite me?" she asked.

I bit her again.

"Fuck. Dominic!"

I grinned and took her nipple back into my mouth, sucking.

She groaned and arched toward me.

"Fuck," I heard her say again.

"It's too late. I was being a fucking gentleman and letting you heal. You came to me, wildcat. So now you're going to take me."

Her eyes widened, and she shook her head.

I pushed most of the paper on my desk down to the floor to make room for her and set her on the surface.

She tried to run away.

I grabbed her hips and held her still, leaning forward and licking her rigid nipple.

She groaned, pushing her hand against my shoulders and trying to get away.

Silly girl.

"Don't try to kid yourself," she said, slamming her hands down my shoulders. "You're not a fucking gentleman."

I laughed and tore the other strap before pulling the romper down, letting it pool around her waist.

"I like this outfit," she said with a slight pout. "And now you've ruined it."

I felt a moment of regret, and then I leaned forward and kissed her softly.

The hands abusing my shoulders slowly moved around my neck, holding me close to her.

"I'll buy a hundred more. In different colors and designs," I promised.

If she likes the weird little romper so much, I would buy her enough to wear each day for the entire year, and then some.

She shook her head, but her lips twitched, a hint that she wanted to smile.

Fuck, but I wondered what it would be like if I could pull a genuine smile out of her. If she smiled fully and looked at me like I hung the moon.

I vowed right then and there that I would make it happen.

"Lift for me, baby," I said softly, indicating her ass.

She did as I asked, and I removed the romper, letting it fall away as I took in her naked body.

She was fucking perfect.

Everything from the soft curves and belly to the swell of her tits, that cute scattering of freckles on her shoulders… fuck me. Everything.

I looked down at her neatly trimmed pussy.

My mouth watered.

I fucking missed the taste of her.

"Spread your legs and show me what's mine."

She hesitated for a moment before she did as I asked and

spread her legs, showing me her pussy. I groaned when I found the lips shimmering from her wetness.

"Haven't even touched you, and you're already wet. Is this for me?" I asked, rubbing my fingers from side to side over her slit.

She nodded, biting her lip as if she was afraid to make any noise.

By the end of this, I would make her scream out my name.

I moved my fingers faster, and pleasure overtook her face.

"Did my pussy miss me?"

"N-not yours."

"You sure? It looks like mine." I leaned down and took a sniff, taking in the potent scent of her arousal. Fuck. "It smells like mine." I used the flat of my tongue and licked up her crease, from one hole to the other, and settled on her clit. Her back arched. I reached up and played with her tits. "It tastes like mine," I growled before I ate her out.

She gasped, her hands settled on my head, as if to find her balance. I was almost tempted to grow my hair out so that she could play with it.

"Mine," I said, in between licks and sucks. "Mine and fucking mine alone."

Her legs trembled on the desk. She was close. "Dominic, please."

I stood and took off my shirt. She watched me with dark, hungry eyes as I unbuttoned my jeans, undid my fly, and pulled out my hard cock.

I stroked up and down my length, squeezing at the tip to keep from coming so soon.

Fuck. Her legs spread a little wider. I didn't think she realized she was doing it, but the sight was enough to almost make me come undone.

I wrapped her legs around my waist and, without saying anything, drove all the way inside her.

She made a small mewling noise, her head moving from side to side and her eyes closing.

"Look at me," I said darkly.

I waited until she opened her eyes before I moved.

"Oh, God."

She reached over her head for the edge of the desk, and I grabbed her hips and pounded into her.

"I want you to know who's fucking you. I want you to see me and know that only I can bring you to the brink of ecstasy. Me and no one else."

She clenched around me, driving me crazy.

"If I-I'm the only o-one for you, then are you the only one for me?" she asked, and the possessive note in her voice nearly pushed me over.

"Only you," I said.

I hadn't even thought about getting my dick wet anywhere but inside her tight little cunt. Did she really think I was out looking for someone else?

"Only you," I repeated.

Her body convulsed from my words, sweat gathering between her breasts.

Fuck. Fuck. Fuck.

I pressed my thumb against her swollen clit, rubbing it as I rocked inside her.

"Come for me, baby girl. Show me just what I do to you."

It was as I promised. She screamed my name as she came, tears collecting in the corners of her eyes.

How fucking beautiful.

Feeling her inner walls trembling around me was enough to push me over. I came shortly after, squirting my cum inside her pussy.

I couldn't fucking wait until she got pregnant with my kid.

Couldn't fucking wait to see the way her belly swelled and knowing she was forever tied to me.

I groaned and pulled out of her. I pushed my jeans off and kicked them to the floor. I turned back to her and took in the sight of her dripping cunt.

I licked my lips and smeared my cum back inside. Some of it dripped down the crease of her ass.

She whined when I pushed it inside her tight little asshole.

"Dominic."

"Shh, hold still and let me play with what's mine."

"But—but *this*!"

I smiled. "Your asshole, you mean?"

She swallowed.

"One of these days, I'm gonna fuck it."

Her mouth opened, but nothing came out.

My smile widened. "Don't worry, before I do, I'll buy some training plugs, yeah? I'm not that much of a monster."

She sputtered something incomprehensible, and I laughed, pulling her into my arms and carrying her out of there. She burrowed into my chest, making me pause.

What was it about this girl that was affecting me so badly?

I didn't know, and a part of me didn't want to know the answer. I wasn't the kind of man who scared easily, but fuck, I had to admit this girl scared me.

In the best way.

I walked us to the room and straight to the bathroom, setting her on the counter before wetting a clean cloth.

"Open," I said, tapping the outside of her legs. She blushed but did as I asked and let me clean her up. I felt almost a sense of regret cleaning away my cum, but that just meant I had to keep dirtying her up.

I could fucking do that.

Once I was done, I quickly wiped myself clean and carried her out of the bathroom and to the walk-in closet.

"You do know that I can walk, right?" she asked dryly.

I grinned at her, tucking a strand of hair falling over her face behind her ear. "Your point?"

She opened her mouth, said nothing, and then closed it once more.

I turned away from her and looked for some clothes for us to wear.

I dressed us in T-shirts and sweats, and once that was done, I brought her back down for some food.

The rest of the night was spent peacefully.

I couldn't even remember the last time I had a night when all the voices in my head quieted down. Perhaps when both of my boys were little and still needed me for every little thing.

But it was never like this.

It never made me want to stay inside this house for as long as I could.

We went to bed pretty early.

I arranged us in the same position we were in almost every night, with my arms wrapped tightly around her, my front to her back, and my face buried in her neck.

"Dominic?" she asked, breaking the silence.

I squeezed her to let her know I heard her.

"I didn't mean that."

"Mean what, wildcat?"

"That you're the monster in my story."

I didn't say anything for a moment.

Then, "Yes, you did."

She nodded. "Yes, I did."

The room was bathed in silence after that. I gave her a chance to gather her thoughts. I was sure she didn't know why she said it. But she had said it, and it was the truth. I was a monster, but I'd also meant it when I said I was her monster, standing between her and everything bad in this world.

I squeezed her to my side when it seemed she didn't have any more to say.

"Go to sleep," I said, my voice gruff with emotions I didn't want to fucking contemplate.

She nodded and burrowed herself into me.

And that was what we did. We went to sleep.

17

DOMINIC

I GOT A LATE START TO THE DAY.

I couldn't remember the last time I had slept in so late, but I had woken up this morning when the sun was already high in the sky, and Emmy was snuggled close in my arms.

I wasn't in a rush to start the day, and even though there was a shit ton for my men to do, we couldn't really do it until we had more information.

My number-one priority was finding the traitors, the men responsible for hunting down my son in the street and traumatizing him. And the moment I found them, they were gonna wish for fucking death.

I looked out the window.

I was in the living room. Lucy was out grocery shopping, and Emmy was upstairs taking a shower after I took her three times this morning to distract her from asking me to wear a fucking condom.

I scowled at the thought.

I wasn't letting anything get between us, so she might as well get that fucking idea out of her head right now.

I glanced down at my phone and waited.

My schedule didn't allow me to talk to Braxton much, considering the time difference between here and New Zealand, but I was expecting him to call as soon as he had breakfast there.

Sure enough, my phone rang with a video call, and I transformed my face into a soft smile that only Braxton and Kai—and even Emmy, to an extent—had ever seen on my face.

"Hey, buddy," I said when I answered the phone.

"Dad! I miss you! Did you miss me?"

My smile widened, and I could feel my shoulders relaxing at the sight of his happy face. Before Jude's death—Jenny's adopted son—she had been a permanent fixture in my kids' life. They were close with their aunt, but Braxton understood why Jenny decided to distance herself from me, and him as well. I was sure he was happy spending time with her again.

"I miss you, baby. So much."

"Well, duh," he said, making me laugh. So confident about his role in my life. The way it should be.

"Are you having fun?" I asked.

He smiled and nodded enthusiastically. Then he told me about everything he had done, including some of the things he had texted me before about. I listened patiently to all his stories, comforted by his voice, chubby red cheeks that were quickly fading with each year that passed, and the light in his green eyes.

I waited until he was done before I spoke. "Are you being good for your aunt?"

"I am always good, Dad," he said.

I laughed. My boy was good, but he also had Madden genes. He was just as wild as Kai had been at his age, and almost as wild as I had been.

"I like it here in New Zealand."

"I'm glad you're having fun, buddy."

Face serious, he asked me, "When can I come home?"

I took in a small breath of air. I could feel my heart hurting at the sight of him. Despite having a good time in New Zealand, he missed home and me and his brother.

I missed my boy so much.

"Soon, buddy. I promise."

"Really?"

"Yes."

"You won't leave me here?"

Fuck. My fist clenched around the phone, and I forced myself not to show any reaction.

"I would never leave you behind," I said gruffly. "You belong with me. Right by my side. With me and your brother. I'm gonna bring you home, I promise. And when have I ever broken a promise to you?"

"Never," he said quietly.

"Never," I affirmed. I might have done a lot of nasty shit in my life, but if there was one thing I was proud of, it was never having broken a single promise I made to my boys. My words count for something with them. They held the weight of the world in them, and Kai and Braxton both knew that.

"You are coming home to me. As soon as it's safe, I'm gonna bring you home. And Braxton?"

"Yeah, Dad?"

"I won't fucking let you go again."

He laughed, his shoulders relaxing. I didn't usually cuss in front of my kids, but I was sure they both heard worse at school, and Kai's colorful vocabulary was attributed to hanging out with the brothers in the club.

"Okay," he said, reassured.

"Is your aunt there?" I asked him.

He looked at something behind his phone, which told me the answer before he said, "Yeah."

"Can I talk to her?"

Jenny must have signaled something because an uncomfortable look came over Braxton's face.

"It's okay, buddy. Maybe next time," I said. I wasn't going to put him in the middle of this.

He nodded, his shoulders relaxing.

"All right. I'm gonna let you go," I said. "You're going skiing today, right?"

He nodded excitedly. It was wintertime there now, so he was probably enjoying the snow.

"Be careful, okay?"

"I will, Dad. Bye. I love you."

"And I love you," I said, and he hung up. I clicked off the phone and noticed my reflection on the dark screen before sighing.

"You know what they say about eavesdroppers," I said. I was aware of Emmy as soon as she'd come downstairs.

"But you weren't talking shit about me," she said, completely shameless that I had caught her. I could feel a small smile tugging on my lips. Turning to her, I held out my hand.

She hurried toward me and climbed into my lap.

I wrapped my arms around her and reveled in the closeness of this tiny girl in my arms.

She buried her face in my chest and wrapped her arms around my middle. "How's Braxton?"

"You've heard. He's having fun with his aunt."

She didn't say anything for a moment, and I could hear the cogs turning in her mind. I squeezed her to me. "Ask."

"What happened between you and your sister?"

"Long story," I said.

"I have time. Since my captivity, I have nothing but time."

I squeezed her for that comment. She scowled at me.

I leaned back against the sofa and took her with me.

Reaching up, I grabbed one tit in my hand and played

with her. She squirmed. "Dominic. We're talking. You can't really be thinking about sex right now."

I laughed. "With you, I'm always thinking about sex."

I rolled her nipple between my fingers, and she ground her pussy down against my thigh, brushing against my hard-on.

"Dominic," she protested.

I let out another sigh. "Fine."

I regrettably let go of her, and judging by the look on her face, she wanted my touch back, too.

"Jenny and I grew up with pieces of shit for parents."

She stiffened in my arms. I squeezed her to get her to relax and continued when she did.

"It has always been my job to look after her. Before Kai and before Braxton, she had been my entire world. Because of that, we grew up close. She's two years younger than me, so you can probably see how protective I was of her. She didn't grow up with the best things in life, and after taking the reins in the club, I thought maybe I could finally give her everything she wanted. But Jenny didn't want me in the club to begin with. She didn't approve of the lifestyle but accepted it because I was her big brother. Jenny met and fell in love with a good man in college. I was fucking happy, and I liked Noah for her. I liked that he was everything I wasn't, and that he could provide a stable home for her.

"For years, we were happy. Jenny was a middle school math teacher, and Noah was the principal. In her second year of teaching, there was this kid in the school. Just one look at him and you know that shit wasn't going well for him at home.

"You know, the kids who come to school every morning with a new bruise and an excuse no one believes. Jenny was the only one who didn't accept his excuses, and by the end of the year, she and Noah were granted guardianship of the boy.

Jude and Kai are close in age, and they were friends at school. They were fucking smart, too. Much smarter than me, with the way they went on and on about technology and shit. Those two got into all sorts of trouble, but I wasn't concerned at the time because it was just good, harmless fun. Until they were gunned down in a fucking alleyway."

Emmy gasped, tears forming in her eyes.

I looked away from her and back out the window.

"Kai lost a lot of blood. I almost lost my boy. I have never felt as helpless as I did then."

That part of my life wasn't something I liked to return to. The image of Kai in that hospital bed, trying to fight for his life, would haunt me for the rest of my life.

"Jude didn't make it," I said.

"And Jenny blames you?" Emmy asked softly.

I nodded. "I don't know who gunned them down. But I'm sure it was club-related."

"What happened to Noah?"

"He died in a car accident earlier that year. So in one year, my baby sister lost both her husband and her kid. Is it really a wonder that she hates me?"

She said nothing for a moment.

I moved my hands to her waist. "Being in this life is dangerous. As you've already experienced. But I'm not the man I once was. I'm not fucking helpless. I protect what's mine. That includes my sons." I looked into her hazel eyes. "That includes you."

She swallowed, then, after a small moment, nodded.

She cupped my cheek, and I held still. She rarely ever initiated anything with me, and any little touches she gave me made me feel like the king of the fucking world.

"Have you ever thought about going straight?" she asked, her voice soft.

"I don't know how," I admitted. And that was the truth.

This was who I was. I couldn't change, even if I wanted to. But that didn't mean I wouldn't do whatever it took to ensure the safety of those under my protection.

Before she could say anything else, I kissed her softly.

I kissed her sweetly.

I kissed her, showing her everything I couldn't with words alone.

18

DOMINIC

It was late, probably past midnight.

Emmy was asleep, naked, beside me, and the streetlight that shined through the window outside my bedroom cast a soft glow around her in the bed.

I hadn't fallen asleep, unable to look away from my little obsession. My phone vibrated on the nightstand. I quickly grabbed it, donned a pair of sweatpants, and walked out of the room to avoid disturbing her sleep.

I'd missed the call by the time I reached the small balcony in the backyard.

I called Micah back. He picked up on the first ring.

"They have properties set up near the border of California and Nevada," he said without a greeting.

"Well, hello to you, too."

Micah didn't say anything for a beat. Then, "Hello."

His voice was dry, and I laughed.

"Did you find out if any of those ugly fuckers have a sixth toe?"

"Not yet, but would you like me to send it to you when I do?"

"That won't be necessary," I said with a smile, before my face turned serious. "Why do you think they have those properties?"

I could already guess.

"They're trying to infiltrate California."

I grunted in agreement. Those sneaky little bastards. And I had no doubt they'd turned one of my men against me. The question was, which man?

Or *men*?

"What do you want me to do?" Micah asked.

"Nothing, for now. Just make a note of all their properties. That will be useful to us later. And when we attack, I'll send men your way."

"Got it."

"Wait," I said before he could hang up. "You okay?"

"You know, you're worse than Roman."

"How?"

He let out a sigh. "I'm fine. Still my chippy self, don't worry about it."

I didn't fucking believe him. I thought it might have something to do with Roman finding Ryleigh, but there was something else going on here. Something he didn't want either of us to know.

I didn't question Micah's loyalty. He wasn't the rat. But there was something going on in his personal life.

"If you want to talk about it..."

"I know where to find you," he finished. "But I'm fine. Just working out some shit in my head."

"Is whatever you're working out here in California? Is that why you jumped at the opportunity to go to Vegas?"

He didn't answer me.

Holy shit.

"Is it a girl?"

"Go back to Emmy, you bastard," he said before he hung up on me.

Fuck.

It was a girl, and the unemotional psycho didn't know what to do about it.

I laughed.

Who was unlucky enough to catch his attention?

Poor girl.

I PROBABLY GOT ABOUT five hours of sleep before I was awakened at five by another phone call.

This one was from Roman.

"Yeah?" I asked softly, looking over at Emmy. She stirred slightly on the bed and mumbled something in her sleep but otherwise didn't wake.

"The rat took the bait," he said.

"Fuck, you're serious?"

"Yup. Just got the news that one of our decoy warehouses is on fire. I'm on my way there now."

"All right. I'll meet you there soon."

I quickly got up and got ready, splashing my face with cold water to wake up.

When I was finished, I went to the bed and gently shook Emmy's shoulders.

"What?" she grumbled without opening her eyes.

I grinned. "Wildcat, I have to go. Give me a kiss first."

She let out a small sigh as if I was inconveniencing her and held out her arms blindly for me, her lips puckering.

I laughed softly as I bent down and pressed a swift kiss against her lips.

She tried to follow my lips with her own without opening her eyes. I watched her, feeling light.

"Be careful," she said softly.

I paused. "I will. I'll be back. Okay?"

"Okay." Another sigh, but this one was soft.

As if the idea of my coming back home to her was something she wanted. I still wasn't sure. Physical attraction was different from emotional attachment.

She could lust after me, but she could also be biding her time until the day I let her go.

Hated to break it to her, but that day would be the day after forever.

I shook my head at my own thoughts and petted her soft hair before I made my way out the door.

It didn't take me long to get to the warehouse Roman was talking about. I found him parked a distance away, and I drove up to him, got off my bike, and stood there, taking in the flames as they engulfed the empty warehouse.

"How long before the cops show up?" I asked.

"Could be soon. The smoke is getting big, and it won't be long before someone notices and reports it."

I nodded.

We now had the list narrowed down to five men.

Trent was at the top of the list. I still didn't know what the Sons of War could offer him to make him turn on me, but he was always resentful that I didn't give him the VP position.

The slimy little fucker wouldn't have lasted one day in the position.

I was almost certain he was the one who gave the Sons of War men the location of this place after I had Roman and Kai tell him and four other men in the group this location.

I didn't think he was the only rat.

He was too stupid to pull off stunts like this, and I wasn't gonna act until I had all the information. It would only be a matter of time.

We got back to the bar a little after twelve, when most employees, including Trent, were coming in and getting ready for their shifts.

Roman nodded to the bastard standing at the bar, doing his prep work. We stood there and watched, and after a moment, he must have felt eyes on him because he looked up and met my gaze.

He raised his hand as if to greet me, and when I didn't react, he slowly let that hand fall.

The fucker squirmed on his feet, clearly more uncomfortable the longer I stood there and watched him.

Good.

He should be uncomfortable.

Because if I found he had anything to do with Braxton, *mere* discomfort would be the last thing he would be feeling.

I turned away and headed to my usual table, ordering beer from the bottle. I didn't drink anything from the tap, not trusting my enemies not to take advantage of that and poison me to death.

Wouldn't that be a fucking pathetic way to go?

Roman sat next to me, looking up at the TV in the bar.

"What's got you so interested?" I asked.

He tapped my shoulder, frowning slightly. "They're opening a new commercial manufacturing company here in Sacramento."

"A commercial manufacturing company?" That was fucking unusual, only because we hadn't had anything that big develop in the city without my knowing about it first. How the fuck was this the first I was hearing about this? I spent a pretty penny to get my people elected as board members for the city to tell me shit like this.

I didn't like it.

Not one fucking bit.

"What are they producing?"

Roman said, "Baby food."

"Should we be worried?"

"I don't know. Have you ever heard of the Blue Paragon?"

I shook my head.

"Apparently, this company is the one to look out for since their stocks and investments are growing near ninth figures annually."

"And let me guess. They're opening this baby food manufacturer."

Roman nodded. "It's all over the news. The governor is pretty excited because he thinks it will bring in a lot of job opportunities."

I didn't get into politics. Too many shiny assholes who only looked polished on the outside. I only got involved if I had to, like when there was a certain policy being considered that would help my business. Then I would hire a lobbyist and donate to whatever slimy assholes would make the policy happen, such as slacking on the rules and regulations regarding shipping goods overseas.

A new company coming in was none of my business unless it interfered with my business, and something about this manufacturer told me it would interfere with my business.

"I'll have Kai look into it," I said.

Roman nodded.

Hopefully, I was being fucking paranoid, and there wasn't more shit raining down on us.

I WAS FUCKING tired by the time I got home.

Emmy thought of me as this energetic monster who

thrived at night, but sometimes even the monster got tired, and all I'd wanted to do all day was get home to her.

Briefly, I wondered if this was how it was with Roman and Ryleigh, but I quickly shook away the thought. I wasn't as fucking gone for a girl as that poor fucker was, and I refused to admit Emmy had the same hold on me as Ryleigh did with Roman, to the point that he risked my wrath.

I walked into the dark and quiet house.

At this hour, I expected Emmy to have already had her dinner, and to be in bed, reading one of her books.

I climbed up the stairs quietly, making note of the lights on in my room. The door was cracked open a little. And sure enough, when I pushed the door, the sight of Emmy sitting on the bed and reading a book greeted me.

I stayed where I was, wondering why my chest felt light.

Things were fucking messy out there in this world. But here in this room, with her, everything was all it needed to be. She was right where she needed to be with me.

She looked up and gasped when she finally noticed me.

We should really work on her situational awareness, but I liked that she was comfortable enough in this house to keep her guard down.

"Jeez, perhaps you should make some sort of noise when you move so you don't scare me," she said, making me want to smile.

I walked into the room and started tugging on my clothes.

"Dominic? Are you okay?"

I didn't answer her. By the time I made it to the bed, I was in only my black boxer briefs, and Emmy was looking at me like I was the tastiest treat in the world.

Fuck me, but I wanted to be devoured by her.

Her eyes tracked my movements, and she didn't say

anything when I pulled the blanket away from her. She was wearing one of my T-shirts and perhaps panties.

Or hell, maybe it was my lucky day, and she had nothing on underneath.

I pulled her toward me and tugged off the shirt, exposing her hard nipples, flushed skin, and baby-pink panties. I pushed her onto her back on the mattress and quickly pulled off her panties as well so she was lying on the bed naked.

I licked my lips.

"How the fuck am I supposed to ever get over the sight of you like this?" I asked, more to myself than to her.

She scowled up at me. "Do you want to?"

I smiled and knew my eyes were soft when I looked at her. "Fuck, no."

I shoved my boxer briefs down and kicked them away. She watched me with hungry eyes.

"I want you to kneel in front of me and suck my cock," I said.

This wasn't my intention when I walked into the room tonight. I had wanted to fuck her hard and fast, to lose myself inside her. But now that the image of her doing that was in my brain...

I couldn't get it out.

She licked her lips, not seeming to be opposed to the idea.

"Do you like that, wildcat? Do you like the thought of yourself on your knees in front of me, making me lose control?"

She hesitated before she nodded.

I reached down and squeezed my dick to keep from coming before I grabbed the pillow and tossed it to the floor.

I helped her off the bed and pushed her down so she was kneeling in front of me.

The little wildcat looked at my cock before moving her

eyes up to my face. Then, shyly, she reached out and grabbed my cock with her tiny hands.

I groaned and buried my fingers in her hair, pulling on it roughly.

"Take me in your mouth," I said.

She did as I asked.

The first feeling of her mouth wrapped around me was like fucking heaven. I tightened my grip around her hair, probably to the point of pain, but it didn't seem she minded because she hummed around me and took more of me inside her mouth.

Our eyes met, and this fucking sight would fucking torment me for the rest of my fucking life, I was sure of it.

"I'm gonna fuck your mouth," I growled. She sucked on my dick harder at my words, making me lose focus and nearly all control.

I thrust my hips, moving in and out of her, slowly at first, before picking up speed and getting more into a frenzy the more I felt her suck.

Fuck me.

I saw stars when she reached up and wrapped her hand around the base, twisting it as the tip of my cock reached the back of her throat, causing her to gag a little.

"Fuck, I'm close. And I don't want to fucking come in your mouth."

She made a slight noise in protest, moving her hands and gripping my hips as if she was afraid I would pull away from her.

I tugged harder on her hair. "Later. I'll fucking come in your mouth later, but right now, I want to lose myself in your pussy."

She moaned, and I took that as agreement. I helped her stand and pressed a hard kiss against her lips, nipping sharply, before I pushed her back down on the mattress.

She bounced slightly, and I crawled my way up her body.

I grabbed my cock and directed the tip to her entrance. We didn't look away from each other when I pushed inside.

I kissed her, stopping when I got to the hilt, taking in the feel of her.

"Baby," I said when I rocked against her. Her hands were splayed on my chest, her nails digging into my skin roughly when I pushed back inside.

"Things are going to be bad for a while, and I need you by my side," I said, and that was the fucking truth. Things might be heading in the right direction, but it was gonna get bad before it got better. I needed her close by.

"Dominic," she gasped.

I moved faster, reaching between us, my fingers seeking out her clit. She arched up when I found it, and I rubbed around the bundle of nerves over and over.

"Fuck, baby. Come for me. Be my good girl and come."

She kissed me again, sobbing as she came.

I swallowed her scream, her orgasm triggering my own, and I released inside her, feeling the beautiful mess we made together.

I flipped us over so I was on the bottom, and she lay on top, my fingers playing around the left side of her rib cage as I imagined my name branded right there.

Fuck, but the image was almost too much to bear.

She hadn't said anything, still clinging to me the way I fucking wanted—needed.

I just needed her.

And I didn't know how to *not* need her.

"Baby?" I said, breaking the silence.

I felt her press a kiss against the skin of my neck. That one little kiss probably affected me more than any other kiss I had combined that wasn't with her.

Finally, she pulled away from me, her hazel eyes clouded.

"Aren't you tired of ruling the world?" she asked, wrapping her arms tightly around me.

I paused. I didn't think anyone had ever asked me that before. "Is it wrong for me to want to be able to give the world to those I love? To my sons." I let my gaze settle over her face. "To you."

Her breath caught. "You want to give me the world?"

"I'd give you the entire galaxy, if possible."

"What if I just want you?" she asked.

I didn't think there had ever been anyone who just wanted me. "You have me."

"You make it sound so easy."

"It *is* easy."

19

EMMY

It is easy.

Dominic's words followed me throughout the next day.

I didn't even know why I told him I wanted just him.

Not because it wasn't true, but because now I worried I'd shown too much of my hand—or my heart.

And I didn't know how to deal with that.

Dominic had left early in the morning, and he had been gone for most of the day. I wondered when he would deem it safe enough for me to get out of this house. I didn't want to leave the safety of his protection. Not anymore. I wasn't stupid. But I also didn't want to be trapped in this house forever, with only him, Lucy, and—rarely—Colt for company.

School would start soon, and I needed to return to my job.

His words from last night came back to me.

He said things were going to be bad for a while. He needed me to stay right by his side, but he wouldn't tell me what the things were.

The bastard hadn't used a condom since he'd fucked me

that first time. I wasn't on birth control. I didn't think I was pregnant now, but that was hard to tell so soon. If things were really going to be bad for a while, did he really think getting me pregnant was the way to go?

And why was he so hell-bent on having unprotected sex? I didn't know. There was almost this light in his eyes as he looked at his cum dripping out of me, and I swore I could see him plotting when he could do it again.

I shivered.

I didn't know when I had become like other girls, turning stupid from lust, but I had.

I felt even stupider when I couldn't bring myself to regret all that we had done.

What was more, I craved it. I craved him.

I couldn't. I had—

I took a deep breath.

I was slowly falling for the terrible man.

I looked down at the piano in front of me. I had been sitting here since Lucy left for home after I had dinner with her and Colt. That was probably about a couple of hours ago. I didn't know why I was sitting here if I couldn't bring myself to play the beautiful instrument.

I pressed my finger down on the F sharp a few times.

It was as I expected. The piano played beautifully.

Using two fingers, I played "Twinkle, Twinkle Little Star," smiling a little when I came to the last note. Playing the piano was like riding a bike. At least, it was for me. It didn't matter how many years had passed since I'd last played a certain song, I still remembered it.

Remembering how to play was never the problem.

It was the physical act of it, and at this point in my life, I had given up hope that I could play again. I couldn't.

I let out a small sigh, then I felt something—or *someone*—

breathing down my neck. I jumped and turned around to find Dominic standing there.

"What the fuck? You scared me."

He shook his head. "Baby, we really need to work on your situational awareness."

"There is nothing wrong with my awareness. You just move like a cat," I accused.

He rolled his eyes. "I made plenty of noise."

"Yes. About as loud as a cat."

His lips twitched, though he didn't smile. Good. I might have slapped him if that was the case. And he might just spank me in retaliation.

Yeah, it was a good idea he didn't smile.

"What are you thinking about, wildcat?"

I shook my head and shrugged, and his blue eyes danced with amusement.

He didn't say anything for a moment. Then, "Do you want to come out with me to the bar tonight?"

I frowned. "Like the bar from last time?"

He shook his head. "No, my bar."

"Your bar? Are you sure that's safe?"

"Things are as safe as they're going to be right now. I just need to make sure you stay by my side all night."

"All night?" I asked.

"All night," he confirmed.

"What if I have to use the bathroom?" I retorted.

"Then I will go in there with you."

My mouth opened, and I wasn't sure if he was joking or not. Then he smiled at me, and I relaxed a little.

"I have a shy bladder," I said.

"Tough," he responded, his eyes still dancing with humor. I stood from the piano bench, tilting my head back to look him in the eye.

He moved his hand up and cupped my cheek, his thumb

swiping underneath my eyelid. "One of these days, you're going to play a song for me, yeah?"

It wasn't a question but a command, and there would only be one answer he found acceptable. I nodded, because despite not being able to bring myself to play, I found I did want to play for him.

Perhaps I could choose an easy and quick song.

"And you're going to tell me who the fuck hurt your hands."

"How do you know someone hurt them?"

"Because that's the only fucking explanation."

"You mean your research on me didn't tell you?"

Very few knew what happened, but Dominic seemed like a pretty persistent man. I was sure if he wanted, he could have found out the whole story.

His hand drifted down, and he grabbed each of my hands in his own. "Your background check only told me so much. I know you have no criminal records, and I know who your parents are and what they do. Your medical record told me what you broke but not how you broke it. I can make you tell me, but I prefer you to tell it to me willingly. There will be no more secrets between us. Got it?"

I opened my mouth to reply when the front door opened and a man I had never met before walked in, carrying a large black duffel bag and a large black case. I moved closer to Dominic, wary of the new man in this house.

Dominic wrapped his arms around me protectively, but he didn't seem worried about the man. He smiled at him. "Thanks, Edger. Why don't you set up everything in my office and let yourself out once you're done?"

"Sure thing, boss," Edger replied, his voice rough. He was a mean-looking man, with bulging muscles stacked upon his large frame and tattoos covering almost everywhere, including his neck and face.

"What's he setting up in your office?" I asked once Edger was out of earshot.

He tapped my nose, and I could have sworn there was a flash of affection in his eyes. But then I blinked, and that affection was gone. All that was left was dark possessiveness and… satisfaction?

"I'll show you later," he said, and I debated on whether I should push him. He did say he didn't want any secrets.

"No more secrets between us?" I asked quietly. He nodded. "That's either a very brave thing for someone in your position to say, or a stupid one."

"See it as brave," he said arrogantly.

"You'll really tell me everything? The investigation?"

I shot him a pointed look. He squeezed me tightly for that comment.

"Not gonna tell you shit about the investigation. You'll only use that as an excuse to leave, and you need to get it through to your head. You ain't ever leaving, baby. As for the other shit, as long as you think you can stomach it."

"Aren't you afraid I might use it against you? I could go to the cops."

He shrugged. "That's a risk I'm willing to take with you."

I couldn't believe he would trust me with all his secrets like that. Did he do this with all the women he was sleeping with?

But no, something told me this was as new to him as it was to me. And something about that thought made my chest light.

"So, do you want to leave for the night? Come meet my brothers? And my oldest?"

I bit my lip. Before he came home, I had wanted to leave the house, even for a little while. But now that he was here, all I wanted to do was spend the time with him in bed.

I wanted to meet his brothers, though. I wanted to see

that part of his life that I wasn't privy to. I nodded. "Okay. Let me change first, and we can go."

We took his bike to the bar, which wasn't that long of a drive, much to my disappointment. It was on the tip of my tongue to ask Dominic to keep driving.

I was getting used to riding.

And I loved it.

But we arrived, and Dominic helped me climb off before I could say anything.

The bar wasn't that much different from the place we'd gone to for lunch, though it was much more lively, and even from the parking lot, I could hear loud rock music from inside.

Dominic grabbed my hand and squeezed. "Ready?"

"Ready," I said, a little excited and nervous about meeting the important people in his life. Especially his son. Technically, I had seen Kai when he went with his dad to rescue Braxton and me, but I had never talked to him.

I was only older than him by a little over a year, which meant I was closer to Kai in age than I was to his dad, my…

I didn't exactly know what Dominic was to me.

My captor? My boyfriend?

I shook my head. He acted with enough possessiveness of me to be either of those things.

We walked inside the bar, and the first thing I noticed was all the people.

There were just so many people around—some crowding around the bar; some on the dance floor, grinding against each other; and some sitting at the scattered tables.

Dominic didn't seem fazed by the scene, though I supposed he was used to it by now.

He maneuvered us through the crowd, and like he was the king of the castle, everyone moved out of his way quickly, some calling out greetings to him.

I caught the eyes of a few women we passed, and none of them looked at me with a welcoming expression.

I hate that my first thought was to wonder how many of these women he had slept with... or was currently sleeping with.

I quickly shook away the thoughts.

He spent most nights with me. I was his only bed partner... right?

I yanked my hand away from his, because no matter how much I tried to reason through it, I didn't actually know the answer to that.

He turned to me, his brow furrowed. "Baby?" he said, loud enough for me to hear through the music.

I opened my mouth, but I didn't know how to explain what I was feeling, not when it felt like the crowd and the music and the *stench* were closing in on me.

Before I could really gather my own thoughts, a rough-looking female biker—probably the female equivalent of Dominic—came up to us, pushing one claw-like hand onto his chest and leaning close to his ear.

"Darling," she cooed. I narrowed my eyes at them, and Dominic never looked away from me to acknowledge her. It didn't make me feel better. "I missed you."

Before Dominic could respond or react, I turned around and walked to the front door.

My heart thudded loudly in my ears as I moved through the crowd.

For the first time since Dominic *took* me, I felt trapped.

There was no choice.

He made me fall for him in the worst way possible, while

he had the freedom to do whatever the hell he wanted, and I still didn't know where we stood.

I was almost to the door when arms wrapped around my waist and hauled me up. Based purely on my body's reactions, I knew it was Dominic. Even when I was angry and confused, I still couldn't disguise how much he affected me.

"No, let me go!" I said, struggling in his arms. Several people looked our way, but no one came to help me. They all took one look at Dominic and turned away, pretending they didn't see this beast holding onto me, or the fact that he was walking us back further into the bar.

We briefly passed the woman who had touched him, and I made eye contact with her.

She shot me a disgusted look, which only made me struggle even more.

Dominic opened the door to the back and walked in, shutting the door behind us with a slam. I could still hear the music from outside, but it was faint. In this small, dark room, it was like we had entered a different world.

I looked around, trying to get my breathing under control.

"Are you calm?" Dominic asked gruffly.

"No," I sneered. "Now let me go."

He let out a small sigh, as if I was an inconvenience he had to deal with, and that just pissed me off more.

If I was such an inconvenience, he should just let me go.

He sat on a couch pushed up against the wall near the door, settling me on his lap. I tried to keep as much space between our bodies as possible.

"What are you doing?" I asked.

"Talking to you."

I didn't turn around to look at him. There was a small lamp in the corner that provided some light in the room, but it wasn't as bright as it was out in the bar. Dominic tightened his arms around me and pulled me closer until my back was pressed up against his warm chest, and his hard cock was nestled snugly between my ass.

I tensed when I felt it. Jesus, was he ever *not* hard?

"What's there to talk about?" I asked, trying to ignore it. I wiggled on his lap, trying to get off.

He leaned forward, his lips grazing my ear. "Hold still, or we'll end up fucking before we talk."

I gasped and turned around to find his dark blue eyes focused intently on me. "When is it ever *not* fucking with you?"

"When I'm dead," he answered seriously.

"Is that what you tell yourself when you're with someone else?"

He didn't say anything. For a moment, I felt naked. Vulnerable. I wished he would stop looking at me like he was.

Then, his lips spread in a wide grin. "Is that what this is about?"

"I don't know what you're talking about," I argued.

"You're jealous," he said, and the bastard sounded way too fucking happy about that.

"I am not. It is none of my business who you spend your time with. But I would like you to do me the courtesy of not touching me anymore. Especially when you always conveniently forget to put on a condom. I don't want to catch anything."

That wiped the smile off his face. "There has been no one but you, woman. And if you can't see that, then you're fucking blind," he growled.

I pulled back from the anger in his voice, even though I wasn't really scared of him. I wondered when I stopped being scared of Dominic and instead began to crave him.

He took a deep breath. "I have been getting shit left and

right from Roman about you. And you think I am going out, fucking someone else? When the hell do you think I could find the time?"

"Oh, my. You are just so romantic," I deadpanned.

He grabbed my breast and pinched my nipple for the comment.

"Hey!" I backed away, clutching my breasts.

His cock twitched. "Fuck, do you have any idea how fucking crazy you drive me?"

"Well, if it's the same amount of crazy you drive me, then I'd say it's a good amount."

He rolled his eyes and cupped the back of my head. I resisted.

"What are you doing?" I whisper-yelled. As if I was afraid someone might hear us.

"What does it look like I'm doing? I'm reminding you."

He slammed his lips against mine.

My hands were pressed against his chest as I tried to push him away… at first.

But the longer he kissed me, the quicker it was to forget why I was even fighting him in the first place.

His tongue came out, and he licked between my lips before molding his lips against mine once more.

He repeated the action until I felt my own lips going slack, and Dominic pushed his tongue inside my mouth, gliding it against my tongue and bringing forth a small moan from my lips.

Fuck.

The hands I had on his chest, the ones fighting him, betrayed me when instead of pushing him away, I fisted his shirt, holding him close.

I was afraid he would pull away, and I wasn't ready for that.

He deepened the kiss, and I lost the battle.

I turned to him fully, and he helped reposition me on his lap. It took a lot of fumbling on our part, but then I was facing him, my legs on either side of his hips, and I was grinding my pussy down on his hard cock.

He let out a low groan in my mouth, the sound vibrating through between us and making more arousal gush out of me.

"Fuck, but you taste so good," he said, backing away slightly. I tried to follow his lips with my own. He held me back. "Can't you fucking see?"

"See what?" I asked, wanting to kiss him again. I licked my lips, and he followed the move with another hard press of his lips against mine.

"You're the only one for me. Do you think I can get this hard for anyone else? You think I would ever let another woman drive me as crazy as you? Let her sleep in my room, in my bed, with me? Do you really think I make a habit of feeding and clothing another woman? How can you not see how fucking obsessed I am with you?"

I didn't know what to say, so I said nothing. It wasn't a declaration of love. But it was as close to one as I would get with him, and perhaps there was something wrong with my brain because I thought his words were sweet.

I hadn't realized I wanted those words from him until I heard them.

Call me crazy, but I believed him. I believed he was like this with me and no one else. A part of me should be alarmed by his actions.

The other part…

"Ditto," I said.

I frowned, unsure why I'd said it like that.

Dominic paused a moment before he threw his head back and laughed, his whole body shaking against me.

I wrapped my arms around his neck to keep myself steady and enjoyed the sight of him so carefree.

Fuck.

Even his laugh had the power to affect me.

Laughter still in his eyes, he leaned forward and sucked on the skin of my neck. I tilted my head to the side to give him better access, feeling the touch all the way down to my clit. Briefly, I wondered if I could come like this alone.

"Should have fucked you before we left. You would have been a lot more compliant and I wouldn't feel like I was fucking dying."

"There you go again with that compliant comment," I said dryly.

He grinned at me and helped me stand up. I quickly smoothed down my shirt, hoping I didn't look like I had just let Dominic have his way with me in the office at the bar, but I was sure that was what most people out there were thinking.

I let out a small sigh as Dominic stood.

"Better?" he asked.

I bit my bottom lip and nodded. Nothing was really resolved between us, but I felt better.

He smiled at me. "Good. Let's go."

I turned away from him and he spanked my ass once as I walked off.

"Hey," I said, rubbing the sore cheek.

"Remind me you're owed a spanking when we get home for that little stunt out there," he said.

I sputtered at him. There were so many things wrong with that sentence, I didn't know which to unpack first.

"No," I said.

We got to the door, but before he opened it, he bent down and looked at me. "It's all right. I'll remember."

He spanked my ass once more and opened the door.

I rubbed at the soreness. He had spanked the same place, and I was sure I would get a bruise there.

The creeper probably would get off on that too.

I shook my head and followed him out.

Dominic led me to the back of the bar. Some people looked at us as we passed, but no one stopped us on the way. They all gave Dominic a wide berth, and if I had ever doubted his influence, that was no longer the case.

He garnered attention, respect, and fear.

I checked out his ass while he walked. One of these days, I would be brave enough to explore it, but right now, I could only admire his swagger, feeling a pounding ache between my legs.

Power was sexy, I decided.

But power in men who were born to lead…

That was a whole different ball game. I had been surrounded my entire life by men who were enticed by power, be it my male piano teachers, my dad, and even my first boyfriend, but never one who exuded it from the very core of his being.

Dominic turned to me suddenly when we stopped at a table in the back, and I didn't take my eyes away from him soon enough.

He shot me a knowing look and pulled me to his side, turning us to face the men and one woman I hadn't noticed sitting at the table.

I recognized Kai right away.

He was the spitting image of his dad, and it was like looking into the mirror of the past. I was sure this was how Dominic looked when he was younger, though there was something cynical in Dominic's eyes that wasn't quite present in Kai's.

I wondered if that cynicism came with age and experience, and I didn't know why the thought of Dominic's cynicism bothered me so much.

I smiled at Kai, and he offered me one back.

"Everyone, this is Emmy. Emmy, these are the bastards. And that pretty little thing sitting next to the ugly ogre is Ryleigh."

It took me a moment to realize he was talking about the only woman there.

I looked at her, waving. She offered me a shy smile and looked down at the table. The man Dominic had referred to as the ugly ogre wasn't ugly at all. Quite the opposite, even though he was scowling at Dominic.

The man turned to me and smiled, and I almost had to stop myself from swooning. If I weren't completely enraptured by Dominic, and if the man clearly wasn't taken by Ryleigh, I might have been interested.

"I'm Roman, by the way. And all the shit you've heard about me is not true."

"Actually, I haven't heard much," I said, sitting when Dominic pulled out a chair for me next to Ryleigh, then sat close to me.

I hadn't realized until I sat down that Ryleigh was heavily pregnant. Her swollen belly seemed to have swallowed her whole. It didn't help that she was so tiny.

Roman clutched his chest and shot Dominic a wounded look. "Ah, prez. I'm fucking hurt. You didn't tell your little obsession about your favorite VP?"

Beside me, Ryleigh giggled, obviously completely and wholly in love with the man. I would have laughed, too, had Roman not just referred to me as Dominic's *little obsession*. I wouldn't go so far as to say that was the case, but I could think of worse things to be than the obsession of a man like Dominic.

"First," Dominic said, humor in his voice, "get over yourself. I only have one VP, and he's a pain in the ass. And second, I ain't thinking about you when I'm with Emmy, thank fuck."

"You love me and you know it," Roman retorted, and I smiled a little at their antics.

"They're always like this," Ryleigh said beside me, and I shifted a little closer to her, glad to meet a friendly and non-intimidating face.

"I'm Emmy," I said.

Ryleigh looked down at the table shyly, and I couldn't help but feel surprised that she had matched up with a man as rough-looking as Roman.

Yet, somehow, the match seemed to work.

Distantly, I could hear Dominic talking about the club with Roman and Kai.

"Do you want to come with me to order a drink at the bar?" I asked Ryleigh. "I mean, I know you can't drink and all—"

She grabbed my hand to stop my mumbling. "I'd love to."

I smiled.

I wasn't shy, but I was reserved.

There was just something about Ryleigh that made me feel relaxed. And I was glad I wasn't the only girl at our table.

We stood, but before I could take another step, Dominic grabbed me by the waist and pulled me into his lap.

I wiggled, trying to get away, blushing slightly when I found Kai watching us curiously.

Oh, God.

I elbowed Dominic in the ribs. Not that it seemed to affect him. The man was made of stone.

His lips grazed the tip of my ear, and I tried not to show how badly that affected me.

"Where are you going?" he asked, his voice low and rough.

"To the bar. Or would you like to pee on me first? You know, get your scent on me."

His shoulders shook as he laughed.

Bastard.

"That won't be necessary. Every stupid bastard with a dick within a mile radius knows I own you. I made sure of that."

It was on the tip of my tongue to ask him how, but I decided against it at the last minute. It didn't matter. The possessive bastard was serious.

I climbed off his lap, looking over at him as Ryleigh stood, a smile on her face.

Dominic just winked at me, and I felt that wink all the way down to my clit.

I swallowed and looked away from him.

We walked to the bar, and a couple of men left their seats immediately. I supposed there were perks to dating the president.

We sat, and the bartender—an attractive brunette with two full sleeves of tattoos—came to serve us.

Ryleigh ordered a lemonade, and I ordered a dirty martini.

Ryleigh stared at me.

I smiled a little. "I can hear you thinking."

She looked down, blushing a little. I had her pegged to be a year or two younger than me.

"Sorry."

"It's okay. You can ask me if you want."

"How did you and Dominic meet?"

"Roman didn't tell you?" I asked. She shook her head. "I saved Braxton from these men chasing him, and then Dominic abducted me. He's been keeping me locked in his house since."

She blinked at me as if trying to assess if I was being

serious.

Then she threw her head back and laughed. "I believe you. Roman stalked me at the beginning of our relationship if it makes you feel better. The bastard even installed cameras in my apartment without my knowledge."

There was a fondness in her voice as she spoke of it.

The same fondness, I was sure, was present in my voice.

If there was something wrong with those men, there might be something wrong with us for being in love—I shook away the thought.

I wasn't in love with Dominic Madden.

I wasn't.

"Are you okay?" Ryleigh asked, and I realized I'd spaced out a little.

I shook my head and smiled at her. "Yeah, just wondering what they put in the water around here."

She giggled. "Whatever it is, we're drinking it."

I laughed.

The bartender came back with our drinks, and we headed back to the table.

Ryleigh was in front of me on the way there, and she was already back with Roman when I tripped up the small platform raised in the back, and hands came out to help me.

I looked up into the blue eyes of a man I didn't know.

He smiled softly at me. "Careful."

"Thank you," I said, smiling back. "I probably would have hurt my ass on the way down."

The handsome man chuckled. "We wouldn't want that, now, would we?"

I shook my head, about to answer, when another familiar voice rang out. "Blue, I suggest you let go of my girl."

The man named Blue let go of me right away. "Sorry, prez. I didn't mean anything by it."

Dominic reached over and took me into his arms.

I glared up at him as Blue quickly moved away from the possessive beast.

"He didn't do anything. He was just helping me. I would have fallen."

Dominic bent and pressed a hard kiss against my lips, and even though I was mad at him, I couldn't help but give in to it.

I moaned around his mouth and pressed harder against him. When he released me, I embarrassingly tried to follow his lips.

He wouldn't let me.

"Fuck. I knew I should have fucked you before we left. I'm gonna make that a rule from now on."

I chuckled nervously, almost half sure he was joking.

"I won't feel better until you wear my brand."

His brand? What the fuck did that mean?

He pressed another scorching kiss against my lips before leading me back to the table.

I followed him in a sort of daze, trying—and failing—not to check out his ass again.

20

EMMY

I WOKE TO THE SUN SHINING ON MY FACE.

I didn't know what time it was, but I guessed it was late morning based on the position of the sun and the fact that I woke up alone in bed.

Did Dominic wake up early to go to work this morning?

It was late by the time we got home from the bar. I had been a little buzzed from the alcohol, but I did remember bits and pieces.

I groaned.

I remember getting home and asking Dominic if he would fuck me.

He laughed, stripped me of my clothes, and pushed me onto the bed.

We didn't have sex, but that would explain why I woke up naked in bed.

I also remember Dominic forcing me to drink water and take some pills before going to sleep, which probably explained why my hangover wasn't as bad this morning as I had expected.

I wasn't even aware of him getting up this morning, and usually, I had some inkling.

Lucy would probably be here already. Slowly, I sat up and wrapped the covers around my naked chest, unsure of what I wanted to do next.

A low male voice from downstairs caught my attention.

Dominic was home.

And he was in the kitchen.

I held still and tried to listen for who he might be talking to, but when no one responded, I assumed he was on his phone.

I didn't hear the usual noise Lucy made when she was here, and I wondered if she had gone out. Probably to the store.

What was he doing at home at this time, and would he stay?

I was excited about the prospect.

So excited, I didn't bother to put clothes on. I wrapped the sheets around me and walked down the stairs. I peeked my head in first to see if Dominic had company, but when nothing seemed out of place, I walked further in.

Dominic was sitting on the barstool by the island, but by himself, and, judging by how clean and empty the kitchen was, I'd say Lucy wasn't even here yet.

How odd.

"Are you going to keep hovering by the kitchen, wildcat, or will you come in?" Dominic asked without turning around to look at me.

"Where's Lucy?" I asked, still standing where I was.

"I gave her the day off with Colt. It's just you and me today."

I smiled a little. "Really?"

"Really."

He turned around, and when he caught sight of me in

nothing but sheets, his eyes heated. I squirmed a little on my feet. The memory of him laying me down on the island and feasting on me weeks before entered my mind.

I wouldn't mind a repeat of that.

I blinked away the memory.

"You look happy this morning," he commented, slowly standing up from his seat.

I paused at his tone, wondering why he sounded so off after observing me being happy. I took a step back, and Dominic tracked the movement intently.

A bad feeling came over me, along with a hefty dose of wariness. How had I missed the mood in the air?

Because right now, it was so heavy, I almost felt suffocated by it.

"Yes," I answered slowly. "Why?"

He smiled. I had never distrusted a smile more in my life.

I took another step back, nearly tripping over the sheets.

"Just hate that I'm probably going to ruin it in a moment."

I eyed him, trying to gauge his expression. He gave nothing away.

"Why?" I asked again.

"Do you not remember what I said last night?"

"You said a lot of things last night," I said slowly. I was feeling a little disoriented now, yet in some sick, twisted part of me, there was also arousal.

Perhaps I didn't believe he would physically harm me. Not like that.

"I told you that you're mine," he said darkly.

I nodded. "Yes, that's been established."

He shook his head. "No, not yet." He paused, and I had never felt a pause quite so full of meaning. The silence of that pause roared in my ear, and my brain screamed at me to get out of there. His eyes roamed up and down my body, and he finished, "But it will be."

I didn't wait.

I ran.

Oh, crap, crap, crap, crap! I thought over and over when I heard him give chase.

Something crashed behind me—the chair, perhaps—then hurried footsteps along the floor had my heart rhythm pounding in a disjointed beat.

"Leave me alone, you crazy, crazy man!" I screamed without looking back.

He answered me with a laugh. The asshole was having a time of it.

Fuck, how could I have let my guard down with the monster?

I climbed up the stairs, nearly tripping in my haste.

Dominic reached out and grabbed my foot. I screamed and kicked him away, and kept it up until he finally let me go with a grunt.

Fuck, if I could do more to hurt him, I fucking would.

I really fucking would.

I didn't think of myself as a violent person, but I found Dominic had the ability to bring out all different sides of me.

He grabbed the corner of the sheets and pulled them away from my body.

I only put up a small fight before I realized all that did was slow me down, and I let go of the sheets. Cold air touched my naked skin, but I didn't have time to worry about that.

The monster was chasing me.

And I didn't fucking know what he was going to do to me once he caught me.

"Emmy," he called, his voice sounding close. Too close.

I moved toward his bedroom and slammed the door shut, locking it. I didn't fucking feel reassured when he tried the doorknob, but it didn't give. I bent down to grab my clothes from the night before when I saw the lock turn.

Fuck.

No time.

I ran to the master bath and locked the door just as the bedroom door was pushed open, making me jump.

"Come out, little wildcat. You know I'm not gonna hurt you, baby."

No, he would not hit me, but I doubted spanking was off the table, and whatever other devious shit he had planned in that messed-up mind of his.

I went to the bath when the lock on the bathroom door twisted open, my hand finding a shampoo bottle. I grabbed it and threw it at him as soon as he opened the door. The sadistic part of my brain reveled in the way the bottle hit him on the chest with a bang, but then the monster turned his blue eyes my way, and I realized there was nowhere else to go.

He walked over to me without a word. If the shampoo bottle hurt him, he didn't show it.

I tried to run past him, shoving him off to the side.

He grabbed my arm and pulled me back to his body.

I wiggled, trying to get away. "No!"

He wrapped one arm tightly around my middle, the palm of the other hand coming up and covering my belly before making its way up and cupping my breast.

I moaned when he played with my nipple. I could feel his erection against my side.

"Do you know what it does to me, seeing you like this?"

Naked and running away from him, he meant?

I squirmed away, and he pushed his hand down between my legs, cupping my pussy.

I ground my hips, trying to push him off, but all that did

was create delicious friction between us. “Look at this, baby girl. Look at how wet you are for me.”

And sure enough, when he pulled away, his palm was slick from me, causing a deep blush to grace my cheeks. He grazed his lips against the flush.

“Dominic,” I said in a half moan, half protest. It should not be this hard, but I was constantly fighting his dominance over me and my sexual attraction to him.

And usually, it was the latter that won out.

He bent down and put me over his shoulder.

“No, let go of me, you freak!” I screamed.

He spanked his hand down my bare bottom.

I groaned. Fuck, that hurt.

“Be my good girl and this will be over before you know it,” he said ominously.

“*What?* What will be over? Dominic!”

He spanked me again. “I’m sure I said you’re owed a spanking for running last night, no?”

I shook my head. “I don’t want a spanking!”

“Luckily for you, I’m not giving you a spanking right now,” he said, his voice light.

“I don’t feel lucky.” I pounded my fists on his back in frustration. He growled and matched each pound with a smack.

Fuck.

I gave up. I did not want him to spank my ass anymore.

I let my arms fall, hissing a little when he cupped one of my ass cheeks, the sting almost unbearable.

“Good girl,” he said, pushing his hand in my crease. I bit my lip to keep from making any noise when he started to rub up and down.

“Fuck, you’re wet for me,” he said, his voice rough. “Is this from the spanking? Are you turned on by a little bit of pain? ’Cause, baby, once you’re healed, we can fucking play as much as you want.”

My eyes squeezed shut when his fingers found my slit, and he delved two fingers inside, pumping in and out of me while he walked. I didn't even know which part of the house we were in anymore until he flipped me over and placed me on a weird-looking chair in his office. The wall in front of the chair was a body-length mirror, but because of the angle, I couldn't see myself in it, thank God. I didn't want to know what I looked like.

"What are you doing?"

He grabbed a fistful of my hair and pulled back until I looked at him. He leaned down and kissed me. "Owning you," he said.

I watched as he pulled out some silk ropes, and when I tried to get away, he simply held me still, tying my body to the chair. I kicked him when he got to my legs, but he overpowered me quickly, and soon I was tied to the leather chair that looked suspiciously like the ones at tattoo parlors.

My suspicion was fucking confirmed when he pulled out the tattoo gun and started setting everything up.

"Dominic, no," I said, panic clearly in my voice.

I shook my head. I already knew what he was planning on doing. The bastard was going to tattoo his fucking name on my skin.

Own me, as he said.

He put the gun down and cupped my cheeks with both hands. "It's all right. This will be done quickly, I promise."

"Do you even know what you're doing?" I asked, my voice hitching at the end. Of all my concerns, this should be the least of it—but fuck, if I didn't have a choice, I didn't want to bear messed-up ink on my skin forever.

He shot me an amused smile and pulled away from me. "I used to be a tattoo artist in Las Vegas. I'm fucking good, too. I would not mess up your beautiful skin, and I would be damned if I let some other bastards see you like this, or hell, touch you."

His heated eyes made their way down my body. I could only imagine how I looked right now, and I regretted not putting on some clothes before I came downstairs this morning.

I wiggled a little, but Dominic must have had some experience with bondage because though the restraints didn't hurt, I couldn't move either.

"You can't tattoo me," I tried to argue. My voice sounded weak even to my ears. I was tied up and completely at his mercy.

His lips quirked in another smile. "No?"

"Dominic, be serious. You can't do this to me."

He moved his hand down and cupped my pussy. "Why not?" he asked as his fingers swirled around my clit. My back arched—or, at least, tried to—and my legs shook from the sensation.

He picked up speed.

"Tell me why I can't do anything to you. I fucking own you, don't I?"

"I'm not a toy to be owned," I groaned, my toes curling.

He delved two fingers inside me. My walls clenched around him automatically as he fucked me.

"No," he agreed. "You're not a toy. You're the woman I am fucking obsessed with. The woman I can't let go. So I am doing what I told you I would do from the very start. I'm keeping you. Now, come for me, wildcat. Be a good girl and come."

Oh, fuck.

His words always had the power to detonate me. He knew which button to push, how to touch me, and how much pressure to use.

I exploded.

Closing my eyes, I let myself get lost in the powerful orgasm, unable to think straight.

I was only vaguely aware of him pulling out of me.

My eyes opened into tiny slits, and, in a daze, I watched him move around the room.

This was probably his plan all along.

Bastard.

He brought out some alcohol wipes and leaned forward, cleaning the skin on my left rib. I flinched when I felt the coldness. He looked me in the eye. "It'll be okay."

I should not feel reassured by his words, but my heart calmed slightly, and I closed my eyes as he continued to swipe.

I opened my eyes when he finished and watched him put on a pair of black rubber gloves.

He had already prepared the stencil, and I watched as he pressed it on my skin. I didn't look down to see the design. I already knew.

I glared at him as he picked the gun up again and set out a small carton of what seemed to be black ink.

I took a deep breath to calm my nerves. I had never had a tattoo before. I didn't know what to prepare for.

"Will it hurt?" I asked.

"No more than you can handle," he said, his voice calm.

Yeah, right.

He moved closer to me with the gun after dipping it in some ink. "Ready?"

"No."

He leaned forward and kissed me. I should pull away. I stayed where I was and let him kiss me, letting that give me the strength to be brave. Fuck. I was still wet from when he had his finger inside me… maybe even from when he spanked me.

I was still in the haze of lust when I felt the first contact with the needles.

I sucked in a sharp breath from the slight pain, and Dominic paused briefly before he continued.

Oh, God. Oh, God. This was really happening. I couldn't believe this was really happening. I was getting tattooed—by a crazy man, no less.

"Okay?" he asked about ten minutes in. I grunted. It wasn't too bad at first, but the more times he kept going over the same spot, the more tender it got, and now there was a burning sensation on my skin.

He continued.

"You're doing great," he praised. "How about I give you a nice little reward after this?"

I sneered at him. "An orgasm is not a reward."

He pulled away and laughed. "You sure? 'Cause I've heard you call out God's name a few times."

"You're an asshole." I hissed a breath of pain when he started back again after dipping the gun into the ink carton once again.

"That's true," he agreed. Then he turned off the gun. The low buzzing noise stopped, and all that was left was the silence in the room, along with our breathing. He covered the wound with some sort of clear jelly and a thin see-through plastic film.

"It's done?" I asked.

"It's done," he said, drawing a small knife from his pocket and cutting away the ropes.

I wasn't sure what I was feeling.

He pulled me up in his lap and swiveled the chair around until we faced the mirror.

I took us in, from my naked skin—a stark contrast against the black shirt and dark jeans he wore—to the sheer size of him that made me look tiny and delicate.

I looked like a doll on his lap.

A naked doll.

I shifted a little, crossing my arms over my breasts, and that was when I caught sight of the ink for the first time.

My breath caught as I stared at the black ink on my red skin, written in beautiful cursive letters:

Dominic Madden

Fuck, he really had marked me as his, and judging by the satisfied look on his face, he was happy.

"Fucking beautiful. Now you're fucking mine in every way possible," he said, gently skimming his hand over the plastic film.

My chest moved in and out with every ragged breath I took, and he kissed the side of my head.

"Now, for your reward," he whispered sensually.

My skin turned from fair to deep red in about zero-point-five seconds. I squirmed and pushed against him, feeling his stiff cock digging into my lap.

Oh, fuck.

"Spread your legs, baby. Show me your pussy."

I swallowed, debating whether I should do as he asked when he lifted my arms and pulled them away. My nipples pebbled noticeably in the mirror as he placed each of my hands on the armrest of the chair.

"You move your hands, and I'll draw out your orgasm," he promised darkly. "Now, spread your legs, baby. Don't make me say it again."

I dropped my head back against his chest but couldn't say anything to that. I didn't want to challenge his words.

Arousal surged out of me, wetting his jeans, and slowly, I spread my legs, leaving them out on the outside of his legs, revealing my wet lips to the mirror.

He groaned, and I felt his cock twitching behind me.

"Fuck. Can't you see how fucking sexy you are? Look at

you. Look at your wet cunt, hard nipples, and flushed skin. And wearing my name so beautifully. The only thing missing is my fucking baby in your stomach."

My eyes widened at his words, and I tried to move off him when he smacked his hand down on my pussy lightly. The sound was a lot louder than the actual pain. Still, I felt myself reacting to it, and I knew Dominic could feel that.

He *wanted* to get me pregnant.

Oh, fuck. How could I not think about that? I—

I yelped when he pinched my clit roughly.

"Look at this," he growled. "Even when I'm mean to your pussy, it weeps for me. You like it when I play rough, don't you, baby?"

He smacked his hand down once more before I could respond.

"Oh, God. Dominic!"

I squealed when he did it again, the slap harder than the ones before. My back arched, and my hand moved away from the armrest.

"Uh-uh," he chided. "Naughty girl. Now you have to take your punishment."

He placed my hands back on the armrest, and I finally caught on to his game. He wanted to punish me.

He brought his fingers up to my mouth. "Open."

Right then, I wanted to play his game just as much.

I opened my mouth, and he made a low noise of approval.

"Suck."

I sucked, my grip tightening around the armrest, and when he pulled his fingers away, I almost let out a small whine.

His hand drifted down, and he cupped my pussy. I held my breath, trying to hold on to some semblance of self-control.

I didn't know how much more I could take as he massaged my pussy.

My hips ground against his hand, trying to find that friction, and he used his other hand to pinch my side. "Hey!" I said, jumping back from the sting.

"Hold still, wildcat. And don't you fucking dare come. Not until you beg me for it."

My mouth gaped, and I didn't know what to say to that. He wanted me to beg him to let me come?

His lips tilted up in a smirk. "Does this feel good?"

He rubbed his finger around my clit in a circle, and I nodded, forgetting I was supposed to be mad at him in the first place. "So good," I said.

So fucking good.

"Please," I pled. I was ready to beg. He didn't need to draw out this torture. I wanted to come, and I wanted him to be the one to make me come. "Please, Dominic. Please. I need you."

And how fucking true that was.

I fucking needed him, and I didn't know how it had happened in the first place.

"Please."

I was on the verge of crying now, and I would probably lose it if he kept drawing it out.

"Shh, baby. You beg so prettily. You know I would give you the fucking world, don't you?"

Fuck.

I spread my legs further, giving him better access to me.

He picked up the pace, and that was all it took. I kept my eyes on our reflection as I came. This fucking image would be what fueled my fantasies for days to come, I was sure of it.

My whole body convulsed under the weight of the release. Never had I come so hard. He tapped my clit several times, prolonging the fall.

I screamed, the image of his expression in the mirror coming in and out of focus.

In one unguarded moment, I could see just how badly he wanted me.

He talked about owning me, but I wondered if he realized I had already owned *him*, and that was without my name tattooed on his skin.

I leaned back and placed a kiss on his jaw.

His hand paused, and he met my eyes.

"Fuck," he uttered. "This was supposed to be about punishing you."

I grinned. "Punish me later. I just need you inside me right now."

I climbed off his lap, feeling brave, and for the first time, it was Dominic with a wary gaze.

I looked down at his crotch area, my mouth watering at seeing him tenting in his pants.

The fact that my ribs were sore only served as a reminder of how much Dominic had gotten under my skin.

I licked my lips as I took in his enormous frame, loving just about everything about his body. I let him see the hungry look in my eyes.

Let him see just how much I wanted him.

I waited until he stood before I stepped toward him. I pushed him down until he was kneeling on the ground in front of me.

"Show me how much you love me," I said, because that was what this was. He could fucking deny it all he wanted, but we both knew the answer.

This monster loved me.

He let out a low groan and wrapped his hands around my hips, pulling me close and taking my pussy in his mouth, eating me out with vigor.

My knees nearly buckled, especially when his tongue

lapped over my clit, and I was so close to coming, it wouldn't take much effort from him.

I looked down at the man in front of me.

He was probably one of the most powerful men in the city, and here he was, worshiping me.

And fuck if that didn't make me feel powerful as well.

My fingers grasped at his head when I wasn't sure if my legs could hold me up much longer, leaning most of my weight on him and letting him hold me.

His hands drifted behind me until he was cupping my ass.

My eyes rolled to the back of my head, and I was seeing stars.

Suddenly, he moved away. I looked down, confused as to why he stopped when he lay on the floor, undoing his jeans and pulling out his cock.

"Ride me," he said, reaching up for my hands and bringing me back down until I straddled him.

I whimpered when I felt his hard cock brush against my thighs. I reached down and grasped his length, stroking up and down a few times, like he had done before, though not as hard.

I watched as pleasure etched around every line of his face as I directed his cock inside me, sinking down.

"Oh, God," I said, as I bobbed up and down on him.

He grabbed my hips, but he didn't try to stop me or take over my movements. He was letting me be in control. My moves were a little unpracticed and out of rhythm, but that didn't stop the pleasurable feeling from taking over.

I slammed harder against him, going faster, driving us both crazy.

My hand reached for the hem of his shirt, and I pushed it up, wanting to feel his skin with my hands, wanting to see as much of him as I could.

Mine.

He was fucking mine, and if he was possessive of me, then I was just the same.

This was my monster.

I paused when my hand moved to a plastic film on his rib, similar to the one he had put on me. My heart felt like it was going into overdrive as I realized what I was seeing.

He got a tattoo.

On his left rib, amid all the other colorful ink, was the word *Wildcat*, written in the same cursive letters as mine.

Tears sprang to my eyes.

The soft look was back in his eyes.

I didn't mistake that.

He was really there.

I slowed my movements. "D-Dominic?"

He cupped my cheek. "Yeah, wildcat?"

"Why?" I croaked.

"Don't you already know? Can't you fucking see how badly I fucking love you?"

Seeing my nickname permanently tattooed on his skin was something else entirely.

Tears fell, and I leaned forward and kissed him.

I picked up the speed as I rode him harder. I wanted us to come at the same time.

"Dominic," I whispered against his soft lips.

He groaned in response.

"I love you, too," I whispered.

And that was all it took. I felt him swell inside me before he reached up and gripped my shoulder.

I kept up the tempo, and it wasn't long before I came as well. I fused our lips together and let Dominic swallow any noise I might have made.

And we lost ourselves to each other.

21

DOMINIC

It wasn't until after we went to bed that night that Emmy discovered the second tattoo I'd had Edger come over and do for me.

Right underneath my right collarbone was her name.

Emmy

She cried when she saw it, though I was told they were happy tears.

I didn't deal well with tears.

Sure, my kids cried when they were little, but those tears were easy to deal with. I could almost always fix what was wrong, and when I couldn't, I would bribe them to stop crying.

That usually worked.

Emmy's tears were something else entirely.

I didn't know how to deal with her crying, and I doubted bribing her with mind-blowing orgasms would get her to stop.

Luckily, she didn't cry all that much.

I rode my bike to the bar after dressing her up in a cute yellow sundress, sans bra and panties, with a promise that if she put on a bra or panties after I left, she would get one hell of a spanking when I got home.

I might do that anyway, even if she was obedient.

I owed her for trying to leave when I took her to the bar. I hadn't forgotten.

I hopped off my bike and shifted on my feet, trying to talk down the fucking hard-on from the image of her over my lap, bare ass, and wet pussy.

Fuck, that thought would be enough to distract me the entire day.

The bar was just getting ready to open. There weren't many patrons around—just the same drunks who liked to come here all day—but that wasn't unusual.

No, what was different was a fucking black Mercedes Benz parked at the far left corner.

The car drew my attention simply because it wasn't the kind of car I expected to see in my bar. Most of the people who came here were dirt poor, trying to drown their sadness and their awareness of the shit hand they were dealt in life.

But this car screamed money, and I was already on alert.

A honk from my right diverted my attention, and I watched as Kai stepped out of his car, his laptop under his arm. He assessed his surroundings like I taught him, and my lips formed a proud smirk when he saw the black car and frowned.

Good boy.

I wouldn't have let my boy join the club if I didn't think he had the grit to survive it.

No one expected to live longer than their kids, and that was the way I wanted it. Ruling one of this country's biggest one percent MC clubs guaranteed there would be people gunning for my head.

Should I fucking leave this Earth, I would do so with a

fucking smile on my face, knowing Kai would take care of my club.

He walked up to me and looked at the car, a question in his eyes.

I subtly nodded, signaling for him to be on alert as we walked through the doors.

Nothing seemed out of the ordinary as we walked in, and I didn't see any men who didn't belong loitering about.

Either they were hiding from me, or…

I looked at my closed office door.

They were there.

How fucking brave of those fuckers.

I nodded to the door, and Kai silently followed me.

My gun was tucked in the waistband of my jeans behind me, but I didn't pull it out. Not yet.

I tried the doorknob, which turned easily, leading me inside the dark room.

Right away, I was aware we weren't alone, and sure enough, when I flipped on the light switch, I saw four men.

One fucker was sitting behind my desk, casually leaning back.

He had a smile on his arrogant face.

I've killed men for being in here. They wanted to risk that?

I looked at each of them as Kai closed the door behind him.

He recognized them on sight. So did I.

I crossed my arms over my chest casually.

"Well, isn't this a surprise?" I said. "What have I done to get a nice little visit from the Four Horsemen?"

Julian Levine's smile never left his face, and if I didn't know any better, I'd say the fucker was amused.

I took in the other three men with him.

Ezekiel Creed, Ezra Aldridge, and Novak Elsher.

All powerful men in their own right, but together, they were unstoppable.

Julian was the one who'd approached me about five years ago, wanting a partnership with the King's Men, though I had only met the fucker once.

Communication between us was done through a secure line and destroyed the moment we no longer needed it.

It was the way I wanted.

I wasn't going to make the same mistake our former Mayor Gallagher made, keeping insurance on his business associates.

It was those insurances my boy had dug up that had led to the mayor's downfall.

"We thought it was time to visit one of our most loyal business associates," Ezra said, his sharp green eyes trained on me. The man was what many would call pretty. With his dark brown hair and tan skin that stood out in contrast to his light eyes. We matched evenly when it came to height and bulk, and even with a smile on his face, there was something vicious about him that he seemed unable to hide—or perhaps he didn't want to. But I could recognize the darkness in a man when I saw it.

Pretty or not, the fucker was lethal, and I would not underestimate him.

"I'm loyal to no one but my club," I said easily. And that was true. I'd agreed to work with the Four Horsemen because I'd recognized the benefit from a business standpoint, even knowing all the nasty shit those little fuckers had their hands in.

"How would you like to change that?" Ezra asked.

I scoffed.

"Perhaps *loyal* is the wrong word to use," Julian said, steepling his hands together and staring at me with his dark eyes. I could see why he'd been chosen as the face of the organization. Compared to the other three, he looked more polished. More refined.

More trustworthy.

He was in an expensive monkey suit I was sure probably cost the equivalent of a month's profit from this bar. His short dark hair was brushed to the side, not a single strand out of place, and he had a beard that reminded me a little of Roman's.

"How about an understanding?" Julian asked. "There is something we want from the King's Men. And there is something you want from us. How about we take this association into a partnership? I'm sure you can find it—ah, *useful*, to have friends like us," he finished smoothly.

I looked behind me at Kai. Right now, I didn't see them as a threat, but I still felt better standing between them and my son.

"I have enough friends. Not looking to make more," I said, getting ready to end this joke of a "meeting."

There was nothing I needed from the Four Horsemen. I took care of my own.

"But you haven't even heard our proposal yet," Novak said, pushing off the wall he'd been leaning against. I narrowed my gaze, and he stopped. Dark blue eyes not unsimilar to my own glinted, as if he wanted to express his sincerity. I wasn't a fucking fool.

I didn't say anything, instead waiting to hear what they had to say.

"You have a traitor in your midst," Julian said.

I didn't react.

The fucker's smile widened. "We can't help you find the traitor. That's club business, right?" When I didn't reply, he continued. "But we can help stop whatever that traitor is planning on doing with the Sons of War to destroy your club."

I finally spoke. "Hmm, I feel like I'm at a disadvantage. You seem to know a lot of shit happening with my club, but I don't know anything about your business."

Novak scoffed, though there was something about his expression that told me he was enjoying this. "You mean your son didn't tell you all about our shit after he hacked into our system and extracted all our sensitive information?"

I smirked. Kai sure fucking did. I wondered how long it took them to figure that out, and judging by the hard look that passed over Julian's face, I'd say way longer than he would have liked to admit.

I turned to my boy, who had been silent up to this point. "Why don't you go home, son?"

He shook his head stubbornly. "I'm not leaving you."

"Oh, we're not going to hurt the boy," Novak said, the begrudging respect in his voice was hard to ignore. "We came here with the intention of forming a partnership. I'm sure Kai would be an asset to us later."

I took a step forward. "My boy is not your fucking asset. I suggest you fucking watch your words before you really piss me off."

Novak put out his hands as if to say he was backing off.

"As I was saying," Julian interrupted. "We can help you with the Sons of War."

"How?" I asked, not really interested. If they thought I needed help to control a fucking chapter barely in its infancy, then they should have gone elsewhere with their business.

"By cutting off their investors," Julian said.

"Who's their investor?"

"Don't you know?" Julian asked. "The people running Blue Paragon. Don't you know they're trying to take over your city?"

Behind me, Kai tensed, and I realized he knew something. Perhaps he had just found it out and hadn't told me yet.

"And why would you help?" I asked.

Ezekiel and Julian shared a look. Up to this point, Ezekiel had been quiet, taking in everything. The huge man was probably as big as Micah, and just as emotionless.

I hardened my gaze. "And try to be fucking truthful. I don't do well with liars."

"The man who heads the group is trying to fuck with us," Ezekiel said. "We're going to get to him first, and that means cutting off his financial resources. You probably guessed the baby food manufacturer is a front to store the narcotics trade they are setting up. He already has contracts with the cartels in the South and with the French-Canadian mob up North. You don't need me to tell you what this will mean for your club, do you?" he asked.

The King's Men would be surrounded on both sides.

Fuck.

"And what do you want me to do?" I asked. How the fuck had we missed how much bigger this was than the Sons of War?

"The contract only exists between Blue Paragon, the cartels, and the French-Canadian mob because the Sons of War guarantee they can destroy your club. We need you to move up the timeline and take on the club. We need you to take them out."

"I would have done that, anyway. Why the fuck would *you* need this partnership?"

"Because we need your numbers. You have been building a fucking army in the U.S. since you took the throne as club president," Julian said.

I crossed my arms and narrowed my eyes at him. I had men under me in the thousands. That was true.

But no one knew of that so-called army, even if there were rumors. How the fuck did they know for sure?

"We need your numbers, and you need our resources. We have connections to some very powerful people—hell, we're powerful men, something I'm sure you will find useful later on. The King's Men are getting into more bad things with each year that passes. We can protect you. And in return, you'll lend us your men when we need it." Julian let out a small sigh when I didn't answer him. "War is coming, Dominic. You might not think it'll affect you here in California, but that shit is going to get big. Do you really think you can protect everyone under your care? Your sons? Emmy?"

My nostrils flared, and I took a step forward. Kai held me back.

"You leave my sons and Emmy out of this."

"They're already a part of it. Kai's the fucking heir, and I'm sure Braxton will join the club later on. And the moment you decided to take the poor piano teacher, you brought her into your world. We're offering you a way to protect them all. With this partnership," Ezra added.

They fucking knew too much about me and my club, and I wondered which fucker sold my information to them. I didn't know, but I would soon.

I took a deep breath, trying to calm myself. What they said made sense, but there was something about forming a fucking partnership with them that fucking pissed me off.

A large part of it was because there would be no backing out once I agreed. I didn't fucking mind, but I wasn't sure if that was what I wanted for my sons.

I looked back at Kai, but nothing in his eyes gave away his thoughts or emotions.

"I have to talk to my VP and my enforcer," I said.

Julian nodded, standing. "Of course. You know how to get in contact with us."

I moved out of the way and watched them leave the office.

Fuck.

"Dad, what are you going to do?" Kai asked when the door closed behind them.

"We'll talk with Roman and Micah first," I said, not wanting to make any decisions until I had their input, though I already knew what I was leaning toward doing.

"Did you find anything on the Blue Paragon?" I asked.

"That's what I wanted to talk to you about before we realized they were here," he said. "I've been tracking Blue Paragon's movements based on their credit card bills, and there has been a lot of air travel for the company to Las Vegas."

Even without the Four Horsemen revealing the connections between the Sons of War and Blue Paragon, this would have made sense. I nodded.

"What do you plan to do?" he asked.

"Tell Roman to send a group of twenty men to Las Vegas. We're gonna go on the offense and start attacking," I said. There was no more waiting around. I still hadn't found the traitor, but perhaps this would be a step forward. I was gonna lure the fucking shitheads out by destroying every single one of their properties. "And we need to tighten security around our properties. I'll put you in charge of this, yeah?"

"Of course," he said without hesitation, like I knew he would. "I won't let you down."

22

DOMINIC

I CAME HOME A LITTLE AFTER SIX, AFTER I CAUGHT ROMAN UP on what was going on and had helped pick out twenty brothers to go out to Las Vegas. The attack would take place tonight, and I needed something to do to take my mind off it until then.

I went home to Emmy.

I didn't think I had ever spent so much of my time at home, but when things went to shit, I needed to go home to her.

To lose myself in her and to remind myself that there were things worth fighting for.

It felt like I hadn't lived for myself in a long time. Everything I did had been for the club and for my boys. But I got greedy, and I took Emmy for my own.

I took her from her life and brought her into the darkness of my world.

I should feel fucking guilty about that.

I didn't.

I would be holding on to Emmy with both fucking hands,

and I wasn't letting her go. I found her by the piano, messing around with the keys but not really playing anything.

"Play something for me," I said gruffly.

She jumped about a foot in the air, turning to me and clutching her chest.

"Jesus, you scared me."

I came up to her and placed one hand on her small shoulder. She didn't flinch.

I looked into her fascinating heterochromia eyes, getting lost in them.

"Play something for me," I said. I still didn't know much about Emmy's life before she came to California. If I wanted, I could probably find the reason her hands were like this, but I wanted to hear it from her.

Obviously, whatever happened still affected her. She didn't talk much about music, even if it seemed to have been a huge part of her life. Hell, she'd still made it into a career despite everything. I wanted to hear the story from her lips.

I wanted her to tell me everything, to give me everything.

I wanted her fucking trust—and how careful I would be with it.

I waited for her to tell me no. To make up some excuse.

She bit her lip, something flashing in her eyes and turning them more brown than green tonight, before slowly moving over on the bench and patting the empty spot next to her.

Wordlessly, I sat, her warmth engulfing me like a warm hug.

She took a deep breath before letting her hands drift to the keys, and then she played a song I had never heard.

The melody was haunting and beautiful. I watched the way her delicate fingers moved across the keys. Her left hand played what seemed to be only two simple notes while her right did most of the work.

She made it look effortless. Easy and so damned efficient. I was in awe of her.

Fuck.

Her head turned, and she looked at me as she continued to play, a sort of happiness dancing on her face that made me realize how badly I wanted to ensure it stayed there. I would do almost anything to make it so.

Then her brow furrowed, and sweat gathered on her forehead.

I frowned.

She looked like she was in pain, and I didn't know why until a sharp note rang out. She stopped playing. I didn't need to be an expert in music to know she had hit the wrong note.

For a moment, we didn't say anything to each other.

This one wrong note was working against all the other right notes she had played, and it was fucking winning.

I didn't know what was going on inside her head, but it couldn't be good. And I didn't know what to fucking say that would make it okay. To bring back the happiness I had seen in her eyes before.

"Emmy—"

She slid off the bench and ran up the stairs without saying anything. The slam of the bedroom door sounded moments later, loud in the empty house.

My fists clenched by my side as I stared at the stairs.

Fuck.

I waited for a beat before I followed her.

She was sitting in her spot in the recliner and looking out the window at the streetlamp.

Her knees were pulled up to her chest, and her arms were wrapped around them, as if she was trying to make herself as small as possible.

I stood at the threshold and watched her. She looked so

fucking sad. All I wanted to do was pull her into my arms, but I wasn't sure if that was what she needed or wanted from me.

"Emmy. It's okay—"

"No, it's not," she interrupted.

I nodded and stepped in front of the recliner, kneeling on the floor.

I grabbed her hands. She let me.

I looked at the scars there. I was sure it was worse when it happened. I was sure the pain had been unimaginable.

"He stomped on my hands because he didn't want me to go to New York without him, after we found out I got accepted to Juilliard on a composer scholarship."

My jaw clenched, and I didn't say anything, even though I wanted to. I wanted to know who the fucking bastard was.

"He was my first boyfriend. My first kiss... my first everything. I had always been so focused on my music, I didn't give myself time to date in high school. But he was different. He was the only one who seemed to really see me. Now that I'm older, I realize it only seemed that way because that was what he wanted me to see. I had just turned seventeen, and he was... he was twenty-eight. Older than me, way more experienced than I was, and I let myself get so caught up in all the excitement of a first love that I didn't realize how fucked up my relationship with him really was."

Seventeen?

Fuck me, but she was only seventeen when she dated that bastard?

"Baby, whatever he did was not your fault. You know that, don't you?"

She shrugged. "A part of me knows that, but sometimes it feels like it. It feels like perhaps I got too greedy. Too arrogant. I had sacrificed almost everything to get into Juilliard, and perhaps this is what I deserved."

"Bullshit," I said vehemently. Unable to stand the distance between us anymore, I stood up and took her into my arms.

I moved to the bed and settled her on my lap. She burrowed her face into my chest, and I tightened my arms around her.

"His parents owned an accounting firm in Nevada, and he couldn't really leave the state," she said, keeping her face on my chest. "He was training to take over the family business soon, and he wanted me to stay and be a stay-at-home mom to our future kids. I had already graduated high school and had my whole life in front of me, and though I loved him, it didn't make a difference to me whether he would be with me in that future. All that mattered to me was New York. I think he could see that, too. Right after he told me how he saw our life playing out, I finally realize how different we saw the relationship going. I broke up with him a week later."

She shuddered, and I had a feeling that what she planned on saying next wouldn't be easy. I moved my hand up and petted her hair, trying to offer comfort in any way I could.

"I was working part-time at a coffee shop, and he waited for me until I left for work. He cornered me by my car, and he—"

She took a deep breath.

"It's okay, wildcat. You don't have to tell me if it's too much."

I felt her shake her head against me. "No, I want to tell you. I haven't talked about that day in seven long years."

She looked up at me, her eyes wet. "I want to tell you."

I leaned forward and kissed her softly, feeling her relax in my arms.

"And I'll listen to what you have to say," I assured her.

She smiled a little before resting the side of her face against my chest.

"He was so angry. So angry. And I didn't know what to

do. I was scared, and the more he talked, the angrier he got, to the point where I couldn't really understand his words anymore. And that was when he got violent."

She shuddered against me.

"H-he hit me. He knocked me to the ground, and then he kicked me. God, it had hurt so bad. So bad. I just wanted to pass out so I wouldn't have to feel the pain. I was already bleeding on the ground when he moved over me. Everything hurt, but then he—when he s-stomped on my hands, I knew what that meant. I knew I couldn't play the piano like I used to, and even if a miracle happened, Juilliard wouldn't wait for me. In just one night, everything was gone."

"Where is the bastard now?" I asked, trying to keep the anger from showing in my voice.

"Last time I talked to my dad, I found out he took over running his family accounting firm."

"He's not serving time?"

I frowned. It made it easier for me to hunt him down, but why the fuck wasn't that bastard locked up?

Emmy let out a bitter laugh. "No. Not with his parents' money and connections. Not when I never told the police who attacked me."

The last part was said in whispers, but even then, I could hear the regret in her voice.

"Why, baby?" I asked quietly.

"My parents asked me not to."

"And why the fuck would they do that?"

She flinched in my arms, and I squeezed her to me—my apology. I was angry, but never at her.

"My dad was working at his parents' firm at the time. That's how we met, at the company's Christmas party. My dad no longer works there. The money his parents sent to me was hush money—I couldn't take it. It felt like such an unfair trade. My future for thirty fucking thousand. But my parents didn't want this to get out. They were afraid it would affect my dad's job prospects. I gave my parents the money and moved away from home."

"Did your parents know about your relationship with him when you first started?" I asked slowly, already seeing the fucking picture.

That would explain why she'd never asked me for her phone to call her parents, even when things weren't so intense between us. In fact, she hadn't mentioned anyone she would call or hang out with, here or back home.

"They encouraged it," she said bitterly. "It made my dad's position at the company a little easier."

Fuck me.

What kind of shitty parents encouraged their seventeen-year-old daughter to date a fucking man almost in his thirties?

I held her a little closer to me. "I'm sorry, baby, but what happened was not your fault or something you deserved. Understand?" I clasped her chin and lifted it until she was looking at me. "I won't have you bearing all that shit on your shoulders, you got me? If anyone is to blame, it's your fucking parents and that fucker."

A dead fucker.

Her eyes watered, and her lower lip trembled. I didn't look away from her. I wanted her to understand exactly what I was saying. It felt like someone was fucking stabbing me when her tears fell and soaked the skin on the side of my palm.

Slowly, she nodded and pressed a small kiss on my jawline.

Fuck.

The kiss was a reminder that I didn't fucking belong to myself. Not anymore. Everything that made me now belonged to this tiny girl with heartbreak in her eyes that I wanted to fucking kill to eradicate.

"What's his name?" I asked.

Her eyes widened. "Dominic, no. Just leave this alone. I don't want you involved."

"It's okay if you don't want to tell me," I said, ignoring her protest. "It won't be hard for me to figure out."

She opened her mouth, but I kissed her, swallowing up any argument she might offer. It wouldn't matter. I was gonna make sure this fucker felt ten times the pain he had fucking inflicted on my girl.

"Don't worry about this anymore," I said when I pulled away. She slowly opened her eyes, the hazel irises soft and clouded from the kiss.

More tears fell, and I realized it would have been a hell of a lot less painful had I been stabbed.

I felt my heart pinch at the sight, and I wondered if there would ever be a time when she didn't affect me so much.

It didn't seem likely.

And I didn't fucking care. Not even a little bit.

23

DOMINIC

EMMY WAS SLEEPING SOUNDLY BESIDE ME ON THE BED WHEN my phone dinged with a text notification from Micah.

Quietly, I grabbed it from the nightstand and silenced it so as not to wake her up.

After I fed her and showered her, we had fallen into bed, where more of her tears had soaked my chest, making me wish I had the bastard chained to the wall in one of my fucking warehouses.

Then, it was as if the tears had drained everything from her because she soon fell asleep, though her rest appeared anything but peaceful.

But my girl was resilient. And I was gonna make sure she had nothing to worry about from now on.

Finding those traitors was more than just ensuring Braxton's safety and getting him home where he belonged.

It was this girl sleeping in my arms, who seemed to get more fragile with each day she spent as mine.

Perhaps it was because the more I loved her, the more terrified I was of losing her.

And I was that.

I was fucking in love with Emmy Wilde.

Soon to be Madden, if I had any say.

I had already bulldozed my way into everything with us. I might as well push for marriage.

She would learn soon enough that when it came to the two of us, there was no such thing as personal boundaries. There wasn't a line I wouldn't cross to make her mine permanently.

I smiled a little at the thought and the phone in my hand vibrated, reminding me there was still so much shit going on.

I sat up and set my bare feet down on the cold floor before looking at my phone at Micah's text.

It's done.

The next text that came through was a picture of a building on fire. I was sure this was one of many buildings on fire in Las Vegas. If the Sons of War were as sloppy as Micah said they were, then it would take the police there no time to connect all the buildings on fire to the MC. I doubted the police could really do anything, but it would cause enough of an annoyance for them for us to build up the attack.

I texted Micah back.

Good. Report back to me on how they reacted. We're gonna fucking get 'em.

I looked back at Emmy. No matter how much I wanted to go back to bed, I wouldn't be able to go to sleep now.

I got up just as my phone rang, this time a call from Kai.

I picked up on the first ring. "Hello."

"Dad," he said, the tone of his voice giving me pause. "There's something I have to tell you."

I PULLED my bike up to the luxurious apartment complex and into a private parking slot.

This place was one of the safest places in the city, and I bet the snobby fucks that lived in the building fucking loved that the son of the King's Men's president lived here.

I smiled a little at the thought, and, hopping off my bike, I made my way to Kai's door.

He opened it before I could knock and I met his blue eyes, bright despite the late hour.

Just because I had trouble going to sleep most nights didn't mean I wanted Kai to be the same way.

"Hey, Dad."

I drew Kai into my arms for a tight hug. I didn't give a shit about upholding whatever reputation other people thought I should have.

I fucking made sure I hugged my kids whenever I had the chance, and holding Kai in my arms right now made my fucking heart ache for Braxton.

Soon.

I would have all of my family soon, and all this shit would be over.

I would make sure of it.

"All right, son?"

He nodded and stepped back, leading me inside to the living room.

I saw his open laptop right away and looked over at him questioningly.

"You asked me to find the man responsible for hurting Emmy," he said by way of explanation.

"I didn't mean for you to do it right away. You should have gone to sleep first."

"Can't," he answered absentmindedly. When I didn't answer him, he glanced up from where he was studying on the laptop. "I'm fine, Dad. You don't have to worry."

"Always worry about you. You and Braxton. You're both my fucking world. How could I not worry?" I asked gruffly, taking a seat on the couch next to him.

He didn't say anything to that. I doubted he would really understand until he was a dad himself.

Fuck me, but the thought of being a grandpa at my age…

Yeah, thirty-eight was too fucking young to be someone's grandpa, even if Kai was a hell a lot older than me now than I was when I had him.

"Why did you call me here?" I asked him.

"I found the bastard. John Moore."

"John Moore," I said slowly. The name of my next victim. Perfect.

Kai shook his head. "That's not why I called you here, though. I did some background research into the man and his family. Did you know Emmy isn't the only person he attacked? He went to a party months after the attack on Emmy and sexually assaulted the governor's daughter. He was trialed and sentenced but only spent two weeks of his four-year sentence in prison."

"What the fuck?"

Kai nodded. "Yeah. And the judge who sentenced him was found in a ditch a week after he got out."

So Johnny boy knew some powerful fucking people. Not fucking surprising, considering Nevada was crawling with corrupted pieces of shit. But who? The Irish mob? Or…

I looked up at Kai and the look in his eyes told me the answer before he did.

"The accounting firm the Moore family owns took on a new client a few years back. Sonny McCain."

"The piece of shit running Sons of War?"

Kai nodded. "Dad, there's a connection between them. I'm not sure where Moore is in Las Vegas now. He doesn't have an address on file for some reason, but I'm sure it's probably with the Sons of War. There are too many coincidences here. Are you… are you sure about Emmy?"

I narrowed my eyes at him. "What are you saying, son?"

"You know what I'm saying."

I stood up and turned from him. "No."

"You have to admit it's a possibility."

"You questioning my ability to read people?" I asked, turning to him.

"Of course not. But I know you've never been like this with another woman." He looked off to the side. "Not even with Mom. And I'm not blaming you for that. I know why you couldn't love her. She's a fucking bitch."

"Don't call your mother that, boy," I said, even if what he said was true.

At least he had the grace to not meet my eyes.

"I'm just saying. You're different with her."

"I know Emmy. And you know her, too. Are you telling me you think she's working with the Sons of War? I'm the one who took her."

"She was there when that shit happened with Braxton. It put her right in your path—"

"Enough."

Kai's lips thinned, but he didn't say anything more.

I let out a small sigh and walked over to him. Cupping the back of his neck, I waited until he looked at me. "I know what I'm doing. Trust me. What you need to do is find out everything you can about Moore's parents."

Kai frowned. "His parents?"

I nodded. "Yup. The slimy little bastard might be hard to find, but I doubt his parents are. And they probably know where he is. Find their location and give me the address."

"What are you gonna do?"

"I'm gonna pay them a personal visit."

I THOUGHT about what Kai said on the ride home.

It wasn't fucking possible.

I wasn't wrong about the kind of woman Emmy was—my woman.

But Kai was right.

There were too many coincidences, and I couldn't ignore them. Had I really fallen into a trap? Was she the fucking reason Braxton was hunted down in the middle of the fucking street? If that was the case, every interaction we'd had was a fucking lie, and I didn't know how to swallow that.

It could be.

It wasn't.

I fucking didn't know.

I hopped off my bike when I reached the house and shut the engine off. I barely remembered the way inside the house, and before I knew it, I was standing in front of the bed, watching Emmy in the middle of it, still sound asleep.

My heart clenched at the sight of her.

It wasn't possible.

She wasn't working with the Sons of War.

If I really thought about it, I could hear the truth in my words, but my mind was a fucking jumbled mess, and I didn't know how to stop the voices.

Just—

"Dominic?"

I blinked, and Emmy came more clearly into view. I could barely make out her face in the darkness of the room, but the streetlight outside was enough for me to see that she was awake.

"What are you doing, just standing there? Are you watching me sleep?" Her question was asked dryly, almost accepting. As if she was surprised at the action itself, but not really.

I shook my head.

I knew her, too, didn't I?

I did.

I climbed on the bed and turned on the bedside lamp.

Looking into her eyes was like looking into her soul. She couldn't fucking fake that.

I reached for her, pulling her up into a sitting position and taking off her shirt. Her nipples tightened when they came into view, and I cupped her breasts, squeezing them tightly. She let out a breath of air harshly as if she'd been holding it.

Her tattoo of my name moved up and down from the small pants. Fuck me, but like every time I saw it, the possessive part of me roared to life in satisfaction.

There was no fucking way she would ever betray the club or me. No fucking way.

"You're mine, aren't you?" I asked darkly.

Her brows pinched a little when she responded, "As much as you are mine."

I smiled a little. "Then every fucking inch of you belongs to me. I fucking own you."

Her chin tilted up, her eyes flashing in defiance as if daring me to deny her next words. "Just as much as I own you."

I shook my head. "Don't you fucking know? Don't you fucking know I belonged to you since the first moment I saw you in that fucking abandoned farmhouse?"

Her eyes softened at my words. "I would call you crazy, but I'm sure that's already been established."

I slapped the side of her tit, watching it jiggle.

Her breath stuttered as she tried to gulp in as much as possible.

Fuck. I slapped it again, and her face contorted in both pain and pleasure.

"Dominic," she whined.

I slapped it a few more times, moving to her nipple after the last one.

"Do you love it? Do you love it when I treat you roughly?" I grabbed her hair and pulled on it. Her mouth opened but nothing came out and I kissed her, taking a bite of her bottom lip and plunging my tongue inside when she opened her lips for me.

I let out a low groan at the taste of her, and her hands settled on my waist.

I pulled back, watching the way her chest puffed in and out.

I slapped her tit again. "Answer me, baby. Do you love being my whore?"

"Yes!" she screamed when I pinched her nipple. "Fuck. Dominic, please."

I grabbed her hips and turned her until she was lying on her front.

She made a small noise in surprise, and a rush of arousal shot sharply through me as I lifted her hips, so her ass was in the air, presented to me.

"So fucking pretty," I said, cupping an ass cheek.

"Dominic? What's going on? Did something happen with the club?"

She was saying that out of concern—but a cynical part of me wondered if she was searching for information.

I shook my head.

No.

I pulled her panties down, letting them rest by her knees when I couldn't go any further, and took in the sight of her bare ass. I used my hands to separate the ass cheeks, presenting me with her tight little asshole.

My cock tightened at the sight.

Fuck, she was a piece of art.

And all mine.

All fucking mine.

Her breath caught when I ran my finger gently over the tight hole, but she didn't say anything. She didn't protest.

"Anyone ever fuck you here before?" I asked.

Her back moved, and she turned her head to look at me. "No."

I smiled a little. "Good. I'm glad I'm your fucking first."

Her eyes widened. "Dominic—"

A small whimper escaped when I dipped one finger inside. Her eyes rolled back as I moved in a slow, steady pace. I wasn't gonna rush this. I was gonna enjoy my time. I was gonna make her enjoy this as well.

Mine.

I pulled out and spanked her ass, one ass cheek, then the next, and over again.

She jumped forward slightly, but held still for me, like the good little girl she was, and I hummed in satisfaction as the pale skin turned red with my fucking handprint.

Her pussy flooded with her arousal, and I licked my lips when some spilled over and ran down the back of her thigh.

Fuck.

My cock twitched.

"Look at you," I said. "So fucking *fuckable*. Hold still for me."

I opened the bedside drawer, taking out a small tube of lube I'd put in there days before in preparation for this.

Her eyes widened when she saw what was in my hand.

"Now? You're going to fuck my ass *now?*"

I laughed. "If not now, then when?"

"This is a fucking inspirational quote time," she grumbled.

I laughed, the turmoil I'd faced in coming back lessening. I wasn't fucking wrong about her.

"Oh, but your ass is fucking inspired. Men would have gone to war for your ass had they had the privilege of seeing it. Too bad for all those little fuckers—they won't see what's mine. Isn't that right, wildcat?" I asked, letting her hear the greedy note in my voice.

When it came to her, I was downright greedy.

I opened the lube and squirted a generous amount on her asshole.

She yelped before it morphed into a moan as I started to rub the lube on her, around her, *in* her.

"Dominic," she said when I used my other hand on her pussy, rubbing over the swollen clit.

She wiggled her hips against me, her legs trembling when I had fingers in both holes.

I fucked her like that, and her back arched.

"God," she gasped. "Dominic."

"That's right. This is mine. Mine to use however I want, and you're fucking lucky I'm feeling generous tonight. I'm gonna let you come. So come for me, baby. Let me feel your cunt drench my hands."

She cried out when she came.

I wasted no time discarding my clothes.

I threw them on the floor and grabbed my cock, playing with myself.

Her little asshole puckered from her orgasm, and I almost came right then and there.

Fuck.

I didn't wait for her to come back down. I pushed inside her tight asshole, almost coming undone from the way it gripped me.

"Fuck," I grunted, pushing further inside.

She tensed and I paused, rubbing the small of her back.

"Baby, I need you to relax, or this will hurt you," I said through gritted teeth.

I heard her exhale before her muscles relaxed.

"Such a good girl," I said, pushing further inside. "My good girl."

I stopped when I had myself buried deep inside her, closing my eyes and seeing a whole fucking galaxy behind my eyelids.

Fuck. Me.

I grabbed her hips and moved.

She made a soft strangled noise when I pulled out until just my tip was buried in her hole, then pushed back inside her.

I did it again, and again, again. Sweat broke out on my forehead, and I had to remind myself to go easy, considering this was her first time, but it was hard. So fucking hard.

She turned her head and our eyes met.

There was no way for her to disguise that fucking look in her eyes.

She was telling the truth when she said she loved me.

She fucking loved me.

She loved this monster.

And I could trust her.

I did.

I pushed harder and her eyes closed, getting lost in the euphoria of it all.

My grip on her tightened as I increased my pace.

"Baby," I said. "How close are you?"

"Close," she moaned, moving her hand beneath her and playing with her pussy.

Fuck.

"Harder," I said as I filled her roughly. "Play with your pussy harder. Until you're fucking delirious. Do it."

She let out a choked breath and moved her hand harder, faster.

I fucked her ass harder as well, and when I felt her tremble violently against me, knowing she was close, I let go.

I filled her asshole with my cum.

She screamed when she came, shaking the entire house.

I pulled out once I finished, watching the white substance pour out of her and down to her pussy, and her legs. The sight was almost too much for me to handle.

I lay down on the bed, wrapping her shaky body in my arms, and buried my face in her neck.

Fuck me, but I loved this girl in my arms beyond reason.

24

DOMINIC

I DIDN'T TELL EMMY I WAS LEAVING FOR LAS VEGAS.

I didn't want her to worry, and hopefully, I would be able to find the piece of shit who hurt my girl easily enough.

I met up with Micah on our bikes at the state line, and after catching him up with everything, we left for the decent two-story house just outside Las Vegas.

I looked around at the nice suburban neighborhood as Micah pulled up beside me.

"You want me to come in with you?"

I shook my head. "No, just keep watch and let me know if there's anything unusual around."

He nodded, and I hopped off my bike, stepping up to the porch and ringing the doorbell.

I waited for a moment, and when no one came to the door, I looked back at Micah. Someone was home. Unluckily for them, I came prepared.

Pulling out a lock-picking kit from my pocket, I knelt and played around with the doorknob a bit before I heard a click. I turned it and pushed the door open, looking into a house that had obviously been professionally decorated.

This entire neighborhood screamed money, so it probably wouldn't be long before someone noticed two bikers who obviously didn't belong.

I walked in and closed the door behind me. A scuffling noise in the back near the kitchen caught my attention, and I quickly walked over, finding two older couples trying to sneak out.

"I wouldn't," I said, making them flinch.

The man turned to me and pushed his wife behind him. I watched with some amusement.

"We don't have anything you want. Okay? We've retired and we don't get into the Sons of War business, so leave us alone."

I crossed my arms over my chest. "I wouldn't say you don't have something I want. And I'm insulted. Do I look like those cockroaches from the Sons of War?"

The man visibly blanched as he took in my outfit. I wasn't wearing my cut since I didn't want to make my presence known in Las Vegas. I had it safely stored in the back of my bike for later because when I destroyed the fucking chapter, I wanted them to know who the fuck was doing it.

"Who are you?" he asked, backing further toward the door. Any more, and he would be pressing his wife into it.

"That's not important," I said. "Where is your son?"

John Sr. looked around. "We don't have anything to do with him anymore."

"You gave him your million-dollar business, didn't you? And now you're telling me you have nothing to do with him?"

Anger flashed in the older man's eyes, and the woman turned away from me.

"We didn't give it to him," he said. "He forced our hands. Him and his *friends.*"

"You mean Sonny?" I asked. The man nodded and wrapped his arms tightly around his wife.

"Where does he live?"

The man hesitated.

"Tell me. And tell me the truth because if I find out you wasted my time with a fucking lie, I'm gonna come back. And I'm gonna come back pissed. We both don't want that."

"And if I tell you, you'll leave us alone?"

I nodded. Looking at the man, it was clear that there was no lost love between him and his son. It worked well in my favor, considering there was no record of where the fuck John Moore resided.

It made me wonder why he didn't want people to know where he lived.

The woman grasped the man's arms, looking up at him. I had a feeling she still loved and cared for her son.

The man shook his head. "It's him or us, and you know that, Susan."

Susan looked down, her eyes filled with tears. I couldn't give two fucks about her feelings, but it was wasting my time. I pulled out my gun and aimed at them. I didn't want to fucking resort to this. I could understand wanting to protect your kid, but their kid messed up.

He fucked with the woman I loved.

John Sr. saw me first and tried to shield his wife's body.

"Okay, we'll tell you," he said. "We don't know if he's still there. It's been over a year since we've spoken."

I looked at him expectantly. "Write it down."

THE BASTARD LIVED on a remote property that I was sure was owned by the Sons of War.

It made things easier for me, considering there wouldn't

be any potential witnesses around to put me at the scene when they found his body.

And hopefully, I would have time for a little fun, and maybe get some information out of him about the fucking Sons of War and the traitors, though I didn't plan on it. I doubted he knew a lot about the club's business since he was still considered an outsider, even if he was working as a fucking accountant for them.

Micah and I parked about a block away from his house, not wanting our bikes to draw attention. I couldn't have him leave before I could get to him, or—if he wasn't home—see our bikes and get spooked.

We walked for about ten minutes before approaching a large house surrounded by nothing but desert land.

We shared a look.

"I'm gonna go in. Can you look around the property?" I asked. Micah nodded, and I walked up to the back door.

I peered through the windows for any movement, and when I didn't see anything, I picked the lock for the back door, and walked into the empty, messy house.

It was littered with takeout containers filling up the trash can, and the ones on top appeared to be recent.

I walked around, careful not to touch anything, and came to an office downstairs.

This room was a little better. Not as disorganized.

I went to the desk that was covered with papers, along with a computer.

It was at times like this that I wished I had my son's hacking skills. It would have been useful.

I flipped through the papers first, a lot of them listing all the properties the Sons of War owned and how much they paid for them, along with the shell companies they used to make the purchases.

How fucking sloppy.

It made my job easier, but I was still fucking disgusted that a club as chaotic as this was causing my club trouble.

It must be fucking old age. I had gotten too lenient.

That wasn't going to be the case anymore. Once I find the fucking traitors, I was going to make an example of them.

I grabbed the papers, quickly scanning each one, and noting the locations. I pulled out my phone and took a photo of each.

I stopped when I got to the bank statements, showing deposits made to a fucking Trent Henderson.

Anger ripped through me, sharp and fast.

I had already suspected Trent was a part of the traitors, and this just confirmed it, taking fucking money from the Sons of War.

But I also knew that dickless weasel wasn't the one in charge. He didn't have the brains for that. So who the hell was it?

I stopped when I got to the last one.

What the fuck?

A doctor's bill.

Not just any doctor. A plastic surgeon.

Now, why the fuck would the Sons of War need a fucking plastic surgeon? I doubted I would be able to find the good doctor now and ask him for the answer. He was probably buried deep somewhere in the desert after providing his services.

It took a little more digging before I finally found my answer.

I stiffened when I came upon the before-and-after pictures, anger coursing through me and making it hard to see.

"Fuck!" I screamed.

A gun clicked nearby. "Who the fuck are you, and what are you doing in my house?"

I turned and saw good old Johnny boy—with a fucking gun.

"Don't you know little boys shouldn't play with guns?" I asked, trying to calm the rage in my heart. It was hard. So fucking hard.

Betrayed by my own men.

And I was gonna kill every last one. This time, I would make sure there would be no resurrections.

John narrowed his eyes at me. "You really want to insult me? I have a gun pointed at you."

Even with the fucking weapon, he still looked unsure. As if he didn't quite know how to use it.

"I know."

I approached him, and he pulled the trigger.

A loud bang rang out, and a small sting spread from my side.

A miscalculation on my part.

My anger blinded me to safety procedures.

Fuck.

25

EMMY

One day had passed since Dominic had left for Las Vegas.

I didn't even know the bastard had left the state until Lucy came over with Colt, and the silent man had passed on Dominic's message.

How rude.

He couldn't even tell me himself.

I was sound asleep after—I shivered—after he took my ass, but he could have woken me up to tell me quickly.

I had to find out from Colt. I shouldn't be worried, but I was.

There had been a heavy feeling at the bottom of my stomach since I found out he had left.

I knew why he went there.

He was looking for John.

I let out a long exhale at the thought. I was worried about Dominic handling John.

It had been seven years since I'd seen the man, but I still remembered his face, as clear as day.

John wouldn't be a match for Dominic, yet the heavy feeling persisted, and I didn't know why.

The front doorbell rang, drawing me out of my thoughts. Lucy squeezed my shoulder as she passed me from where I was sitting in the kitchen by the window on her way to the door.

I listened for Lucy's voice and heard the soft greeting of another woman.

I smiled, recognizing the voice right away, and watched as Lucy walked back in, Ryleigh behind her.

"Hey," I said, watching the way the small girl waddled over to me. "What are you doing here?"

"Roman said Dominic left you here alone, and I thought you could use some company. Do you want to go to Dominic's bar with me?"

I eyed her up and down. "You sure you don't want to go somewhere else more... pregnant-friendly?"

She rolled her eyes. "I'm not going to drink there. And Roman's been getting more and more, ah, protective of me as this pregnancy progresses. He doesn't want me anywhere he can't see me."

I laughed. "Protective or crazy?"

She grinned. "It's not like you don't know. I imagined Dominic to be much more insane."

"Downright neurotic," I agreed with a laugh. Lucy smiled at us from her place by the island, chopping up some vegetables for dinner. "Is he out there?"

"Roman?" she asked. I nodded. She gave me a sheepish smile. "Yeah, I can't drive anymore. This belly makes it impossible."

I nodded, wondering what I would be like pregnant. It was a high possibility now, considering Dominic had been actively trying to get me pregnant since the first time. I should be freaked out about that. Or angry.

But the fucker had really worn me down because all I was feeling right now was curiosity.

I'd never imagined myself as a mother, but the seed had been planted.

I stood. "All right. Let's go."

I turned to Lucy, about to ask if she needed anything, but she made a shooing motion with her hand.

"Have fun, Emmy. I hope this will take your mind off things."

I shot her a grateful smile and hooked my arm with Ryleigh, walking to the door.

She looked sideways at me. "You have a lot going on?"

"I just miss Dominic," I admitted.

Things would be better once he got home, and I could see for myself that he was okay.

She nodded in understanding. "Yeah. I would miss Roman, too, even if it had only been a day."

The man in question was standing by his truck, his arms crossed over his enormous chest and his eyes on his surroundings. I wondered if there was ever a time when he wasn't on guard. Probably around Ryleigh when it was just the two of them.

And sure enough, he turned to us as soon as we approached, and I could see the way he softened.

Whoa.

If I didn't have Dominic, I would have been jealous of the way he was looking at her.

He smiled at us. "Ladies. Your chauffeur awaits."

Ryleigh giggled like a woman in love, and I rolled my eyes at them, grinning.

God, she had it bad.

Roman opened the back door for us and helped me in, then Ryleigh, before reaching in and buckling her up.

She slapped at his hands. "I can do this, you know. I'm not an invalid."

He ignored her and did up the belt before turning to me. "Do you need help, too?"

I shook my head with a smile and pulled on my belt, and Ryleigh laughed.

"God save us from overprotective men," she muttered, and I nodded, missing Dominic so much at this moment, my heart ached.

Ryleigh waved excitedly at Kai when we walked to the bar and found the man in his usual spot in the back, a laptop in front of him.

He closed it quickly as soon as we reached him, and I couldn't help but feel he did it because I was here.

I didn't know why, though, and it was probably just my mind messing with me.

I had been feeling a little emotional lately, and I wasn't sure if it was due to the lack of sleep or something else.

I blinked.

No, I wasn't pregnant. I couldn't be.

My period had never been regular, so I doubted I was fertile at the moment.

No.

I shook away the thought.

I might have thought about it back at the house, but something about it being a very real possibility at this moment made my heart race.

Ryleigh looked back at me curiously, and I realized I had stopped walking.

I shot her a small smile I didn't exactly feel and took a seat.

"How are you?" I asked Kai.

"Good," he answered me carefully.

I nodded, unsure why there was a sudden tension in the air. "Have you heard from your dad?"

Kai shook his head, and his shoulders relaxed. "No, but don't worry. Dad can take care of himself."

He glanced at my hands, and I realized I had been wringing them together as I asked him.

"I don't think I can just not worry because you say it," I said.

He chuckled softly. "Fair enough." He turned to Ryleigh. "Are you just about ready to pop, Ryleigh-girl? I feel sorry watching you do the duck walk."

"Kai Madden, that is such an insensitive thing to say!" she said, punching him in the arm.

I doubted it actually hurt him, which he confirmed when he laughed and looked at her as if he thought she was cute.

I smiled a little too. Ryleigh was cute. She reminded me a little of a younger Mila Kunis, and I could see why Roman had fallen for her at first sight, even if he had done it all wrong by stalking her first.

Roman's phone had rung as soon as we'd arrived, and he'd told Ryleigh and me to go inside without him. Now, the door opened, and the big man walked in.

There was something about his expression that had my heart throbbing painfully. I sat up, and Kai must have noticed, too, because he stood when Roman approached.

"What is it?" Kai asked.

Roman glanced briefly at me. "Let's talk outside."

I stood too. "No, this is about Dominic, isn't it?"

Roman didn't answer me.

Kai walked closer to the man, fear tight in his eyes. "Roman. Is it about Dad?"

My mouth felt dry as I waited for his answer.

A gasp from across the bar caught my attention, and I glanced over at the waitress, who was staring up at the TV in shock.

I ignored Roman yelling at me to stay where I was and walked over to get a better view of the TV.

"Turn it up," I said to the bartender, who did as I asked without protest. I watched the new anchor wearing a dark shade of burgundy lipstick speak words I refused to understand.

I blinked as her voice got louder, but—but she wasn't making any sense.

What the hell was she talking about?

"A body found in the Colorado River in Nevada has been only identified as a man in his thirties. Authorities are working diligently on the case, which is suspected of foul play. However, there has been speculation that the man is a member of the King's Men Motorcycle Club here in Sacramento, though nothing has been confirmed—"

The anchorwoman pressed a finger to her ear, obviously listening to whoever was talking to her.

She turned to the camera with wide eyes.

I felt Roman, Kai, and Ryleigh move close to me.

Ryleigh wrapped her arms around me.

There were King's Men in Nevada besides Dominic, weren't there? Why did it feel like she wouldn't be saying the name of those men?

"I'm getting some new information that a bystander had witnessed officials pull the body out of the river. The victim's face was mutilated beyond recognition, but he was allegedly wearing a motorcycle club garment that belonged to the president of the King's Men." She looked to the camera, her wide eyes set in disbeliefs. Then she uttered the words that had my heart shattering in a million little pieces. "Dominic Madden is dead."

Everything went fuzzy. Arms wrapped around me when I felt my legs giving out. I looked back at Kai's blank face. I realized, a little distantly, that Kai was the one holding me up.

Dominic Madden is dead.

Impossible.

Dominic was invincible.

He was a monster.

My monster.

And monsters didn't die. It just wasn't possible.

A terrible noise filled my ears, and I realized after a moment that it was me. I was making that terrible noise.

"Emmy," Roman said.

I shook my head. "She's lying."

"It's possible it's not him," Roman said. "But we need to leave right now, okay? She shouldn't have fucking said it until they have a confirmation on the"—he took a deep breath—"the body. It doesn't matter. The news has hit, and things are going to be bad for a while. I need to get you and Ryleigh somewhere safe."

I shook my head. "I'm not leaving until we know for sure."

Tears streamed down my face, and my heart hurt. So bad. So fucking bad. My heart was breaking from the inside out, and I didn't know how to make the pain disappear. I didn't know how to give in to it. Not when I—

I let out a choked sob.

Roman shook his head and looked at Kai. "Keep your head on straight, kid. I need you to be strong. Got me?"

I didn't know why he was being so harsh with Kai, but I couldn't worry about that.

Roman wrapped his arms around a red-eyed Ryleigh while Kai grabbed hold of me, and they both led us out to Roman's truck.

Everything happened in a blur.

I didn't even remember climbing in. Ryleigh sat close to me, burying her face in my neck. More tears dripped down my cheek, and I wiped them away.

Dominic Madden is dead.

No.

No, he wasn't. He wouldn't leave me. He was too neurotic, too possessive, to leave me alone. Not after he branded me and made me fall in love with him.

"He's not gone," I said. Roman looked at me in the rearview mirror and stepped on the gas, speeding us through Sacramento.

"Where are we going?" Kai asked.

"To Big Bear Lake."

Big Bear Lake?

That was about seven hours away.

"Why?" I croaked.

"I need to get you three to safety," he answered.

Kai, in the front passenger seat, turned to the man sharply. "I'm not fucking leaving."

"You're not arguing with me, kid, so don't try, or I'll fucking drug you and chain you in my fucking cabin."

"Damn it, Roman. I'm not leaving the club the way it is."

Roman shook his head. "If Dominic is dead, who do you think all those other bastards will be gunning for next?"

Kai punched his fists on the dashboard. "Then let them fucking come."

Roman tightened his grip around the steering wheel. "I need you to protect Emmy and Ryleigh. Got it?"

"No," Kai answered, his voice in a low growl that almost sounded like Dominic. I closed my eyes as pain pierced my heart sharply. "We're not fucking leaving with our tails tucked behind our fucking legs. We're gonna fight."

"Damn it, Kai. I can't—"

A car slammed against the truck, sending it spinning. Luckily, we were on a small, deserted street.

Ryleigh screamed as Roman pumped on the brakes.

One black truck and several bikes surrounded us.

Oh, fuck.

My heart slammed against my chest, and Roman pulled out his gun.

"Once I start shooting, you gun the gas and drive the fuck out of here, got me?" Roman said to Kai.

"You're fucking outnumbered. How the hell am I supposed to just leave?"

"You protect Ryleigh and Emmy. And my unborn son. You got it? You protect them all with your fucking life, and you don't turn back for me."

Someone shot the back of the truck. I flinched and bit my bottom lip, trying to keep from making any noise.

I looked out the window and saw the man in the middle aiming his gun at us. His voice was drowned out by the growl of the motorcycle engine, along with us being in the truck, but it was easy to make out the words he was mouthing.

Get out of the fucking car!

"Roman!" Ryleigh cried.

He turned around and reached over, cupping her cheeks. "Shh. It's gonna be okay, baby."

She grabbed his arms, pulling on him desperately. "Come with us."

He shook his head. "We can't outrun them. But I can buy you guys some time."

"No!"

"Baby," he said sharply. "Be a good girl for me and protect our son, yeah?"

"I don't want to leave you," she cried.

My fists clenched. How the fuck did things come to this?

I looked out the window and saw a familiar-looking man hop out of the truck. I frowned.

"What the fuck?" I said out loud. The man was wearing a King's Men cut. And now that I was looking around, I realized all the men here were.

Traitors of the club, I realized.

These men betrayed Dominic. And off to the side were two very, very familiar faces.

"Roman," I said. "Those are the men who chased Braxton and me."

The other man's face darkened.

"Fucking rats," he spat out. "Axel betrayed the club."

Roman looked at Kai, whose eyes were red and wet now. "Remember what I said, kid. I'm counting on you to protect my world."

Another shot came out at the truck. I flinched.

He leaned over and kissed Ryleigh quickly, and I looked away from them, blinking back tears.

The king is dead.

No.

It looked like Axel was sending someone over to pull us out of the truck, but Roman exited the car first, and Kai moved to the driver's side.

The men around aimed their guns at our truck. Even if Roman was able to distract some of them, I didn't know how we would outrun all the men.

"No!" Ryleigh screamed. "We're not leaving him!"

"Emmy, hold Ryleigh!" Kai commanded.

I looked at him, then at the struggling girl beside me, unsure of what to do. We couldn't just leave Roman. We couldn't—

Engines growled from a distance.

I paused. More than a dozen bikes came into view.

Kai looked, too, and Ryleigh stopped fighting.

Tears continued to fall down my cheeks as I watched the scene unfold.

I gasped when the bikes got closer, though it was probably drowned out by all the noise.

Because the King's Men had arrived. And in the middle, leading the charge, was Dominic.

My monster was alive.

26

DOMINIC

WE SURROUNDED THE FUCKING TRAITORS.

I took in the scene, from Roman standing in front of his truck protectively to Kai getting out from the driver's side, his gun drawn. Fucking Axel's surprised face.

Blade stood off to one side, defeat set in his dark eyes. Fucker knew it was over. Next to Axel was—surprise, surprise—fucking cunt-face Trent, all the blood draining from his face.

He had been the one selling out the club's information. The one who told those bastards where to find my Braxton.

My eyes moved back to Axel, the fucking leader of this insurgent group.

My jaw clenched.

I was gonna have a good fucking time messing up his face so badly, no plastic surgeon could fix it—again.

Not that he would have a need for it.

After all, dead men didn't need shit.

Bet he was fucking surprised I was alive. He would be even more so to know John fucking Moore was the body they recovered from the Colorado River, wearing my cut, while the news anchor, on my payroll, let it slip about my *death*.

Though that had been necessary, I was still fucking stiff that my cut was gone.

My eyes went back to my VP and son, noticing the relief on their faces.

Neither man moved away from the truck, which told me they were guarding something infinitely precious in there.

My guess?

My girl and Roman's girl were there.

My fists tightened around the handlebars before I pulled out my gun and aimed at Axel.

My men took my lead and pulled out their guns, pointing them at all the traitors. Ten, by my count, and two fuckheads I had never met before. I assumed these were the men who chased after my boy and Emmy.

All the traitors got off their bikes and surrendered their weapons, except for Axel.

They knew they wouldn't win in this fight. Their best bet was to surrender and hope I was feeling generous.

I wasn't feeling generous. I was feeling murderous.

I narrowed my eyes at the fucker trying to run off and leave his men behind.

Axel.

Better known as Brooks Tanner.

The former fucking president of the King's Men. The man infiltrated my club using a dead man's identity and took a page from my playbook as he recruited men for an insurgent group.

Fucking pathetic that he only got ten men to join him.

When I rebelled, I had more than half the men in the club standing behind me, including his VP.

But this was ten men too many.

And they were gonna wish they hadn't worked for a man like him.

"What do you want to do?" Micah asked beside me through the growl of the engine.

"Gather up all the fucking men and take them to one of the warehouses. You can pick one and have your fun. You deserve it. I'm gonna chase Tanner," I said, knowing the little fucker was about to run.

Sure enough, he ran to one of the abandoned bikes and took off.

"Don't shoot," I yelled to my men. "The fucker's mine!"

I revved my engine and chased him, catching up after a block.

He turned slightly around to look at me. He blindly shot his gun behind him and missed me by about a mile.

I smiled and sped up, quickly driving up to his side.

He tried to drive me off by clipping me on the side. I pressed on my brakes to get him off my side before I sped up once more. I got behind him, and before he could react, I kicked his bike with one leg.

He lost control of the back wheel, and that was enough to send him spiraling off the road. The bike fell, and he fell with it. I turned my bike around and stopped in front of him.

I watched him lie there, looking at me with wide eyes.

I smiled.

He knew what was gonna happen next.

He tried to move out of the way. I rolled the throttle back and drove the bike straight for him.

His scream was cut off short when I ran him over with my bike.

I stopped and looked back at the fucker. His eyes were wide, blood and guts pouring out from his middle, his mouth open in a soundless scream.

He wasn't dead.

Not yet.

I fucking hoped he felt all the pain in the world.

I hopped off my bike and walked over to him, pressing my foot down on his stomach. I would have to replace my boots later.

"You can rot in hell with your bastard son and your fucking accountant," I said.

He gurgled on his blood, and I took satisfaction from the sound.

Pulling out my phone, I texted the location for a cleanup. I had men nearby in case things got messy, and moments later, a white van pulled up.

Three minutes was all it took for him to die.

The men in the front saluted me, and I drove away. They would take care of the body.

27

EMMY

RYLEIGH AND I CLIMBED OUT OF THE TRUCK AS SOON AS ALL the men were tied up.

It wasn't long after that when two vans arrived, and they shoved all the men in there, closing the door. I didn't ask where the van was taking those men. I didn't care.

My eyes had been on the road Dominic had taken off on when he chased that man, anxious for when he would return to me.

Ryleigh was in Roman's arms, crying in his chest while yelling at him, and I half laughed, half cried at the scene.

Kai hugged me.

"He's okay," I said, my lips trembling.

Kai nodded, wiping away the tears on his cheeks. "Yeah, he's okay."

We stayed there for a while, until I heard the bike engine once more, and I knew for sure it was Dominic.

I cried harder when he came into view, and he quickly shut off the bike and hurried over to us.

His eyes were filled with emotions as he saw Kai and me standing together—then he wrapped us tightly in his arms.

I broke down.

"Don't ever fucking do that to me again!" I yelled.

He nodded and chuckled. "I won't ever do this to you again. I promise."

He stepped away from us, looking from me to Kai.

"How could you ever think I would leave you two? You two and Braxton are my fucking world, and I will stay breathing for as long as possible to protect you all. Okay?"

I nodded, more sobs coming out.

"Wildcat. It's okay. No more crying."

"No, it's not," I said. "But it will be as soon as you promise never to leave my side."

His shoulders relaxed, and he chucked my chin affectionately. "I promise."

I shook my head. That didn't make me feel better.

He was okay, and he was back with me.

My hands trembled as I placed them on his shoulders, clutching him in my grips.

He looked over at Kai, cupping the back of Kai's neck with his other hand. "I won't ever leave you."

Kai leaned forward and briefly laid his head on his dad's shoulder before pulling away. He shot me an affectionate look and walked over to Micah, though there was something haunted about his eyes.

It was going to take us both a while to really be okay with this.

I turned back to my monster, taking in the way his blue eyes glinted in the afternoon sun.

I burrowed closer to him, not wanting to let him go.

"I love you," I said, and I felt his shoulders relaxing.

"I love you, too, wildcat. So fucking much."

It was close to five o'clock in the morning.

Dominic was sound asleep next to me on the bed, shirtless.

The dawn light outside provided just enough for me to make out his beautiful body.

To count the breaths he took while he slept.

There was a small bandage on his side from when he got hurt in Las Vegas.

I closed my eyes. I didn't want to think about it. Had the bullet been a little higher, a little deeper, and I would have really lost him.

I wanted to reach out and touch him, but I was afraid he might wake up, and the last thing I wanted to do was explain why I wasn't asleep because of a nightmare about him dying.

A week had passed since Dominic did his coming back from the dead bid.

Though it wasn't that long of a time when the news reporter said Dominic was dead to him making an appearance, there was still something so utterly terrifying, so utterly traumatic about believing he was dead.

I was still affected by it.

He had left only once this week, to take care of the traitors of the club and to make sure his club brothers knew the club was as strong as ever. The rest of the time was spent at home with me.

We got Braxton home a few days before, and if the little boy was surprised to see me here and living with his dad, he didn't show.

I was sure Dominic told him about us beforehand, though what he said was a mystery to me.

I had been having nightmares.

Of Dominic leaving me, and I couldn't find him anywhere.

I was glad he stayed home because I wasn't ready for him to leave and go back to his business as if everything was fine.

Everything was not fine.

And sure enough, my newest problem made itself known.

I quickly, but quietly, jumped out of bed and ran to the bathroom.

I opened the toilet lid and hurled last night's dinner into the bowl.

Tears stung my eyes, and I felt absolutely miserable.

I was pregnant.

Fuck Dominic and his breeding kink, and fuck him for making me love him so much, to the point where I didn't think I could breathe.

To the point where I had already forgiven him for getting me pregnant on purpose.

I still haven't told him.

I didn't want to see the smugness in his eyes.

I might just punch him in the throat if that were the case.

I noticed movement from behind me then, when I was no longer throwing up and instead just dry heaving.

It seemed I couldn't keep this little secret anymore.

I was surprised he hadn't noticed all the signs before.

I hadn't taken a pregnancy test yet, but I had all the signs, from being overly emotional to the morning *and* evening sickness, to being more tired than usual, and even to my tender breasts.

A terrible symptom, considering how much Dominic loved waking me up most mornings by sucking on my nipples—

I shut the lid off and turned, leaning against the toilet and leveling him with a glare.

"You knew."

He smiled, that possessive look coming into his eyes.

It was becoming a common look for him whenever he looked at me.

"Yup."

"Why didn't you say anything?"

"I was waiting for you to tell me."

"Are you happy now?" I asked meanly. "Now I'm pregnant and miserable."

He didn't say anything for a moment. Then he reached down and pulled me into his arms. I rested my head against his chest, taking in his scent because as mad as I was at him, I still craved him.

I still fear that he might be taken away from me one of these days.

He set me on the counter and passed me my toothbrush. I quickly brushed my teeth as Dominic watched me with intense blue eyes.

I pretended not to notice.

Once I rinsed my mouth, he pulled me back into his arms and carried me to our bed.

He settled me on his lap, one hand moving up and grabbing my boob.

I let out a sigh but didn't stop him. At least he wasn't playing as rough as he normally would. In fact, he had been gentle with me all week—which made sense now.

"I'm sorry you're miserable, wildcat."

I paused. "Come again."

"I said I'm sorry you're miserable, baby."

I couldn't say anything to that.

He looked down at me, smiling a little at my reaction before he chucked my chin gently.

"Close your mouth, baby."

I closed my mouth.

Then, "Did you just apologize to me?"

He laughed. "Yeah, I know. What the hell am I thinking?"

I slapped his chest.

He retaliated by twisting my nipple slightly. I squirmed on his lap.

"Are you really sorry?" I asked.

He nodded, looking serious again. "I am. I fucking love that you're pregnant, baby. But I hate that you're miserable because of it."

I deflated a little. While he was happy about our child, I was too busy feeling sorry for myself.

Was I a horrible mother?

Alarm suddenly entered his eyes, and he cupped my cheek. "Baby, why are you crying?"

I sniffled. "I'm a terrible mother, aren't I?"

"What?" he asked sharply.

"All I've been doing this week is cursing you in my head while feeling sorry for myself. I didn't give myself time to even be happy about our child. I *am* a terrible mother!" I wailed.

He pulled me tighter into his arms. "Fuck, no. Emmy, look at me."

I shook my head.

He firmed his voice. "Emmy."

I let out a sigh. He couldn't even let me be miserable on my own.

"What?" I said, looking at him.

He frowned, swiping his thumb under my eyes. "How could you possibly think you would be a terrible mother? That's not fucking possible."

"You don't know that."

"Really? You think I don't know? You're over here, worrying yourself to tears that you might be a terrible mother. Would a terrible mother really be doing that?"

I looked down at his chest, to the kneeling angel tattoo.

I shrugged.

"And let's not forget you risked your life to save Braxton. Who in their right mind would do that?"

"Everyone," I said, looking at him. "Why wouldn't they? Braxton's a child."

He shot me a soft look.

"Only you would think everyone in this world is good. You have a big heart."

My lips trembled, and I placed my hand on his chest, trying to get closer to him, to his warmth.

"A heart big enough to love a monster. Don't you think you can love our baby?"

Well, when he said it like that...

"You really think I will make a good mom?"

"I know so," he said confidently.

I relaxed against him. Dominic was so strong, so confident in everything he did, so if he thought I wouldn't be a terrible mom...

I blinked. "I am happy about our kid. Do I wish you would have at least worn a condom? *Yeah.*" He smiled at the sass in my voice. I rolled my eyes. "But I am happy."

"Good," he said, leaning down and kissing my temple. "I'm happy, too. And I will do everything I can to protect my family. I can't protect my family if I'm dead. So stop looking at me like you're afraid I would disappear on you, wildcat."

Of course, he caught on to that.

Dominic was one of the most astute men I had ever met.

"I just don't want anything to happen to you," I whispered.

His job—who he was—was just so dangerous.

And I didn't know what to do to ensure he would always come back home to me.

"Hey, listen to me," he said. "Nothing is going to happen to me, okay?"

My lips trembled. "You don't know that. Everyone wants to take you away from me. I c-can't—"

"It's okay. No one is going to take me away from you."

"You don't know that," I said.

If there was one thing I knew, it was how unpredictable life was.

He pulled me in closer to his arms. "You're right. I don't know that. But I do know that no matter what happens, I will always try to get home to you."

He cupped my stomach with his huge, scarred hand.

I looked down at it.

"You and our little one."

"Promise?"

"Always."

I closed my eyes. I knew nothing was resolved, but somehow, this small promise made me feel better.

"I love you," I said softly.

"I love you, too, wildcat."

EPILOGUE

DOMINIC

Seven and a half months later...

Emmy hissed in pain before stopping and pretending nothing was wrong.

I rolled my eyes at her.

When would she learn not to hide anything from me?

Did she really think I hadn't noticed her going through contractions all morning?

I had been timing them all day, and though they were getting closer together, it wasn't close enough for us to go to the hospital yet.

I smiled and reclined back on the couch, holding her, pretending to watch some cheesy, romantic shit she had picked out earlier.

I had not been paying attention, but the movie was clearly nearing the end because there were tears in Emmy's eyes as she watched the man in the movie chase the woman and beg her to stay with him.

I scoffed at that.

She turned to me. "What?"

"Why the hell would that spineless dick beg? I know what I would do if I were him."

"Yeah, me too," she deadpanned. "You'd abduct the girl and make her delirious with orgasms until she submits."

I chuckled and reached my hand down, cupping her pussy. I squeezed it through her leggings, and she squirmed, looking up at the stairs.

"Dominic, Braxton is home."

"Yes. And Roman is on his way over with Ryleigh."

Emmy frowned. "Why?"

"Well, I thought Braxton would like to help babysit Ryker. You know, get some practice for when the twins are here. And it's better to have someone here with him when I take you to the hospital. Judging by your contractions, I'd say now would be a good time."

She looked at me with wide eyes. "You knew!"

I laughed. "Baby, I've known since the first one."

"How come you didn't say anything? How come you aren't freaking out?"

"I wanted you to tell me when you're ready. And the reason I'm not freaking out is because this isn't my first time."

She sputtered, and I smiled, leaning forward and kissing her lips while rubbing my thumb over her clit.

She moved against me. "Dominic."

She moaned, first in pleasure before it morphed into pain. Another contraction hit.

I stood. "All right, baby. It's time I get you to the hospital."

I helped her stand just as Braxton bounded down the stairs. "Is it time?" he asked excitedly.

It was a fucking miracle that what happened to him and Emmy didn't affect him more than it should have.

My little boy was still the happy boy he was before everything happened, and the time spent with his aunt had been good for him.

I had done what I promised Jenny and hadn't reached out to her since I got Braxton back.

She was happier without me in her life.

It was a hard thing to admit, but I had to let my baby sister make decisions about her life, and she had decided to not have me in it.

That didn't mean it didn't break my fucking heart in two.

But I was finding it easier to live with when I had Emmy, my boys, and soon, the two newest additions to the Madden clan.

I ruffled Braxton's hair and nodded. "Yeah. I'm gonna take Emmy to the hospital. Roman, Ryleigh, and Ryker are on their way. They'll be here soon. You be good for them."

I couldn't believe my VP was now a dad, considering the lost man he had been when he first came to Sacramento as a prospect for my club.

Fuck, but that felt like a lifetime ago.

Braxton's smile widened. "Oh, I love Ryker. I hope Emmy has boys."

We chose not to learn the sex of the babies. All we knew was that the babies were healthy, and there were two of them.

Emmy grunted again, reminding me we needed to hurry.

"Be good, okay?" I said to Braxton, kissing the top of his head. He grumbled a little about that, but he wasn't really upset over my show of affection.

Fuck me, but it was good to have my boy back, in my house and under my protection.

We used the SUV.

I didn't drive my car often, preferring the bike over the humongous beast I had parked in the garage, but ever since we found out Emmy was pregnant, which wasn't long after my little resurrection act, I had been using it.

I was afraid to take her out on my bike.

Afraid she might fall off, even though it was unlikely.

We took off for the hospital, and I followed every single traffic law to the fucking T. Something Emmy seemed to find amusement from, despite the obvious pain she was in.

When we got to the hospital, one of the nurses came out with a wheelchair. I had called in advance to let them know we were coming, and I'd booked a private room.

When Kai was born, I barely had two dimes to rub together. Things had been tough with him for a while, but now that I had the resources to give all my kids better things in life, I was going to make sure they wanted for nothing.

I jumped out of the car and ran to the other side to help Emmy out.

"I got this," I said, taking control of the handles on the wheelchair from the male nurse. He smartly stepped back and let me push my baby inside to have my babies.

Fuck me—I wasn't nervous all day today, but now that we were here, the reality of the situation finally penetrated.

My knees felt fucking weak, and it was a miracle I was able to stay standing.

We got to the room, and her doctor greeted us just as I got Emmy situated on the bed.

"How is Mommy doing today?" Dr. Bryant asked. The doctor was a small-statured, dark-skinned woman with a no-nonsense attitude that I respected, along with an impressive list of credentials. More importantly, Dr. Bryant was a woman.

"I'm doing good," Emmy said.

I frowned at her.

Her skin was getting pale, and it wasn't as if Emmy had

naturally tan skin on a regular day. If she got any paler, I'd be afraid people would mistake her for Casper.

"Baby, tell the doctor the truth."

She glared at me. "I am fine, you big mule. I'm only like this because of you and your breeding kink!"

Dr. Bryant barely batted an eye at our conversation. After seven months of my harassing her, I was sure she was used to us by now.

"Dominic is right, Emmy. It's important to be honest with me so I can provide you with the best care possible."

Emmy pouted, her eyes shimmering. Fuck me, but I couldn't handle her tears right now. I would probably tear this whole damned building to shreds.

"I'm in a little pain," she whispered.

"Baby," I said, moving closer to her, pushing the strands of her long dark hair out of the way. "What can I do?"

I didn't feel helpless all that often, but I was now.

"Just your being here helps," she said, offering me a sweet smile.

"Fuck, of course I'll be here. I'll be glued by your side, so much so, you'll probably get fucking sick of me."

She let out a light laugh that had my heart clenching in pain and making me feel like I could hold the weight of the fucking world on my shoulders.

I would fucking do it for her.

Fifteen long and grueling hours later, Emmy gave birth to my twin boys, Maddox and Caleb.

Along with my two oldest boys, these little boys were the most precious in the world. Fuck me, but they were so tiny. They were born premature, which we had prepared for since that was common with twins, and they would have to stay in the hospital for several weeks to grow a little more.

They were so perfect.

And I fell at first sight.

Emmy was resting on the bed. I went to her side after the boys were put down to sleep.

I glanced over at the ridiculous bouquet the Four Horsemen had sent in congratulation. The fact that they knew Emmy was in labor and arranged for the flowers to be sent told me they had eyes on my city.

Fuckers.

This partnership better go my fucking way, or I would be burning a trail of inferno all the way to Chicago.

At least they kept their word. After the elimination of the Sons of War, Blue Paragon was hit with a tax audit that resulted in a cool ten-million-dollar fee, along with the CFO sentenced to ten years in prison for fraud.

The Blue Paragon was no more.

Not when all of the investors pulled out, and there wasn't even enough left of the company to buy toilet paper.

"Lie down with me?" she asked.

I couldn't deny her anything when she looked at me like that, so I didn't. Carefully, I climbed on the bed and held her gently against me.

"Once you feel better, we're going down to the courthouse to get married. I want you to have my name."

She laughed. "I shouldn't be surprised anymore by the outrageous things coming out of your mouth, but I am."

"I'm being serious," I said, and if I had to fuck her to get her compliant, I would.

She slapped my chest. "No way, you neurotic man. I want a big, expensive wedding."

I watched her for a moment, letting her see my love for her in my eyes. "Then that's what I'll give you."

"And maybe we can invite my parents?" she asked quietly.

Emmy's relationship with her parents was pretty much the same. They rarely talked, which was fine with me because it was me, Kai, Braxton, our twin boys, and the rest of the men of the MC that were her family.

"If that's what you want. I'll make every one of your dreams come true, wildcat."

Emmy had quit teaching at the school. She was still deciding what she wanted to do with her life, though she told me she wasn't in a hurry to decide. Whatever it was that she wanted, I would move the Earth to make it so.

She snuggled closer to me. "You already have."

I swallowed down the emotions and nodded, kissing the top of her head.

Everything was going to be okay with us.

I would make sure of it.

"I love you, wildcat."

"I love you too, my monster."

Sweetest words a man like me could ever fucking hear.

end.

Made in the USA
Middletown, DE
22 May 2025

75873144R00199